C. Lloyd Morgan, Theodore Compton

A Mendip Valley

Its inhabitants and surroundings, being an enlarged and illustrated edition of

Winscombe sketches

C. Lloyd Morgan, Theodore Compton

A Mendip Valley
its inhabitants and surroundings, being an enlarged and illustrated edition of Winscombe sketches

ISBN/EAN: 9783337094294

Printed in Europe, USA, Canada, Australia, Japan

Cover: Foto ©Andreas Hilbeck / pixelio.de

More available books at **www.hansebooks.com**

A MENDIP VALLEY,

ITS INHABITANTS AND SURROUNDINGS,

BEING AN ENLARGED AND ILLUSTRATED EDITION

OF

WINSCOMBE SKETCHES,

BY

THEODORE COMPTON,

WITH

ORIGINAL ILLUSTRATIONS BY EDWARD THEODORE COMPTON,

AND A

CHAPTER ON THE GEOLOGICAL HISTORY OF THE MENDIPS

BY PROFESSOR C. LLOYD MORGAN, F.G.S.

LONDON: EDWARD STANFORD,

26 & 27, COCKSPUR STREET, CHARING CROSS, S.W.

SWINDON: W. C. EDDINGTON, VICTORIA PRESS.

1892

The cottage homes of England,
By thousands on her plains ;
They are smiling o'er the silvery brook,
And round the hamlet fanes

Through glowing orchards forth they peep,
Each from its nook of leaves ;
And fearless there the lowly sleep,
As the bird beneath their eaves.

And green for ever be the groves,
And bright the flowery sod,
Where first the child's glad spirit loves
Its country and its God

PREFACE.

THE Second Edition of WINSCOMBE SKETCHES having been some time exhausted, an opportunity has been given for enlarging and revising the work, and issuing it in an illustrated form, and under a new title.

The illustrations will speak for themselves. They have been a "labour of love," like the rest of the book. I have also to thank Professor Lloyd Morgan for his kindness in freely offering to contribute a paper on the Geology of the Mendips, and for the interesting chapter from his practised pen. To Canon Church, the sub-dean of Wells, I am indebted for an inspection of the Register in the Cathedral Library, from which the history of Winscombe Church has been corrected. References to other friends and neighbours will be found in the body of the work.

The delay in publication having been occasioned by the illustrations exceeding the number expected, will not, I trust, be any cause of disappointment or regret.

WINSCOMBE,
16th June, 1892.

ERRATA.

Page 2, line 8, erase the (,) after placid.

,, 7, line 6 from bottom, insert (-) between top and heavy.

,, 9, for *Trifoliata* read *trifoliata*.

,, 79, line 11, from bottom, *for* Cottages *read* Cottagers.

,, 85, line 13, from bottom, *for* inigratiou *read* immigration.

,, 151, line 14, from bottom, *for* perch *read* perching.

,, 184, line 6, from bottom, *for* Manger *read* Maugei.

TABLE OF CONTENTS.

—o—

LIST OF ILLUSTRATIONS.

LIST OF ILLUSTRATIONS *(continued)*.

I.—THE VALLEY.

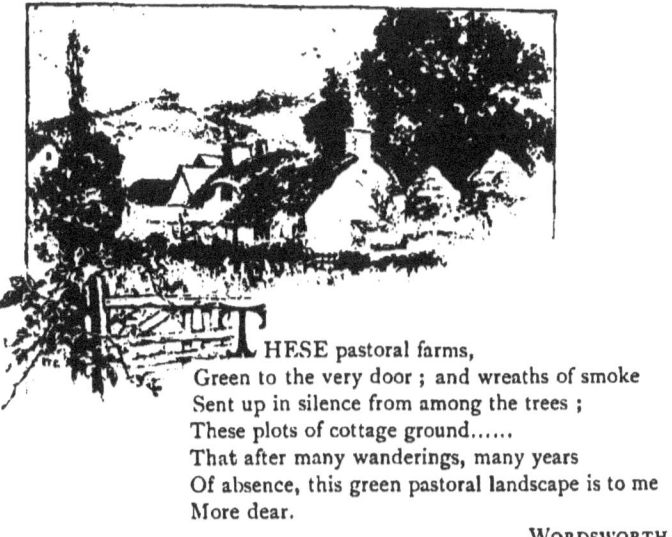

THESE pastoral farms,
Green to the very door ; and wreaths of smoke
Sent up in silence from among the trees ;
These plots of cottage ground......
That after many wanderings, many years
Of absence, this green pastoral landscape is to me
More dear.
                                        WORDSWORTH.

THE Laureate of the Lakes could hardly have been
more disturbed by the projected railway through his
beautiful country, than some of us were when our valley
was first threatened by the railway people. With him
we exclaimed

Is there no nook of English ground secure
From rash assault ?

B

Must our unpretending valley, as yet unknown to
tourists and overturners of every kind, be ravaged by
the invader who has tapped the Lakes, disfigured the
Rhine, and pierced the heart of the Alps ?   " Forbid it,
heaven ! " Must we have our quiet meads and rural lanes
disfigured, the field paths stopped by cuttings and embankments, the frisking lambs disturbed in their sports,
and placid, cows in their ruminations, and the feathered
songsters of the grove scared away by the engine's
frightful squeal ?

> Baffle the threat, bright scene from Winscombe hill ;
> Plead for thy peace, thou beautiful romance
> Of Nature !

Such were our dismal reflections five and twenty years
ago, when we thought of the good old times when the
world to us was young, and the evil days had not yet
come when we should have no pleasure in coaching. We
remembered the old winding ways, up hill and down dale,
with companionable coachman and guard, and scarcely
less companionable horses ; the ever-varying incidents
of travel as we passed through country towns and villages
and rural scenes—and then thought of the hard new
way, with noisy machinery, along flat, unbending rails,
where all is rigid and lifeless as iron, harsh and unfeeling
as rock.

Five and twenty years have passed.   The railway
navvies have done their worst.   Bowery lanes and green
meadows have been cut through and disfigured, the
rural walks are not as they were ; but Nature has again
spread her mantle over man's rude works.   The bare
embankments and rocky cuttings are covered with herb-
age ; the lambs frisk in the meadows each returning

spring; the cows ruminate as quietly as they did before; the feathered songsters have not been scared away, and the most conservative of Nature's gentle lovers finds the passing train, with its following cloud of steam, little more annoying than the old coaches and wagons with their clouds of dust. In fact, the rural spirit of the valley, which has reigned here for ages, instead of being over-come by the railway people, has come over the railway itself.

Our Mendip Valley is the Pass or *Col* through which the Cheddar Valley Railway crosses the Mendip Hills, from Sandford and Banwell in the North Marshes, to Axbridge and Cheddar in the south. It is a quiet rural line all the way to the city of Wells, passing through rich grazing land dotted with cottages and village churches. A rather steep incline from Sandford, brings it to the higher level of our valley, which is almost entirely occupied by the extensive parish of Winscombe, in which Sandford is also included.

The name of Winscombe, however, is not to be found in the list of places in the Postal Guide, except as the Tele-graph Station for "*Woodboro', R.S.O., Somersetshire.*" Woodborough is in the centre of Winscombe Valley and parish, and the Post Office and Inn as well as other indus-tries being there, the name is more familiar to drivers from Weston-super-mare than that of the parish itself. Our letters are brought by mail-cart from Weston, through Banwell, to Woodboro', though of late, there has been an afternoon arrival and despatch by railway at Wins-combe Station. The station is itself in Woodborough, and was at first called by that name; but there being another Woodborough station in Wiltshire, and mis-takes having been made, our station received the more distinguishing, comprehensive and correct name of the parish and valley. It is the only Winscombe in the whole island, perhaps in the whole world !

A pleasant prospect of the valley is seen from the railway platform, looking westward, towards the Church, about half-a-mile off, and the village, which an American visitor said was the prettiest he had seen in England. His views of English villages might be limited, but Winscombe may fairly be considered one of the most picturesque.

Before railway times, our valley was reached from Bristol by the road over Red-hill, and through Churchill. This road enters the parish of Winscombe at Pattenham,* and skirts the valley from Sidcot to Shutshelf ; whence it descends as a shelf road to Compton Bishop and Cross, where the coaches used to change horses. This road along the hill-side, without hedges, commands views of the vale of Winscombe and surrounding hills, and, after leaving our valley, the more distant Quantocks and Polden hills, with Brent Knoll, Glastonbury Tor, and other points of interest. The road, however, is comparatively modern. A much more ancient one exists, leading from Woodborough to Shutshelf, which was, no doubt, the old bridle-way from Axbridge to Banwell. Being too narrow for carts, it has long been left to decay, and is now almost impassable, even for horses. It may serve to remind those who venture upon it, of the difficulties of travelling in " the good old times," even as late as those of the poet Cowper, a hundred and fifty years ago ;—

> Oh, this lane ! now it is plain
> That struggling and striving is labour in vain.
> Come, wheel around, the dirt we have found
> Would buy an estate at a farthing a pound.

* Called also Pakenham and Paddingham.

But if you should have ventured on wheels, you may
find wheeling round impracticable.   Our old way is like
the " Devonshire Lane " of the poet—

> Howe'er rough and dirty the road may be found,
> Drive forward you must, there is no turning round.

On horseback, and, in very dry weather, on foot, the
road is practicable for those who do not object to mud
and water ; but those impediments are inevitable here and
there from the local springs, which rarely, if ever, entirely
stop or freeze.   The lane is so singularly picturesque
that it is worth an adventure.   It is one of the rural
solitudes cut through by the railway.   Near the point of
crossing is a small cottage farm, with a duck-pond by the
lane-side, overhung by a pollard oak, the branches
spreading over nearly the whole pond, or pool, as such
waters are called here.   It is a spot that recalls some of
Bewick's and Birket Foster's rustic gems, of which there
are many in our valley.   The lane grows deeper and
narrower as it tends upwards ; having worn its way, for
a thousand years and more, between banks now covered
with greenery.   Pollard oak and ash, bedecked with poly-
podies, lean over the road ; old crabs scatter their sour
apples beneath, and brambles and briars spread across
the way, festooned with woodbine, bryony, bindweed
and the pencilled vetch.   These in their different seasons
garnish this ancient green lane, as you walk, or wade,
through thick grass, water-cresses, mud, or snow and ice
as the case may be, till you emerge at Shutshelf on the
open common, prepared to enjoy the fine air and view
toward the south.   So completely disused is this narrow
way of our forefathers, that the entrance from Shutshelf
is generally closed by a hurdle ; presumably as a cheap

substitute for a shepherd, to prevent the hill sheep from straying down the verdant lane.   It is not uncommon in our rural parish to find a right of way, or even a well-used church path, effectually barred to all but active climbers, and the few who care to trouble themselves to assert the public rights by main force.

The usual road from Weston-super-Mare to Cheddar is over Banwell Hill and through Woodborough, missing the best view of Winscombe valley, for the sake of the more level road.   But a " Syntax in search of the picturesque," would be well repaid if, at the cost of leading his *Grizzle* down the pitch of the hill, he chose the steeper descent from Banwell Castle by Winthill to Max Mill and Winscombe Church.   The steep part is but short, and leads to a lovely view of the vale below, lying in pastoral beauty—

> Embosomed in the silent hills,
> Where quiet sleeps and care is calm,
> And all the air is breathing balm.

Descending the hill the road winds between banks of primroses and violets, with meadows on either side, enlivened in early spring with frisking lambs, and then amongst apple orchards, whose " blooth " in early summer fills the air with sweetness.   At the bottom of the valley a clear babbling brook is crossed, up the course of which the road continues as far as Max Mill, where the water falls from the mill-dam on the higher level.   The road here rises to the higher ground, and crosses the brook by a low bridge.   On the left is a shady orchard, through which the stream flows in a wider channel, amongst a profusion of marsh marigolds, purple loosestrife, and

other water beauties. As you pause on the bridge, the
trout glide beneath you, and the galinule hides among
the sedges ; the green woodpecker and the jay laugh in the
orchard, and the goldcrest's cradle hangs from a fir just
over the stile by the roadside.

On the right, across the meadows, seated under a crag,
is the secluded hamlet of Barton, where Bristol benevolence has established a summer camp for poor city
children. Turning to the left, and soon after to the right,
the lane brings us to Winscombe " Square," near the
church ; whence it climbs a steep hill along the south
side of the valley, till it joins the Bristol Road at Shutshelf. The hill is not unreasonably shunned by drivers,
those especially of hired carriages, who prefer the
easier, but less interesting road through Woodborough
and Sidcot. Winscombe Hill, however, should be taken
by those who care for scenery. The steep part is short,
and affords an opportunity for seeing the church and
yew-tree. The road all the way is very pleasant, with
views of the vale below, and, in clear weather, the Monmouth and Welsh hills across the Bristol Channel.

Winscombe Vale is purely rural. Without park or game
cover, without baron, or squire, or knight of the shire—
the holy friar only represented by absent commissioners,
and soulless corporations—we can boast of no forest
scenery. The churchyard yew is almost the only ancient
tree spared by the ruthless axe. Of hedge-row timber
there is no lack, but, stript and top heavy, it stands
where chance and tempest leave it. A few copses and a
small part of a fir wood are all that remain to represent
the two miles of wood set down in the Norman Survey.
With small enclosures, divided by quick-set hedges and
hedge-row elms, the effect of the valley in summer is

leafy enough.   Small farms, orchards, and scattered
hamlets compose the scene, with

> Trim cottages that here and there
> Speckling the social tilth, appear.

Perhaps in appearance as well as reality the valley is as
pleasant with its cottage homesteads and small plots of
ground as it would be were its four thousand acres
owned by one man, and peopled with pheasants or deer ;
even though the illustrious stranger, invoked by Gilbert
White a hundred years ago, should come and

> Expand the forest sloping up the hill,
> Swell to a lake the scant penurious rill,
> O'er the gay lawn the flow'ry shrub dispread,
> And with the blending garden mix the mead.

Could the " penurious rill " be swollen to a lake, or the
numerous springs be induced to lay their heads together
and form a shining river, the aspect of the valley would
be charming indeed.   Its chief defect is the absence of
visible waters.   With plenty of springs we have neither
lake nor river ; nothing more to be seen than the tiny
brook whose meanderings through meadow and orchard
scarcely form a part of the landscape.   This little stream,
however, is not without interest.   It is a river in minia-
ture, traceable from its source to outflow, with its several
small tributaries draining the valley.   Its head is East
Well, sometimes wrongly called Ice-well ; but that name
is inappropriate, for the water in this and all the springs
in the valley is warmer than the air in frosty weather ;
never freezing, and sometimes giving off visible vapour.
Except in dry weather the spring may be seen rising
from the bottom of a shallow basin, and throwing up

Whimscombe from the hills

jets of sand and small pebbles. The brook, which, like Tennyson's, abounds in water-cresses, runs rapidly through copse, orchard and meadow, winding about, and in and out—

With many a blossom sailing,
And here and there a lusty trout ;

but not, for rhyme, a grayling ; till it reaches the road or " street " of Winscombe village. Here it is now bridged over ; but within the memory of old villagers it was crossed by a ford, with a plank bridge for foot-passengers. The land on the north side of the ford was a separate manor called Ford-juxta-Winscombe. The brook, now increased by another spring, to be mentioned again among the springs of the valley, turns a corner under a dwelling-house, crosses another lane, and, entering the meadows, winds its way amongst cresses and ranker vegetation, often hidden under hazels and brambles, till it meets another brooklet in a marshy copse, where the bog-bean, *Menyanthes Trifoliata*, puts forth in May its fringed and fragrant flowers. Strengthened by this small meeting of the waters, and by other springs, the widened brook flows on, through " brambly wildernesses," where the kingfisher still finds a refuge, and where, on

Fairy foreland set
With willow-weed and mallow,

the moor-hen rears her brood. The brook, now wider and smoother, turns to the left, and running quietly between meadows and orchards, reaches Max Mill, already mentioned.

Our Max miller does not grind philology, and has never sifted, or parsed, or analysed the name of his mill. It may have been the *Mola Maxima* of the valley ;

for it probably superseded a smaller and more ancient mill higher up the stream. The ruins of this old mill are still to be seen, and are familiar to lovers of wild flowers as a spot where wild snowdrops are earliest found. This is believed to be the mill mentioned in Domesday Book ; where the Manor of Winscombe is described as comprising "a mill of five shillings* rent, sixty acres of meadow, with one mile of pasture in length and breadth, and a wood two miles long and one mile broad." It would seem as if this old mill was still used a century ago ; for Collinson, writing in 1791, says the brook turned two grist mills.

The mill-dam still remains, and is well supplied with clear water by powerful springs, which throw up the sand, and form basins like volcanic craters at the bottom of the pool. The overflow forms the brooklet already mentioned, which joins the other brook in the marshy copse, before it reaches the present mill.

After turning the *Mola Maxima*, the stream runs by the roadside till it is joined by two other brooklets at a small "waters meet," where the confluent waters curve into a bowery nook, and then wind through the meadows, till, following the bend of the valley, the stream, now called the Lox Yeo, finally quits it between the hills of Loxton and Crooks Peak, and soon afterwards joins the River Axe, which discharges its muddy waters into Weston Bay.

I have sometimes wondered whether the author of *In Memoriam* may not have rambled from Clevedon to this quiet valley, and in his familiar lines immortalized our Winscombe Brook.

---

* A shilling at that time would be about the value of a sheep.

Of the springs of the valley we have already mentioned East Well, those in the old mill-pond, and the spring at Winscombe Ford. This last needs further description. Before the brook was bridged over at the bottom of Winscombe street, the spring, no doubt, overflowed into the brook from East Well, and increased the stream which then crossed the road and had to be forded. Since the raising of the road by a bridge, the spring, which rises on the east side, has been enclosed in masonry, and is carried under the road to a stone tank on the west side, from which it perpetually overflows into a brooklet that joins the main stream further down. The water never fails nor freezes ; ·its course under the road is marked in winter by the thawing of the frost and snow over it. This is the principal fountain in the neighbourhood. During the long droughts of 1864, 1865, and 1871, when many parts of the country suffered severely, and even East Well failed, as had rarely happened before, the spring at Winscombe Brook supplied the whole neighbourhood. A picturesque and touching sight was the gathering of villagers round the unfailing fountain ; some with the familiar brown pitcher, dear to painters of rustic life ; others with carts and water-casks that looked as if they never could be filled from the little road-side tank, but two feet deep in water : but all the vessels were filled day by day, and the fountain failed not.

Another spring supplies the pool at Slough-pits on the Sandford road, and another the deep pool called Fullers' Pond ; from which, however, there is seldom any considerable overflow.

Another spring had the ill fame of being haunted by a spectre ; but the march of intellect has laid this ghost as well as many others. The appearance was, perhaps, caused by moonlight falling on vapour rising from the warm water and condensed by the evening air. A more lively appearance is sometimes seen in the water itself, through which jets of air-bubbles rise in bright and quick succession, like reflections of the showers of light from rockets.*

The eastern end of the valley has other springs; notably the picturesque Hale Well, a favorite resort of Sidcot scholars and of the author of *Rambles of a Dominie*, who has immortalized it in his account of " Sleepy Hollow."

* This spring is now enclosed, and supplies Burnham with abundance of pure water.

II.—THE HILLS.

Therefore am I still
A lover of the meadows, and the woods
And mountains, and of all that we behold
From this green earth.

WORDSWORTH.

THOUGH rich in ancient remains, as well as in minerals, and as renowned as the northern lime-stone hills for caverns and underground streams, the Mendips are but little frequented by tourists. The scenery and fine old churches do not combine variety and interest enough to attract many strangers from a distance. Cheddar Cliffs and Caves, indeed, draw hundreds from Bristol and Weston for a summer day's excursion ; but even these remarkable rocks—said to be more like the Gorges of Circassia* than anything else in England—are not very generally known, and are seldom attempted by landscape painters.

* See an interesting article in the *Standard* newspaper, 26th Oct., 1874.

The Mendip Hills are a small range of mountains, chiefly limestone and conglomerate rock, with the base of old red sandstone appearing in some places. Their greatest height but little exceeds a thousand feet; but as they rise abruptly from a plain barely above the sea-level, they look higher in proportion than many loftier hills ; while the rocky character, from which they take their name, gives them a more mountainous aspect than their mere height might suggest. They are in fact the denuded relics of ancient mountains, probably a mile or more in height, whose crumbled remains form the fertile plain which has driven the sea from their feet.

The sunny side of the hills facing south-west, between Winscombe and Wells, may remind a traveller from the Rhine country, as he skirts them by road or railway, of the Bergstrasse between Darmstadt and Heidelberg ; but we must grant to our German visitor that our hills are as inferior to his Odenwald as the scanty remains of the Mendip forest are to the Walds of Baden. This country, however, was well-wooded in ancient times, and a great hunting-ground of the Saxon Kings. Long after them, in 1220, Henry III. granted out of his forest of Cheddar "sixty great oaks" for the building of Wells Cathedral. The forest was cleared by Edward III., and now affords cover for no nobler game than the fox and badger.

The Mendip Hills are rocky and bare compared with the Quantocks, and still more so contrasted with the Carhampton and Dunkery range, in whose forest combes the red deer still remain, the last and noblest of the wildlings of the ancient forest.

Of the hills immediately enclosing Winscombe Valley, the best known by name is Crooks Peak, a prominent headland forming the western end of a long ridge called Wavering Down, which divides the valley from the plain on the south, and reaches eastward from the Peak to Shutshelf, where the high road and railway pass out of the valley. On the east side of the pass rises Shutshelf Hill, more generally called Callow, and in the old charters of Banwell Abbey, Calleva. It is nearly a hundred feet higher than Wavering Down, and three hundred feet lower than Blackdown, which lies behind it and is the highest of the West Mendips. Beacon Batch, the highest part, is by Ordnance survey 1087 feet above the sea, and is supposed to be the part of Somersetshire said to be sometimes visible from Windsor Castle.

It was on Callow Hill that Hannah More and her sisters, in 1791, gave what was then a rare, if not unheard of entertainment, a school treat to five hundred and seventeen children of the rural schools they had lately set up in the neighbourhood. So strange was the sight that a great multitude gathered together to witness the miracle. Opinions were divided. Some praised the good women who had thus laboured to teach poor children to read ; others, and amongst them several of the clergy, condemned their efforts as Methodistical and revolutionary, undermining distinctions of rank and the British constitution itself. The scenes of the benevolent sisters' labours, as related in the Mendip Annals, are embraced in the views from Callow and Wavering Down. Just over Sandford Hill, looking north-east, is the richly timbered vale of Wrington—the fine church tower backed by the wooded hill ; and on the hillside, a little to the right, is Barley Wood, a name well-known the world over as the abode of the benevolent and gifted Hannah More. Cowslip Geeen, her first residence after leaving Bristol, is

in the vale below, to the right, near Aldwick Court.   In
the vale of Langford, on this side of the Yeo, is Langford
Court, formerly a hunting-seat of the Earls of Essex;
then, in succession, the property of Dr. Whalley and the
Rt. Hon. J. H. Addington, and now the residence of
Evan Llewellyn, Esq., M.P.   On the hill above, but not
visible in our view, is Mendip Lodge, built by Dr.
Whalley, who planted the trees on the hill.   Here Mrs.
Siddons was a frequent visitor.   In one of her letters she
says her " castle in the air " was a cottage near her be-
loved Langford.   Some of her letters are addressed to
Dr. Whalley at Winscombe Court, then the residence of
his mother and brother.

Amongst the Mores' friends were, as is well known,
David Garrick and the Macaulays.   Zachary Macaulay's
wife, Miss Mills, though of Quaker family, had been a
pupil of the Mores at Clifton.   Lord Macaulay was
thus early known to Hannah More, who quickly saw his
talents and predicted his future fame.   Some of the
happiest days of his youth were spent at Barley Wood.
The Mendip Hills and their caves must have been among
his earliest recollections, and their traditions might have
furnished his genius with materials for lays of Ancient
Britain in times long before the Mendip miners could
meet any Armada stronger than a Norseman's fleet.

A few years before the death of Macaulay, Barley
Wood was visited by Madam Bunsen, who wrote to her
daughter about the delightful drive from Blaise Castle.
"The way there and back is wonderfully beautiful.
From the exquisite valley of the Avon we ascended a
Wasserscheide, from the other side of which we gained a
sight of the Mendip Hills—a beautiful range, and the
exquisitely rich and varied expanse of country, ending

with Weston-Super-Mare on the shore of the Channel. The flower garden at Barley Wood, and the manner in which the cottage is decorated with choice climbing plants, is a pattern for imitation. We sat out on the grass under a tree planted by Mrs. Hannah More herself."

Barley Wood is associated with many celebrated characters, including Elizabeth Fry, who visited Hannah More in 1823; but it is best remembered in the annals of benevolence and the advancement of general education, in the face of opposition, at this day almost incredible. It is well-known that Hannah More extended her benevolence beyond her means, and that her servants and others made free with her hospitality. Some years ago I fell in with a man who, in his youth, had been one of the many entertained in the kitchen at Barley Wood. He said Miss More used to like to have the lads of the village to sing to her, and her favorite song was, " In my cottage near a wood." She was extremely considerate of her servants, especially of her old coachman, Charles. One hot hay-making day, when he was at work in the hay-field, his mistress sent to him to tell him to come out of the heat, and receiving the reply that the hay must be made, she went to him herself, and told him to come in, and let the hay make itself. So kind and generous a lady, Charles thought, could not object to her benevolent example being imitated by her servants. While she charged them never to waste even a crumb, they were never to let anyone go away without some refreshment ; and no one ever did. Open house was kept in kitchen and parlour, and at such a " bountiful old rate " that our fine old English lady was eaten out of house and home, and " left Barley Wood for ever." My honest informant was less indignant at Charles' abuse of confidence than at

C

the ingratitude of those who had shared in his plunder.
When he was no longer Mrs. More's coachman, the people
he used to regale at Barley Wood "turned round upon
poor Charles and would have nothing to say to him :
t'were too bad." And so it was.

Close to Wrington Churchyard, where the mortal
remains of Hannah More and her sisters are buried,
stands a cottage with this inscription, "John Locke was
born in this house, A.D. MDCXXXII." Francis Bacon had
departed this life but six years before. Great, indeed,
has been the "Advancement of Learning" and the
"Conduct of the Human Understanding" since the days
of those philosophers. Times much more remote are
recalled by the neighbouring hill of Dolbury, with its
ancient British camp and later Roman walls conspicuous
in our distant view ; while modern history recurs in
Churchill, where, tradition says, Sir John Churchill
lodged a troop of soldiers on their way to Sedgemoor.
The church tower appears amongst a row of tall poplars
at some little distance from the village. Further north
is seen one of the few Somersetshire examples of
Shenstone's

> Village marked with little spire,
> Embowered in trees, and hardly known to fame.

Congresbury spire is a pleasing feature in the landscape. According to Camden the name is taken from
a hermit, one Congarius, "a son of the Emperor of Con-
stantinople!" * It is said that coins have been found
there with the inscription, "Constantinopolis." Perhaps,
as probable a derivation might be found in Congar,
a chief or king ; whence may come the royal title of the
conger eel. The same root, König, a king, is a frequent

---

* A.D. 711. A Bishopric is said to have been here since 167.

origin of the names of places, such as Kingston, Conis-
ton, and others, and agrees with the local traditional
name here, which, until the railway people brought it
to book, was pronounced Coomsbury or Koonsbury.
In one M.S. of Asser's *Life of Alfred*, the name is
Cungresberie, and is so spelt in the Domesday Book.

Further north, again, is Yatton's spireless steeple ; the
stump recalling that of Redcliff, so many years a distinguishing feature in every view of Bristol. Like Redcliff, Yatton has been lately restored, but the steeple
waits for a fresh outpouring of zeal to raise its spire, and
point it to the skies. Cadbury Hill,* the site of another
ancient British camp, is seen a little to the right, between
Yatton and Congresbury. It commands a fine view, and
is remarkable, like the famous Glastonbury hill, for
winter flowering hawthorns. Are these also descended
from the Pilgrim's staff? Or is their celebration of Christmas due to the sun and wind prematurely developing the
ripened buds in anticipation of Spring ?

North of Yatton is Clevedon, on the " lone hill that
overhangs the Bristol Channel," where the remains of
Arthur Hallam and his heart-broken father lie buried ;
and where Coleridge dwelt for some time, in a cottage
still to be seen very much as he left it,—Myrtle Cottage,
a home he always held in pleasant remembrance.

> Low was our pretty cot ; our tallest rose
> Peep'd at the chamber window. We could hear
> At silent noon, at eve, at early morn,
> The sea's faint murmur.
>   The little landscape round
> Was green and woody and refreshed the eye,
> It was a spot which you might safely call
> The Valley of Seclusion !

* One of several of the name, which is Keltic for Battle Hill.

Brockley Combe, a favorite haunt of the poet, is nearer Congresbury. Coleridge describes it well :—

> From the deep fissures of the naked rock,
> The Yew-tree bursts. Beneath its dark green boughs
> I rest—and now have gained the topmost site.
>
> Ah ! what a luxury of landscape meets
> My gaze ! proud towers, and cots more dear to me,
> Elm shadowed fields and prospect bounding sea.
> Enchanting spot !

Between Brockley Combe and the Vale of Wrington is Cleeve Combe, with Cleeve Toot, a remarkable crag or conical rock, the top of which may be seen above the Brockley woods, from the railway between Nailsea and Yatton. It is supposed to be one of the " Toot Hills," used by the Ancient Britons for sacrifices to their god *Taith* or *Teutas.* There are Toot-hills in different parts of England, as Toot-hill in Yorkshire, and in Norfolk, as well as other places supposed to be named from the same deity, such as Totton, Tottenham, Tutbury, Tooting, Tothill-fields, and many more ; to which might possibly be added Chewton Mendip and Chew Magna ; near which is the Druid temple of Stanton Drew. The Keltic deity *Teutas* was identified by the Romans with their god *Mercurius*, the Greek *Hermes*, the Egyptian *Thoth*, and Phœnician *Tautas* or *Taute**. This Keltic derivation, however, is disputed by a late learned writer, who considers *Toot* to be Danish for a Look-out ; from which comes *Tout*, to look out for customers.

Returning to the immediate boundaries of our valley, —the north side is shut in by Banwell Hill and Winthill, as the western part of the hill is called. The eastern

---

* An interesting paper on this subject will be found in
Hone's Year Book, July 24.

part, called Banwell Park, contains the remains of two ancient British camps, the larger one in an open space called Banwell Plain ; the smaller nearer Banwell Castle. The western and higher part of the hill is distinguishable from a distance by the tower erected by Bishop Law, while engaged with William Beard in searching the now celebrated bone-cavern discovered at the west end of the hill. Banwell village, with its beautiful church, lies hidden behind the hill, but we can hear the softened sound of the bells whenever the wind comes from the north. Beyond Banwell, the flat country, or North Marsh, extends to Clevedon and Worle. The Bristol and Exeter Railway crosses it on a dead level, and in a perfectly straight line. The " Flying Dutchman " and other trains can be watched and heard, as they dart at full speed between Worle and Yatton, leaving trails of steam behind them, which, in some states of the atmosphere, hang as a stratum of cloud a mile or more long, before becoming absorbed in the air.

The western end of our valley is closed by Loxton and Bleadon Hills, which turn the water-course toward the south. Between Bleadon and Banwell Hills appears Worle Hill, above Weston-super-Mare, noted for the remains of one of the oldest and most remarkable of the many ancient British camps within our view.

Across the Bristol Channel is seen the fleet of shipping lying off Penarth Point, near the thriving port of Cardiff. Further up the Channel are Portskewet, Port-y-coed, where Earl Harold in 1065 began to build a hunting-lodge for King Edward, and Chepstow, with the Wyndcliff near Tintern. Beyond are the Skirrid, or Holy Mountain, above Abergavenny, and the Sugar-loaf, near Crickhowel. In clear weather the Brecknockshire Beacons are distinctly seen, at a distance of sixty miles. Looking westward down the Channel, we see on the Welsh side, Nash, or Ness Point, and possibly the high promontory beyond the Mumbles. Towards the south are Exmoor, and the hills above Porlock Bay, the scene of *Lorna Doone*. In front of the extreme distance are North Hill and Minehead, the hills above Dunster—all historic ground—and towering above them, Dunkery Beacon (1707 feet), from which may be seen Dartmoor in South Devon, and the Malvern Hills in Worcestershire, a hundred and fifty miles apart. Brendon Hill is a little to the south.

The country between Porlock and Dunster, with the wooded slopes of Dunkery Beacon, is the most beautiful part of Somersetshire, and amongst the most picturesque of English woodland scenery.

> Porlock ! thy verdant vale so fair to sight,
> Thy lofty hills which fern and furze embrown,
> Thy waters that roll musically down
> Thy woody glens, the traveller with delight
> Recalls to memory.

These hills abound with ancient barrows, camps and beacon hearths. Many a signal fire had blazed on Dunkery beacon ages before Popes were heard of. On the approach of the Spanish Armada it would be one of the principal signals, when

> Far on the deep the Spaniard saw along each southern shire,
> Cape after cape, in endless range, those twinkling points of fire.
> The fisher left his skiff to rock on Tamar's glittering waves,
> The rugged miners poured to war from Mendip's sunless caves.

The poet conveys the signal to London by easy stages:

> The sentinel on Whitehall gate looked forth into the night,
> And saw o'erhanging Richmond Hill that streak of blood-red light.

But if the beacon on Blackdown can be seen from
Windsor Castle, the Queen might be told of danger at
Plymouth almost as soon as the Mendip miners had been
warned from Dunkery Beacon.

It was at Porlock and at Watchet, midway between
Minehead and the mouth of the Parret, that the Danes
attempted to land in 918, and being driven away, took
refuge in one of the Holm Islands, where they were
nearly starved. Watchet was harried again in 988 and
997. The Holms are remarkable objects in our landscape. With the smaller islands lying between them and
the Welsh coast, they connect Wales with the Mendip
Hills at Brean Down. They and Brean Down have been
lately fortified, to protect the Severn Sea from any future
attacks of Northmen or others.

Due south of Worle Hill is Brent Knoll, another
ancient camp. At its southern foot is Battlebury, where
Alfred fought the Danes, and on the east side is seen the
spire of East Brent church, connected with a different
kind of contention.

Beyond Brent Knoll, looking south-west, are the
Quantock Hills, with more relics of barbarous times and
contention of races. Danesborough Hill has the remains
of an ancient camp, probably occupied by the Danes,
but formed long before their inroads. It is said to have
been taken by the Romans from the Belgæ or Ancient
Britons. But the Quantock Hills have more agreeable
associations; they were a favorite haunt of Wordsworth and Coleridge, before they became "Lake Poets."
Coleridge lived among them when at Nether Stowey,
"Beloved Stowey," and Wordsworth at Alfoxden. Here
were written many of Wordsworth's lyrical ballads,
Coleridge's *Ancient Mariner*, and the first part of

that "singularly wild and beautiful poem," as Lord
Byron called it, *Christabel.* Wordsworth thus alludes
to those days :

> Upon smooth Quantock's airy ridge we roved ;
> Unchecked we loitered mid her sylvan courts ;
> Thou, in bewitching words, with happy heart,
> Didst chant the vision of that Ancient Man,
> The bright-eyed Mariner, and rueful woes
> Didst utter of the Lady Christabel.

It was here, if I remember right, that the poets
experienced the difficulty with the horse-collar, almost
as great a puzzle as Peter Pindar's apple-dumpling.

Midway between the Quantocks and the Mendips, and
a little to the south, are the Polden Hills, on which is
conspicuous a monument to Admiral Hood, "with
Keppel and with Rodney trained," when battle and murder were not so nearly related as rifles, secret rams, and
torpedoes have since made them.

These hills interfere with our view of Bridgwater, and
shut out more completely the historic ground of Sedgemoor and the Isle of Athelney. Near together as these
places are on the map and in the distant landscape, how
wide apart are their historic traditions ! the one associated with a name ever since distinguished as "*the*
infamous," the other with one as justly called The Great.
All the country southward in our view abounds with
traditions of King Alfred. Though tradition is out of
fashion since accurate science has come in, there may be
as much danger in fashionable doubt as in vulgar
credulity. Athelney at any rate is a spot where Alfred the
Great found refuge ; on yonder rising ground he surely
must have walked. But a still more important and
indisputably historical spot lies nearer within the range

Crooks Peak & Compton Bishop

of our view. Just over the slope between us and Glastonbury is Wedmore, where the famous treaty of peace was made in the year 878 ; " Weadmore," says Camden, "a village of King Alfred's, which he gave by his last will to his son Edward." Not far from the village is Mudgely, where the Saxon Kings had a summer residence, and where Alfred entertained his conquered and converted foe. Whatever the pagan's conversion to the Christian faith might be worth, he was certainly a believer in his enemy's Christian charity. He was impressed with the goodness of the Christian king, and seems to have respected it in deeds as well as words. Perhaps this is the only faith that answers the rule of *Quod semper, quod ubique, quod ab omnibus* (What has always, everywhere, and by all men, been believed). The treaty of Wedmore was a turning point in the history of England, and the spot where it was made should be at least as interesting as the site of a decisive battle. The Danes were baptised at Aller, near Athelney and Langport, but the " Chrism-losing " was held at Wedmore, and it was here, at Mudgley House, the site of which is still traceable, that the Danish king and thirty of his worthiest men were feasted for twelve days, when, according to the Saxon Chronicle, Alfred's steadfast heart beat high with solemn triumph that his greatest enemy had become a Christian, " and he honoured him and his freres with mickle fee."

Beyond Wedmore, toward the south-east, and rising abruptly from the plain, like Brent Knoll, is Glastonbury Tor, whereon the last of the abbots was hung by order of the first " Defender of the Faith." Abbot Whiting had educated nearly three hundred sons of nobles and gentlemen, sent to the Abbey for training in morals and

manners ; with what results would be an interesting subject of inquiry. At the foot of the Tor hill the town of
Glastonbury is partly visible, but the remains of the
famous Abbey are hidden by houses and trees. The Tor,
or Tower of St. Michael, originally a small oratory, was
rebuilt by St. Patrick, and beautified by his successors ;
but nothing remains of this ancient fabric. Arthur's connection with Glastonbury is rather poetical than historical.

> From this blest place immortal Arthur sprung,
> Whose wondrous deeds shall be for ever sung.

Here, it is said, were laid his mortal remains, in

> The island valley of Avilion,
> Deep-meadowed, happy, fair with orchard lawns,
> And bowery hollows crowned with summer sea.

So sings the bard who has last and most sweetly sung
his wondrous deeds.

The traditions of Glastonbury take us back far beyond
the days of King Arthur and the Knights of the Round
Table. According to Monkish legends—which may be
sometimes true—Joseph of Arimathea and a band of
Christian pilgrims came through Gaul to Britain. Perhaps they fell in with ships trading along the coast and
up the Bristol Channel ; but somehow or other they
found their way to the shallow bay between the Mendip
and Polden Hills, and landed on an "island in the blue
waters," called by the natives Ynys—gwydryn, and
also later Avalon or Apple Island, afterwards by the
Anglo-Saxons, Glaestingabyrig.

Hence Camden calls Glastonbury the "rise and
foundation of all religion in England." It was on
Wyrral, corrupted into Weary-all Hill that the saint
is said to have planted his staff, which grew into the

thorn-tree that for sixteen centuries afterwards bloomed at Christmas, and is still represented by a descendant of the parent staff which

> The good saint
> Arimathean Joseph, journeying, brought
> To Glastonbury, where the winter thorn
> Blossoms at Christmas, mindful of our Lord.

Southward, beyond Glastonbury, the view stretches away into the blue distance, including the famous Cadbury Hill, or *Camelot*, the last stronghold of Arthur and the Ancient Britons; and, on a clear day, the pointed hills of Montacute, near Yeovil, backed by more distant hills. *Mons-acutus* is the hill on whose top was found, in the Confessor's time, "the holy rood of Waltham." The higher hills beyond include another pair of twin heights, Lewesdon Hill and Pillesdon Pen, the highest ground in Dorsetshire (934 feet above the sea),

> That rival height south-west,
> Which like a rampire bounds the vale beneath.

It was on the side of this hill, near Crewkerne, that Wordsworth and his sister lived, from 1795 to 1797, and where they were visited by Coleridge, before they removed to Alfoxden. Miss Wordsworth was enraptured with "the lovely meadows, the combes, and the scenery on Pillesden, Lewesdon and Blackdown Hills."

When the air is clear, and the light is reflected from lines of cloud, casting their shadows across the scene, the variations of light and colour, and the soft aerial effect as the landscape fades into thin air, are beyond description exquisite.

> Peaceful as some immeasurable plain
> By the first beams of morning light impressed.

Hills have their own beauties, and so have plains. Both require clouds, as much as the heights and levels of human life.

The middle distance of our landscape is the rich alluvial land, once sea, then swamp, and now a land flowing with milk, and famed for Cheddar Cheese. Along the line of the Mendips are Shepton Mallet, a rich cheese district ; the City of Wells, hidden behind the bend of the hills ; Wookey, celebrated for its ancient hyæna den, and the " Hole " through which the river Axe emerges from its underground course from Priddy on the hill above. Priddy was a great mining centre, and, at the close of the last century, was the principal seat of the Mendip lead-mining industry. The Roman road from Sarum to Uphill is still traceable near Priddy, and many ancient remains are found in the neighbourhood.

From Wells, northward, following the line of railway, come in succession, Westbury and Lodge Hill, with the Ebbor Rocks, Stoke Rodney, Draycot, Cheddar, and its famous cliffs, and lastly, the old town of Axbridge, with its old charter, old church and old houses, so shut off from the north and east, under Shutshelf Hill, that it is said to be as safe for delicate lungs as Torquay or Madeira. Axbridge, we learn from the Wells register, was granted by the Crown to the Arch-deacon in 1209, and sold to the Bishop in 1226 for 100 marks.

We have now glanced at the panorama from Wavering Down. In some respects the higher hill of Callow commands a better view, especially of our own valley. It was a happy instinct that led the Mores to the hill-top with their schools and the multitudes they were trying to lift above the narrow views of the village. On high ground, the mind, as well as the body, "breathes a freer air," being raised above the small objects that surround the folk below. Their cares, their squabbles, and their schemes sink into littleness when seen from above ; parochial differences, happily rare in our valley, even the greater affairs which worry political life, and fill the daily newspapers with their dismal pictures of human frailty, look smaller from the mountain top. Can the greatest of them ever be worth the risk of turning scenes like these into fields of battle, with all the unutterable horrors of " mad war's dreadful strife ? "

As we look from these hills over one of the most purely rural scenes in England, without a single smoky town in all the wide view around, and contrast its pastoral beauty with the seats of manufacture and busy town life, the question arises, Will the simple healthy life of the rural swain be banished, or smothered, by the increasing power and smoke of iron and coal ? Will "the country" be all turned into town, or covered with the refuse of mines ? Will no open fields be left for health as well as food ? Will " the breezy call of incense-breathing morn " no more convey the scent of new-mown grass or fragrant clover ? Will hay-makings, and harvest homes, daisy-chains, and cowslip-balls, primrosing and Maying, black-berrying and nutting, be but traditions of the past, to be read by the future children of England amongst the curiosities of literature in the nursery books of their grandmothers, but no more to be seen in real life ?

Already the swallow twitters but seldom from the straw-built shed ; for tiles are cheaper than thatch, and the straw is turned into newspapers. The echoing horn sounds out of tune with steam whistles and winnowing

machines, and the cock's shrill clarion, which roused our
rude forefathers, is less welcome to their refined descendants.   If the farmer's usual estimate of Chanticleer be
true, he will soon be heard only in fanciers' pens and
poultry shows, where he and his owner together try to
crow over their neighbours.

The sleepy spirit of the rude forefathers has indeed
been roused by such rivalry.   Their sober wishes have
learned to stray sometimes beyond the bounds of sobriety.
Early rising and industry are measured by a different
standard now : the farmer and his equipage are not what
they used to be.   But though all were still willing along
the cool sequestered vale of life to keep the noiseless
tenor of their way, and help to scatter plenty o'er a
smiling land, there is not room in the smiling land for
the ever-increasing plenteousness of its population.   On
yonder channel ships are passing laden with the works
of British industry and skill, and bringing back the productions of foreign lands.   Some of them carry emigrants
to lands only known to our grandfathers as the abodes
of savages.   In those distant regions changes have taken
place greater and more rapid than our forefathers
dreamed of.   Great cities have sprung up where, but a
generation ago, were only forests and boundless wildernesses ; farms and plantations are supporting in comfort
and affluence thousands who might have been unborn, or
struggling with hopeless poverty in the land of their
fathers.

Hopeful visions of the future, the spirit of the song of
" Cheer, boys, cheer," may haply chase the sadder thoughts
of those who, from yonder ship, are taking a last long
lingering look at these familiar hills, the scenes of their

childhood, where their forefathers have dwelt, and their names have been known for many generations.

> Good bwye to the cot—on thy drashel, a-ma-be,
> I niver naw moor sholl my voot again zet ;
> The jassamy awver thy porch sweetly bloomin',
> Whauriver I goo, I shall niver vorget.

The strong men leave us, the weak remain behind. It is right that brain and muscle, as well as corn and cotton, should go where they are most wanted ; where they fetch the most money, for money is the world's criterion of value. Yet there may be good things which cannot be bought and sold for money. Increased means do not always mean increased happiness. Even earthly ease and contentment are no more at the command of the rich than of the poor. Selfishness is as dissatisfied in one as in the other. Useful employment is itself the right object of pursuit, and he that cannot find it at home should seek it abroad. But to refuse the work which "lieth nearest," with its customary reasonable reward, not for the sake of being more useful, but merely for the sake of more wages, is of a piece with the selfishness of *strikes*, and, like them, generally loses more than it gains The labourer, we are told, has a right to sell his labour at the best price he can get for it. Undoubtedly, and the best price will naturally be given where the thing sold is most wanted. But let the labourer look to the coin in which he is paid, He may find the higher price, paid under pressure and in a spirit as selfish as his own, will prove in the end a poorer reward than the old wages paid and received in the old kindly way. The offerings of mutual love and respect cannot be looked for where the old relations of master and man are ex-changed for those of buyer and seller of labour. If you

like the spirit of *Shylock*, have the bond : if you prefer
duty to promotion, follow the dutiful *Adam*.

> O good old man ; how well in thee appears
> The constant service of the antique world,
> When service sweat for duty, not for mead !
> Thou art not for the fashion of these times,
> Where none will sweat, but for promotion,
> And having that, do choke their service up
> Even with the having.
>   *As You Like It.*

WHERE are the mighty thunderbolts of war?
The Roman Cæsars and the Grecian chiefs,
The boast of story?

THE name of our Mendip Valley has had several supposed derivations. Collinson, in his *History of Somersetshire* (1791), says " the name signifies in the Saxon
language the Valley of Battles, the Danes and Saxons
having frequently encountered in these parts." But the
valley had probably a name long before the Danes in-
vaded it, and, though it may take its name from the Saxon
Winnan, strife, there are Keltic derivations, which seem
as likely. Of these, some authorities prefer the Cymric
Gwy or *Wy*, water, from which we have the rivers Wye,
Lludgwy and others, including, probably, the Conway,
Solway, and the rivers Wey in Dorsetshire, Hampshire, and Surrey. The Welsh names of water-fowl
are from the like source, as the goose from *gwydd*, and
the duck from *hywdd*. Wyns-combe would thus

D

mean a Valley of Waters or Springs, which would be an appropriate name; for although the valley cannot boast of any navigable stream, it abounds in springs of excellent water; and in ancient times, if not a watery valley, which it may have been, it was certainly situated between watery marshes.

Another, and equally probable derivation is from the Keltic *Gwent*—open, from which come Gwentchester, now Winchester, and Caer-went in Monmouth, in the ancient kingdom of Gwent, a name still used in that district.

It may be objected that a name descriptive of an open country is not applicable to a valley shut in by hills; but a *combe* is not a *glen*; it is a Keltic or Cymric name *Cwm*, for a bowl-shaped vale or basin, which is quite the character of the Vale of Winscombe. We must notice, also, that the name of the Hundred is Winterstoke, and it contains Winterhead and Winthill, which last name, in the Ordnance Map, is called Vent-hill, and is the latinized form given by the Romans to other Keltic names, as Venta for the ancient British Gwent, Venta-Silurum for Caer-went, and Venta-Belgarum for Gwent-chester or Winchester.

Win-ter-stoke may possibly come from *Gwent*, open, and *Dwr*, water, and mean an enclosure surrounded by open water, Win-ter-head being the head of the valley. But Collinson derives it from Winthill, where, he says, "according to tradition, a battle was fought between the Saxons and Danes."

We have therefore three not unlikely interpretations of Winscombe—Battle Valley, the Valley of Springs, and Open Vale; to which may be added a fourth, which Wins-combe folk will hardly repudiate—Winsome Valley, from the Saxon *Wynsum*, cheerful and fair.

Whatever may have been the real origin and meaning of the name, whether taken from strife or water, openness or pleasantness, there can be little doubt that contention came before contentment, and that our valley suffered with the country on either side, when the camps on the surrounding hills were full of armed warriors, and when

> The Norseman's king was on the sea,
> The leader of the helmets, he.
>
> .   .   .   .   .   .
>
> Whistles the war-axe in its swing,
> O'er head the whizzing javelins sing,
> Helmet and shield and hauberk ring ;
> The air-song of the lance is loud,
> The arrows pipe in darkening cloud.

But there are no Somersetshire sagas to commemorate the deeds of our Mendip Valley heroes. With plenty of priests to shrive them, at least in Christian times, they had no scalds to celebrate their fame. They rest among the unhonoured dead, until the spirit of a Scott or Macaulay shall breath through Fame's trumpet, and summon them to live again in some new *Tales of a Grandfather*, or *Lays of Ancient Britain*.

Long before Christianity was brought to our shores, Keltic settlers had established themselves on the Mendip Hills, and, with or without Phœnician help, had discovered those metallic treasures which long afterwards attracted the Romans, as they had the Phœnicians, whose ships the Romans are said to have followed.

With the decline and fall of the Roman Empire came the Saxon barbarians, driving the Keltic Britons westward, " from the Axe to the Parrett, and from the Parrett

to the Tamar," * and then the more barbarous Danes
whose exploits are part of English history. During
their inroads, Winscombe may well have been a battle
valley, though there appears to be no record of a fight
nearer than Battlebury, near Brent, where the Danes, who
had taken possession of Worlebury, in attempting to
join some newly arrived bands, were defeated by King
Alfred, and compelled to surrender the Camp to the
Saxons, A.D. 998.

This famous Worlebury camp is, however, of vastly
greater antiquity than the times of the Saxons and
Danes. Even the Roman remains in it are found near
the surface. Beneath them are the bones and weapons
of a much more ancient people, with evidences of fierce
conflict, and under these again, have been found burnt
fir-wood, roofing and thatch, shewing that previous
occupiers had been burnt out before the iron-armed people
took possession. Still deeper, at the bottom of the pits
occupied in succession by these three nations, lay a quantity of sling-stones, chert arrow-heads, rude pottery, stone
cooking plates, and heaps of remains of pulse and other
food used by the primitive inhabitants. Who these
primitive people were, whence they came, how they got
here, and why they came at all, are questions easier asked
than answered, but not on that account less interesting.

An old implement of un-warlike character was found
at Max in 1865—a stone hammer-head, seven inches
by four, weighing 2½lbs, and having an eye-hole for the
handle. The point is broken off, and the edges are
much worn, which may possibly indicate that the tool
was worn out and thrown away. It was turned up in

* Prof. E. A. Freeman's " Old English History."

·draining some boggy ground, and is still in the possession
·of the owner of the Max estate. This implement belongs,
I presume, to what is called the Neolithic or New Stone
Period. Its rounded form and polished surface indicate a
more civilized race than that of the Palæolithic or Flint
Implement Period ; of which relics have also been found
"in the valley of the Axe, in a place now covered by
twenty or thirty feet of sand and gravel."* These ruder
implements are believed to be the weapons of a race of
hunters even more barbarous than the Cave men, and,
perhaps, the earliest of the human race in this country.
What is very remarkable is, that similar implements are
found not only in all parts of Europe, but in Asia, Africa,
and even in America.†

Remains of two ancient races of men are found in the
tumuli or barrows on the Mendip Hills, the round-shaped
barrows containing the skulls and bones of a round-
headed race, with bronze spear-heads, amber beads and
·coarse clay cups ; the long shaped barrows containing
relics of a long-headed tribe, with only stone implements.
A skull and other relics of this tribe have been discovered
in a recently opened cave at Uphill.‡ They appear
to have been overcome by the Roundheads with their
bronze weapons, whose burnt ashes and spear-heads are
found in the barrows on Blackdown.

The Longheads are believed to be of the Iberian or
Basque race, called also Euskarians, a name still trace-
able in the Basque provinces of Spain, as in Viscaya and
Biscay. These people are supposed to have come from

---

* Prof. Boyd Dawkins, Archæological Proceedings, 1883.

† Idem.

Natu·al History Journal, March 1882.

Asia at a very remote period, taking much the same course as that followed ages afterwards by the Moors, skirting the shores of the Mediterranean Sea, or Valley, as it may then have been, and bringing their flocks and herds with them; for they are believed to have come before Britain was separated from the European continent, and to have brought from the East the original ox, sheep, goat, swine, and dog.

The Iberian or Euskarian race appears to have been overcome by a more modern tribe of Kelts, who were in turn overpowered by the Gauls or Belgæ, who encountered the Romans. These were a well-armed and warlike race, and so well-skilled in the management of their war-chariots as to be no mean opponents of Julius Cæsar himself. They were not the wild savages some have supposed. The Romans, however, introduced a higher civilization, with improved buildings, cities, and roads, and took possession of the ancient British camps, especially that of Dolbury; which was afterwards used by the Danes, of whom there are still lingering traditions, as "the Redshanks."

The Roman road from Old Sarum to Uphill is still traceable in several places in this neighbourhood. It passes over a wild district on the sides of Blackdown, and then by Shipham and across the present Bristol road at the 14th mile-stone, following the lane to Slough Pits, which was a British station. Thence it runs along the sides of Winthill and Bleadon hills to Uphill. At Charter-house—so called from a cell there of the original Carthusian monastery at Witham — are some ancient lead-works, where the refuse left by the Romans has been, till lately, smelted with profit by modern improved means There is reason to believe that these lead mines were taken by the Romans on their first coming into the country, and were probably part of the mineral wealth that first made them wish to possess these islands. The Romans seem to have carried the lead to Sarum, and thence to their seaport in the Isle of Wight ; as is shown by pigs of lead found on the road, with the Roman marks upon them. But the mines were worked before the Romans seized them, and the Belgæ whom they plundered may have taken them from an earlier race, who possibly learned the art of mining, as well as the value of the metals, from the Phœnicians.

There was an ancient British track before the Romans improved it into a road, leading from Blackdown, by Dolbury camp, and along the hills of Banwell and Bleadon to Kewstoke. The oft-quoted tradition—

> If Dolbyri dygged ware
> Of golde should be the share,

is supposed to have meant that Dolbury was a store-place for metallic wealth, waiting disposal to the merchants. If so, the metals stored there would be the zinc or calamine of the neighbourhood, and possibly lead from Blackdown. The export merchants might be the Phœnicians, who are believed to have come from their colony at Cadiz, to Cornwall for tin, and may probably have rounded the Land's End, and found their way along the coast of Devon and Somerset, as the Northmen did ages afterwards. The men who could sail from the Levant and through the Pillars of Hercules to the Tin islands of the Atlantic, would be likely to extend their navigation and discoveries in search of traffic and wealth. From the Cassiterides they might, intentionally, or by chance, sail along the north coast of Cornwall, and find their way into the Severn sea, and to the port of Kewstoke, connected with the ancient British Camp of Worlebury. There they might hear of the Mendip metals, and open a trade with the native miners.

The brass or bronze of the ancients was made of copper and tin, and it is doubted whether they were acquainted with zinc, a metal said to be unknown before the sixteenth century ; but ancient coins are said to have been found containing zinc. Probably there may have been but little knowledge of the difference between the various white metals known to the merchants of Tyre and Tarshish—" With silver, iron, tin, and lead they traded in thy fairs."* A silver ring of Phœnician work similar to those still met with in Palestine, was recently found at Worlebury.

Sir C. Hawkins, in his account of the tin trade of the ancients, mentions a mirror composed of copper, tin and lead, and Aubrey speaks of pewter having been ploughed up near the ancient barrows at Amesbury. Of the Phœnicians coming to Britain for tin, there is little or no doubt ; may we therefore venture to suggest these notes and queries—Was the Colossus of Rhodes in part a Cornish tin man ? Were Tyrian tankards made of Britannia metal ? Did King Hiram drink out of native pewter ?

Relics of ancient inhabitants—we dare not say aborigines—have been discovered in the caves of this neighbourhood. In one of these in Burrington combe, explored in 1795, and again by Dr. Buckland in 1820, were found in a recess near the entrance, fifty human skeletons lying in regular order, the heads against the

---

* Ezekiel xxvii.

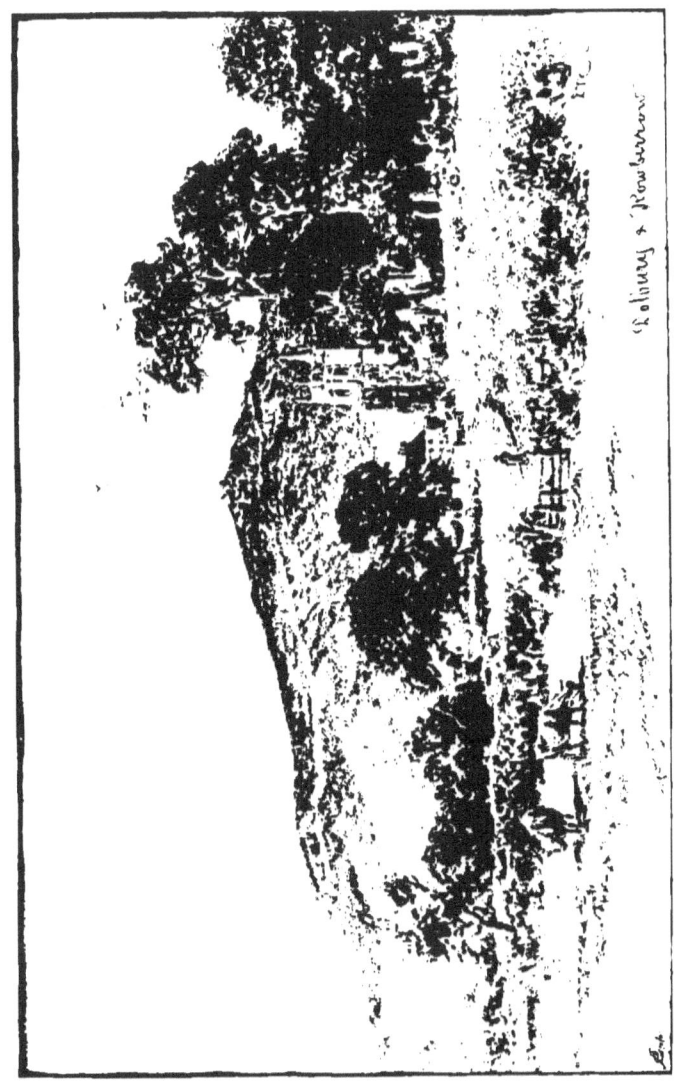

"Johnny + Rowburn"

side of the cave, and the feet towards the centre. The
bodies do not seem to have been buried; but some of the
skulls and bones were encrusted with stalagmite, and
the same substance had nearly closed the cave's mouth.
The later search discovered traces of charcoal, mutton
bones, flint knives, and what is more curious, a set of
counters, dice, or *tesserœ*, used by the Romans and other
ancients in games. The skulls collected by Dr. Buckland
have been lost, and no account has been given of them
to show to what race of men they belonged. The flint
knives would indicate an early date, while the *tesserœ*
show a connection with men more advanced in çiviliza-
tion. The discoverer of the cave seems to have considered it a catacomb, used, like those of Paris and Rome,
for both living and dead. It is difficult to understand
how fifty unembalmed and uncoffined bodies could have
been entombed in such a way, unless at the same time.
The account seems rather to suggest the idea that the
men had their dwelling in the cave, and, after playing
at counters by their charcoal fire, with the door shut
to keep out the cold and hyænas, had fallen asleep and
been stifled.

Another of the Burrington caves was explored by
Mr. Boyd Dawkins and others, and called by them Whit-
combe's Hole. It is at a height of 135 feet from the
bottom of the combe, and is well fitted for a place of
concealment, being invisible both from above and from
below, while it commands a view down the combe. It
contained bones of wolves, foxes, badgers, hares, rabbits,
goats, stags, and the Keltic short-horned ox. These
might simply indicate a wild beasts' den ; but the bones,
with one exception, had evidently been broken by the
hand of man, and not by the teeth of beasts. Besides

this evidence of human occupation, there were found fragments of a rude urn of coarse black ware, with a bent piece of iron resembling those used to strengthen the corners of wooden chests or coffins in the Gallo-Roman graves on the banks of the Somme. Supposing the urn to be sepulchral, and of the Roman period, the occupation of the cave must have been long anterior ; for the interment was made in the mass of earth mixed with bones and charcoal, the relics of the former occupants. These ancient cave-dwellers appear to have lived at some unknown period, between the Roman conquest and the time of the great elk, rhinoceros, and their contemporaries.*

Traces of human inhabitants have been found in other Mendip caves, in Burrington combe and elsewhere, and there can be no doubt of the fact, that "when the caverns at Wookey Hole were dens of hyænas, savages with their rude missiles of chert and flint, hunted the Irish elk, the rein-deer and the bison, on the slopes of Mendip ; or defended themselves against the cave-bear and the cave-tiger, or the fury of the enraged mammoth and rhinoceros.†"

Whether these savages were degraded wanderers from more civilized tribes ; whether they wandered from the east before "the age of great cities," or even before the "golden age," are among the questions which make pre-historic speculations so entertaining. Prof. Boyd Dawkins, to whom we are indebted for a most able and interesting account of the "evidence of caves respecting the early inhabitants of Europe," says "the Palæolithic

---

* *Vide* Som. Arch. Soc. Proceedings, 1864, and Dawkins's Cave Hunting.

† Boyd Dawkins, Somerset Archæological Proceedings, 1864.

people or peoples arrived in Europe along with the peculiar fauna of that age, and after dwelling here for a length of time, which is to be measured by vast physical and climatal changes, finally disappeared, leaving behind as their representatives the Eskimo tribes of Arctic America. There is no evidence that they were inferior in intellectual capacity to many of the lower races of the present time, or more closely linked to the lower animals. The traces which they have left behind tell us nothing as to the truth or falsehood of the doctrine of evolution."*

There are, however, two very curious facts, that seem more consistent with the supposition of a degraded race, than with the theory of evolution from a lower to a higher kind of life. Some of the most ancient of these primitive cave-dwellers had a surprising talent for delineating animals on bone and ivory. This would seem more like a traditional or hereditary art, descended from a civilized state of society, than an original talent evolved from a state otherwise barbarous. On the theory of evolution we might expect such a faculty to be further developed in succeeding races; but that is not the case. "The later stone-using pre-historic races did not inherit it.†" It seems to have been preserved amongst the Esquimaux, but not improved. The other fact is of a different kind. The later Cave men appear to have practised cannibalism, which can hardly have been hereditary or instinctive. It is contrary to the nature of the higher animals, including the apes, and is only explicable on the ground of desperate need, or moral degradation.

* Boyd Dawkins's Cave Hunting.
† Stevens's Stone Period.

Another familiar but important fact is the loss of instinctive and hereditary knowledge even of his proper food and of the simple arts of walking and swimming, which man has to learn with difficulty, while no other creature needs such instruction.

> Reasoning at every step he treads,
> Man yet mistakes his way,
> While meaner things whom instinct leads,
> Are rarely known to stray.

The human race may have begun very much as the individual man does now, the animal part first developed,* and the mind by education; but the capacity for mental and spiritual development must have existed, and there is no evidence of any such capacity in mere animals. Assuming the truth of the tradition of the *Golden Age*, there is no need to imagine it a state of luxury, or what is now called refinement, with its manifold forms of selfishness and pride. Men might then care less for mineral gold, than for the golden rule of life. The Golden Age would be ages before the age of great cities. If no traces of such a people should ever be found in the regions where they would probably dwell, the inference would be, not that they never existed, but that they dwelt in tents—as in after ages some did who entertained angels†— building neither palaces for the living, nor sepulchres for the ashes of the dead.

There seems to be no doubt that central Asia was the cradle of humanity, by whatever process the human being was created. From that centre, as population increased, it would spread, and would follow the means of subsistence.

---

* That is not first which is spiritual, &c —1 Cor. v. 46.

† Genesis, xviii, 1, 2. Hebrews, xiii, 2.

Hunters would pursue venison, fishers would trace the rivers, herdsmen and shepherds would accompany their herds and flocks wherever pasturage was found. These wanderers would turn their backs upon the rising civilization of the east : while Nineveh and other great cities of antiquity were building, they would still follow their primitive habits, or lapse into ruder life, amid the dangers of the chase. While game and pasturage remained unlimited, necessity, the mother of invention, would give birth only to means of capture and destruction, and the preparation of food and clothing. Europe would thus be gradually occupied by more or less barbarous people, until they reached Ultima Thule on the shores of the Atlantic. As population increased, and land became limited, disputes would arise between hunters and herdsmen, tribe and tribe ; the caves which had sheltered the few, would give place to camps of refuge for the many, and in this way may have begun the hill camps, afterwards occupied by the historical Kelts, Belgæ, Romans, Saxons, and Danes.

The counterpart of these may be seen in the *Oppida* of Gaul, familiar to readers of Cæsar's Commentaries, and which appear to have been large camps of refuge, capable of receiving within their fortifications, in times of disturbance, the whole population of the neighbouring district.

* *Vide* Cæsar's Seventh Campaign in Gaul, with Notes by Rev. W. Cookworthy Compton, M.A.

IV.—MONKISH TIMES.

silent life of prayer,
Praise, fast, and alms, and leaving for the cowl
The helmet in an abbey far away.

THE HOLY GRAIL.

THE Norman Survey, or "Domesday Book," prepared in the eleventh century, has a long chapter, headed, *Terra Sanctæ Mariæ Glastinburiensis*, in which, among the possessions of the rich abbey of Glastonbury, the manor of Winscombe is included. It was given to the monks by Queen Ælswithe, under Dunstan's influence, about A.D. 970, and remained in their possession about 250 years. How it came to the Dean and Chapter of Wells is a curious piece of ecclesiastical history. When Richard Cœur de Lion was captured in Austria, on his return from Palestine, and kept prisoner by the Emperor Henry VI., the Chancellor Sabaric or Savaricus, a cousin of the Emperor's, obtained from the captive king, in return for various services, the promise of the bishopric of Bath. Not content with this, he persuaded the Emperor to demand, as a condition of the king's release, that the abbey of Glastonbury should be added to the bishopric, making the see Bath and Glastonbury. To this, also, the unfortunate king reluctantly consented. The Pope's sanction was obtained "by hook and by crook,"—that is, by the captive king and the Archbishop of Canterbury— and the abbot was caught with a hook baited with the see of Worcester. After the death of Savaric, who was succeeded by Jocelin in 1206, the monks of Glastonbury applied to King John and Pope Honorius III. for the restoration of their independence ; which they obtained on the 17th of May, 1219. They had leave to elect their own abbot, and the Bishop of Bath and Glastonbury took the title and see of Bath and Wells. The independence of the convent, however, was gained at the price of surrendering the manors of Wynscombe, Blackford-in-Wedmore, Pucklechurch, and Cranmore, all of which remained with the bishop.

Jocelin was then busy completing the cathedral at Wells, which was dedicated to the Apostle St. Andrew on the day of St. Romanus, October 23rd, A.D. 1239. On "the morrow of that day, Wynescombe manor and church were given to the *Communa*, reserving a payment of five marks to the vicar, to be appointed by the Dean and Chapter." *

In 1241, on the resignation of Walter of Cossington, the Dean and Chapter were inducted as perpetual rectors

---

* A mark was valued at 160 pennies, or 13s. 4d. At this time a sheep was worth from 5d. to 1s.

of Winscombe, and so continued in spite of many at-
tempts of the monks to regain possession. In 1256,
other parcels of land and wood were given to the church,
and the charters contain the names of Stephen of Sandford, Henry of Wynterton, Victor de la Hale, Robert
of the Mill *(de Molendino)*, Henry of the Barton, Helias
of Ford, and Edward of Sidecote.*   Wynterton may be
the same place as Wintreth or Winterhead. Hale and
Sidcot, as well as Sandford and Barton, are familiar
places.   Robert de Molendino would be the old miller
of Max, and Ford was the manor or lordship of "Ford-
juxta-Winscombe;" conveyed in 1474, as Collinson tells
us, by Sir Stephen Glover and others to Reginald
Stourton and others, and in 1526, to John Mawdley,
whose son conveyed it, in 1576, to John Cocke.   Thirty
years later, we read of the estate as "the manors of
Foord and Woodborough, alias Foord-juxta-Winscombe."
   During the Wars of the Roses, Winscombe was the
demesne of Sir John Tiptoft, or Tibetot, and his son, who
became Marquis of Worcester in the reign of Edward IV.
As a zealous Yorkist he was executed on the restoration
of Henry VI., being one of the few persons of note who
suffered on that occasion.   Hume speaks of him as "an
accomplished person, in an age and country where the
nobility valued themselves on ignorance as their privilege,
and left learning to monks and schoolmasters."
   The hamlet of Winterhead, called in the Norman
survey Wintreth, was part of the vast possessions of the
Bishop of Coutances,† and was afterwards "held under the

---

* Somerset Notes, Vol. I., page 50.

† *Terra Episcopi Constantiensis.* The Roman name was modernized
                    by the Normans into *Coutance.*

Crooks Peak from Chinaman

king " in the reign of Edward I., by the family of Arthur
of Clapton in Gordano. Later it came to the Berkleys,
Botreaux, and Chedders. The last named family also
held of the Dean and Chapter of Wells the chief estate
in the hamlet of Sandford, "sometimes called Sand-
ford-juxta-Banwell," but belonging to the parish of
Winscombe.

At a more remote date, namely, in the time of
King Alfred, we read that the king granted to his
tutor and biographer, Asser, "the monasteries of
Kongresberie and Banwille," otherwise Congresbury and
Banwell.

The Banwell convent is believed to have stood on a
site known as Chapel Leaze on the south or Winscombe
side of Banwell hill, there called Winthill. The founda-
tions of a large building, and many skeletons, lying east
and west, were discovered there some years ago, but before
much scientific interest in these subjects had been
aroused. The original building was destroyed in one of
the Danish inroads, and the convent removed to Banwell
on the other side of the hill.

From the original monastery, Crooks Peak would be
so striking an elevation as to suggest a site for a cross or
crucifix ; either as a sign of Christianity to the invading
Danes, or as a place of pilgrimage or penance, like the
Calvarienberge, or Mount Calvaries, still common in
Roman Catholic countries. We may therefore, without
extravagance, picture *Crux* Peak, whither pilgrims of
pleasure now resort, as the scene of pilgrimages of a
different kind, with processions of monks, or, it may be, of
nuns, with crosses and banners from Banwell abbey, on one
side of the valley, and the Fraternity of the Blessed

E

Virgin on the other; perhaps, also, from Cross on the
other side of the hill.*

I have ventured to suggest that Crooks Peak may have
had its name from the monks, but there are several other
possible derivations.   It may have been a resort of the
shepherds with their crooks; or the name may, more
probably, come from the Cymric *craig*, a rock or crag, or
from the Saxon *cruc* or *cryc*, a creek, which may be the
common root of creek and crook, the radical idea being
curvature.   Crooks Peak, as it is usually called, or Crook
Peak, as it is oftener printed, is a conspicuous landmark,
and would be a guide to the creek leading into the valley
at its foot.   But the commonest interpretation may be
the true one, though that is not always the case.   The
prevalent belief is that the name comes from the resemblance of the crest of the hill to the crooks, formerly
used for loading pack-horses.   This resemblance is striking enough from some points of view, and may have
been more so in the days of pack-horses.   Objects
familiar to travellers have given names to other hills, as
in the well-known name of Saddleback, the common
name of Blencathra in Cumberland.   On the other hand,
there is a tendency to invent meanings, and to modify
names to suit them; as *Wirral* hill, near Glastonbury,
has been turned into Weary-all-hill, and *Maen-hafod*—
Manheve in Domesday Book—into Minehead, where no
mines are to be found.   Similarly, *Mendip*, from the
same root—meaning rocky, has been supposed to mean

---

* Cross is a hamlet in the adjoining parish of Compton Episcopi, the
church of which was consecrated by Bishop Jocelin in 1236, and endowed
with ten acres of the moor enclosed.   He granted Helias, chaplain, canon,
and parson of Compton, the right to run eight oxen with the bishop's oxen
in the pastures of the bishop's manor.   *Vide* Canon Church's *Jocelin*.

Minedeep, an inappropriate name where the mines are shallow " groves," and the miners were called " grovers."

Of the monkish times, or middle ages, are the old stone crosses numerous in Somersetshire, and more or less preserved in many places in this neighbourhood. Crosses, or fragments of them, remain at Loxton, Bleadon, Compton-Bishop, and Weare. At Burrington, only the socket is left, and that in a different place from the original site. The parish register states that the steps, being in a ruinous state, were taken down in 1805, by order of the vestry, and given to the parish clerk " to make groins in a house erecting for his residence."*

At Axbridge, the destruction of the old cross has been still more complete, nothing being left of it but a fragment of the shaft, now in the rector's garden.

These crosses are probably of the fourteenth century. A more ancient relic is preserved at Rowberrow, supposed to be of the eleventh, but believed by Mr. Pooley to be much older. It is a remarkably perfect example of the serpentine ornament, called *Schlangenzierath*,† a stone slab with a well-cut figure upon it of a lizard-like creature with many convolutions of a long tail. It was dug up in the church-yard, and has been fixed in the outer wall of the church porch, where it is much exposed to the weather, and is not very conspicuous.

At Congresbury are the remains of a church-yard cross of the fourteenth century, and a more complete village cross of later date, and at Yatton are the socket and steps of a cross of unusual size and elaborate structure, of which a record remains that "the New Cross was erected

---

* Pooley's " Old Crosses of Somerset."
† Pooley.

A.D. 1499, and cost eighteen pounds," equal to about £200 at the present day.

There are traces, or traditions, of other old crosses, including three at Wrington, which have gradually disappeared ; the last having been used in building a bridge about sixty years ago. Complaints had been made to the vestry that the cross was "a meeting place for idle boys." *O tempora, O mores !* There were no School Boards in those days !

It is worth remembering that the river Wring, from which Wrington takes its name,* has long been called the Yeo, the name of several other streams in this county, and meaning simply, "the river." It is the Saxon *ea,* which probably comes from the same root as the Keltic *gwy,* and is the origin of the Norman *eau,* all meaning *water*: gwy, wye, yeo, yo, yow, ea, eau. Old Somerset folk still call ale *yal,* acre *yacker,* early *yarly,* earth *yarth,* and what the Normans called *eau,* they would call *yo.*

We have the principal stream, or Yeo, at Congresbury, with the water-courses in the Marsh, called in the ordnance map, Bale Yeo, and in our parish map, the Liddy Yeo ; and in the south, falling into the Axe, are the Mark Yeo and the Lox Yeo, the lower end of our Winscombe Brook.

---

* According to the late learned Prebendary Scarth. Wring-bridge is mentioned in Abbot Beer's *Terrier,* A.D. 1514

A little, lonely church in days of yore,
For so they say, these books of ours.
                              THE HOLY GRAIL.

WINSCOMBE CHURCH, viewed in connection with its surroundings, is one of the most beautiful of the many fine churches of Somersetshire. Standing on the north side of a green knoll of Wavering Down, it is a strikingly picturesque object from many points of view, the picture being completed by the grand old yew tree and the landscape around. The variety of form and colour in the architecture and masonry of the tower, nave and porch, are as pleasing to the artist as they are interesting to the archæologist. Few scenes of the kind can surpass the

view of Winscombe Church and Yew Tree on a moonlight evening, when

> The silver light, which, hallowing tree and tower,
> Sheds beauty and deep softness o'er the whole.

The architecture of the church, Perpendicular Gothic,
has been a subject of much discussion, from the difficulty
of reconciling the style with the reputed date of the
building—the middle of the fourteenth century. For it
is stated on the high authority of Bishop Godwin, that
the church was entirely rebuilt by Bishop Ralph de
Salopia, who died in the year 1363. The transition from
the Decorated to the Perpendicular style had then begun,
and it is not denied that Winscombe may possibly be an
early example of the change of style. Bishop Edyngton,
who began the alteration of Winchester Cathedral into
the Perpendicular, died in 1366, by which time, it is said,
" the great principles of that style were fully established."*
But the other similar churches of this neighbourhood,
Axbridge, Banwell, Cheddar, and Wrington, are generally
dated a century later, and that would be taken as the
probable date of Winscombe, were it not for the statement of Godwin that Ralph de Salopia, who died in 1363,
" *Ecclesiam prœterea condidit de Winscomb.*"
This statement of Godwin's, which has been appended
to Ralph's tomb in Wells Cathedral, for the information
of visitors, appears to be founded solely on the documents in the library of the Dean and Chapter; in which
we read of Bishop Ralph, " *Hic, etiam, construxit de novo*
capellam de Wynescombe, et totam curiam de Claverton,

---

* Parker's " A B C of Gothic Architecture."

et unam cameram honestam valde sumptuosam apud Evercrich." All these works would therefore seem to have been improvements of the bishop's own manor-houses, and we learn from Collinson, that his palace or manor-house at Wiveliscombe, originally built by his predecessor, John de Drokensford, was greatly improved by Ralph de Salopia.

The Wells record goes on to mention the death of the Bishop at *Wynelescombe*, or *Wyvelescombe*, where it is well-known the bishop lived and died. The names in the manuscript look so much alike as to suggest the probability of an accidental omission of the letters *le* in the first, and that the two names are really the same. This is confirmed by other documentary evidence. In a charter of Henry III, 1256, Wiveliscombe is spelt *Wynelescombe*, and in 1331, a visit of the archbishop to the same place, is recorded by Walter de Hemingford, who spells the name variously, *Wenelliscombe*, *Wynescombe*, and *Wivescombe.** It is now commonly pronounced *Wils-combe.*

It would seem, therefore, that Godwin's incorrect quotation may be safely rejected. *Capellam* is not *ecclesiam*, and there can be little doubt that the *capella de novo constructa*, was the bishop's chapel at Wiveliscombe, and not the church at Winscombe.†

It is, moreover, certain that Ralph did not re-build the *chancel* at Winscombe, for that part of the walls of Jocelin's church, in the Early Lancet period, remained when the chancel was restored in 1864. Some fragments

* See " Archæological Proceedings," 1883, page 24.

† See also " Somerset Notes and Queries." Vol. I., page 93 and 147.

were then found of a still older Norman church, to which the Early English Chancel appeared to have been added.

The documents belonging to the Dean and Chapter of Wells record that on the 26th of August, A.D. 1236, "Wynescombe Church was dedicated by Bishop Jocelin, in honour of St. James," and, at the same time, endowed by Henry de Lovesestre with 4½ acres in the manor of Sandford, and a meadow to the parson of Wynescombe, with an adjoining alder coppice, "*alnetum suum.*"* Whether the church had then been newly re-built, or only dedicated on its transfer to the bishopric, does not appear. However that might be, the present edifice is not of that period. No records appear to have been yet discovered of the building of the present tower and nave. The tower is of much better masonry than the nave, which would seem to be of a later date, as its walls abut on the finished buttresses of the tower. It was, however, not unusual to build the tower apart, that the jarring of the bells might not shake the whole fabric. Possibly, the present tower may be of the time of Bishop Harewell, 1366—86, when the south-west tower of Wells was built, and the nave, as it stands, may be of the time of Bishop Beckington, 1443-64, who is supposed to have built the church, as well as the bishop's palace, at Banwell.

On the south side of the tower of Winscombe church, lying on the grass outside, is an empty stone coffin, on which lay a slab dating from the fourteenth century, but not the proper lid of the coffin, which was quite empty and uncovered when found under the pavement of the

* See Canon Church's account of Bishop Jocelin in the "Proceedings of the Society of Antiquaries," 1888.

Winscombe
1889

church, near the spot where the pulpit now stands. It
may have contained the mortal remains of some person who
had edified the church in one way or the other, or, possibly,
of a superior of the convent hard by, whose memory has,
unfortunately, not been perpetuated. Or can it have been
the coffin of Henry de Lovesestre ?

The church tower is 95 feet high, in four stages of remarkable elegance ; the gradual lessening of the stages
with inclined buttresses, giving Winscombe the advantage
in lightness and " soaring " effect over Banwell and Cheddar, which bear much resemblance to it.

The eastern face of the tower, over the nave, has the
image of the patron saint, St. James, dressed as a pilgrim
and looking eastward. On the west side is a tankard
with lid opened upon the handle, and holding a lily, the
flower of the Blessed Virgin.

The west door was blocked up at the restoration in
1864, as well as the west entrance to the south aisle,
where a modern vestry had been built, which was in use
until that date.

The porch is large, and had a room over it, the floor of
which has long since disappeared, and nothing is known
of the use of the room. It might have been a vestry, there
being no other, or a depository for parish records. It
has been suggested that the room might be occupied
by an anchorite, or penitent, or a leper; but that is mere
conjecture.

The Font, now placed under the tower in front of the
closed west door, is the original rough stone structure of
the early church.

There are several old windows in the church, of considerable interest, and some beautiful memorial windows
of recent date. They are briefly described in Canon

Jackson's excellent Handbook to Weston-super-Mare, from which the following particulars are taken :—

> CHANCEL, *north*, a very beautiful window ; centre, St. Peter with keys ; *west*, figure with staff (St. John, almoner ?) ; *east*, St. Benedict with aspergillum or sprinkler—a design seldom seen. NORTH AISLE, Catherine of Sienna, the Virgin holding her Son, crowned ; on the east, St. James the Less, as pilgrim, with staff and scallop shell. *East* end of same aisle a fine four-light window, St. John with book ; a crucifixion with *Filius Dei*, *ora pro nobis* ; the Mother of our Lord, her hands folded in prayer ; and Anthony, the Hermit, with his swine, bell, book, and staff. On the *South* side, the costumes should be observed, and the central figure of a bishop compared with the arch-bishops on either hand, all being in characteristic canonicals.
>
> The large modern window in the Tower, and the Munich window in the chancel, are justly admired as beautiful specimens of their class.

Winscombe bells are often spoken of with affection by old villagers in distant lands, and by old scholars of Sidcot School.

> Those Winscombe bells ! those Winscombe bells !
> How many a tale their music tells
> Of youth, and home, and that sweet time
> When last I heard their soothing chime !

The church music was of a rustic kind until modernized by recent vicars. Sixty years ago, the singing was led and supported by a village band consisting of two clarionets, a bassoon, and a serpent. An old villager, who gives this information, regrets the change. " Ah ! " says he, " that wer a quire, *that* wer : I wish we had the like o' he now." The performers were his own kindred, and, perhaps, kept up a greater interest in the music than is the case now. They were succeeded by a seraphine, the gift of Vicar Cobley, and that was followed by a harmonium, which survived the old vicar, but was in turn superseded by a small church organ, obtained through the exertions of Vicar Harkness, who also improved the choir under a competent teacher. The organ was played by ladies of the congregation until 1889, when it was succeeded by the fine modern instrument at present in use under a professional organist.

The choir, now surpliced, is creditable to a village church ; but the usual difficulty is experienced in keeping it up, and securing regular attendance at the choral practice. People long used to the simple old country ways may not like the introduction of surplices, and the procession of clergy and choristers; but where the singers are seated conspicuously apart from the rest of the congregation, it seems more orderly that they should appear in a suitable costume *as choristers*, rather than come in promiscuously, and not always reverently, as the village boys and tradesmen familiar to us in their working-day personality. Even cathedral choristers, whose surpliced forms in the middle distance harmonize so well with their voices, are apt to betray the frailties of mortality when stripped of their sacred vestments. If that be so in cathedral cities, what is to be expected in a rural village ?

At Easter in the present year, 1892, a reredos of carved oak, in three panels, with a new altar cloth, a brazen cross, and a pair of brass vases, have been presented to the church and added to the chancel, chiefly through the exertions of the curate, the Rev. A. F. Drake.

That yew-tree's shade,
Where heaves the turf in many a mouldering heap,
Each in his narrow cell for ever laid,
The rude forefathers of the hamlet sleep.

PRETTY poetry ; but what does it mean ? The empty stone coffin that lies outside the church is a curious comment upon the poet's text.

There is a calm for those who weep,
A rest for weary pilgrims found—
They softly lie and sweetly sleep
Low in the ground.

"Ashes to ashes, and dust to dust," is said over the graves ; while on the tombstones, and in poetry, the dust and ashes are mistaken for the immortal men.

Perhaps such thoughts as these may sometimes arise in the minds of some who sit under the yew-tree's shade, as their forefathers have done for many generations ; and who may like to think of their departed friends, and their own approaching departure, with pleasanter views of the coming state than the prospect of lying under the turf for ages of useless unconsciousness. Perhaps some of them as they enjoy the friendly shade of this ancient tree, and observe its evergreen boughs still full of life, may regard it rather as an emblem of immortality, than as a

> Cheerless, unsocial plant that loves to dwell
> Midst skulls and coffins, epitaphs and tombs.

Other some, perhaps, while fondly thinking of their departed friends as living, intelligent, loving souls, rather than dust and ashes, may haply wonder why skulls and coffins, epitaphs and tombs, should be connected with temples consecrated to the worship of the living God, and why religion should be associated with death rather than life.

Others, perhaps, whose thoughts turn more to the stirring scenes of this world, if

> Knowledge to their eyes her ample page, .
> Rich with the spoils of time,

may have unrolled, will reflect on the long course of human history since this tree was planted in the monkish days. It was probably rooted here when the Domesday Book was written. It has grown with the gradual growth of the English constitution and people ; through the successive periods of crusading, fighting, burning, reforming, preaching, scoffing, printing, debating, philanthropic and muscular Christianity, and may live till a

new dispensation of Truth and Love shall have prevailed
over the religion of creed and greed, and He who told
His doubting disciple, " He that hath seen Me hath seen
the Father,"* shall be worshiped as " The mighty God,
the Father of Eternity, the Prince of Peace."†

Our yew must have been a great tree when the
Protestant Reformation gave Henry VIII. an excuse for
annexing the property of Glastonbury Abbey, and hanging the abbot on Glastonbury Tor.   The yew remained
unhurt when the signal fires on Dunkery Beacon and
Beacon Batch announced the approach of the Spanish
Armada, when

> The rugged miners poured to war from Mendip's sunless caves.

Unharmed by Puritan, and unshorn by Dutch taste,
like its sisters at Sandford, the church yew has spread
its umbrageous boughs, while Shakespeare and Bacon,
Milton and Newton, Addison, Pope, Cowper, Johnson,
Garrick, Hannah More, Maria Edgeworth, Robert Burns,
Scott, Campbell, Byron, Moore, Wordsworth, Coleridge,
and Southey, Tennyson, Dickens, and many others have
peopled the world with new thoughts and characters,
and while modern engineers, explorers, and men of
science have supplied it with new facts and knowledge, as unknown to the fraternity of Winscombe
Court, as the continents of America and Australia.
"During all this time," says the author of *The Gentle
Life*, " Truth lives, and must at last conquer . . . . .
Christianity is about to take a new development ; this
half-hearted faith, this imperfect mode of life, has long
been weighed in the balance : the young Samson is born."

* John xiv. 9.   † Isaiah ix. 6.

Though far from the oldest or largest of English yews, the Winscombe tree is one of the most perfect. Its sheltered position has preserved it from the shattering suffered by most of its kindred from the storms of centuries. Its trunk is not split, but remains a solid mass of timber five yards round. The branches spread on all sides over a circle of twenty yards diameter. Each year it bears abundance of powdery blossoms, but no berries, for it is of the masculine gender. Many an old monk of the Winscombe Fraternity may have told a younger brother, as they sat under its shade :

> O, brother, I have seen this tree *smoke*,
> Spring after spring, for half a hundred years.

According to De Candolle's mode of reckoning the growth of trees, the Winscombe yew cannot be less than 600 years old, and may probably be 1000, which would date it back to the first possession of the manor by the monks of Glastonbury, who held it from the Saxon times till the end of the reign of Richard Cœur de Lion. Even if planted as late as the thirteenth century, when the church was dedicated and endowed, the yew must have been a large tree when the present fabric was built, and it may have been one reason why the south aisle is crowded into the hill-side, in preference to destroying a fine tree of centuries' growth.

Behold the village rise
In rural pride, 'mong intermingled trees.

COLERIDGE considered the characteristic charm of Somersetshire to be "its rurality." Our village, we have said, was described by an American visitor as the prettiest he had seen in England. Comparisons are odious, and tastes differ; but if still prettier villages can be found in England, it would be hard to find one more thoroughly rural. Though it boasts of a "street," and even a "square," there is not a row of houses in the village. The street is without shop, foot-path, or lamp-post, and the square is simply a meeting of lanes, with a cottage or farm-house at each corner. The nearest approach to a shop is a small cottage with a few pipes and lollipops in the window, and an intimation over the door that the occupier is licensed to sell tobacco. There is not even a public-house or beer-shop in the village! An attempt was made some years ago to supply this uncommon want, and a vermilion sign swung for a while from a small farm-house in the street, heralding the "Rising Sun;" but the vermilion faded, the sign broke down, and so did the publican: the Rising Sun set, to rise no more.

The old village smithy, with mossy thatch, under a spreading pollard oak, has also gone. We miss the picturesque scene in winter evenings, when the red light of the forge, seen between intervening trees, shone upon the rustic figures, and the horses standing to be shod. We miss, too, the music of the harmonious blacksmith; for George, or Jarge, as he was called, could blow the flute as well as the bellows. He "played the waits" at Christmas time, and sacrificed, occasionally, to Bacchus, as well as to Vulcan and Apollo. The old brown thatch, which for many years had proved, with the certainty of man's inheritance of trouble, that sparks fly upwards, and do not come down alive, at last gave place to flaming tiles; the old ivy-grown oak was beheaded and felled, and the harmonious blacksmith went with his family to America, where they are doing well.

Another thatched roof, on whose deep green mossy carpet the Virginia creeper used to spread its autumnal splendour, is also gone. Time cures the rawness of even red tiles, and our village is not often disfigured by restorations. We lose more by neglect. The last twenty years have seen the end of many picturesque country objects: tumble-down cottages and sheds, fit only for sketching; old barns with dovecotes, ferny mossy walls, and rustic gates, the very originals of the old lithographic copies of our childhood. A wall of the old tithe barn is

F

still standing, but the village pound has been improved away. Winscombe Court, the former abode of the Fraternity of the Blessed Virgin, has been gradually rebuilt, but without being ever uninhabited, or losing its identity! The fine old elms that used to shade it, spreading their boughs across the road, were felled some years before, in fear of their falling on the old house. Opposite the Court, on the ascent of the hill, is the vicarage; its pretty gardens and sloping lawns adjoining the churchyard: which brings us to the end of the village, and its crowning glory, the village church.

From the brook, looking up the street, with the church and its yew tree at the end, backed by the steep green hill, the village is a picture worthy of any artist's skill. A more general, and equally picturesque view,* including Crooks Peak, may be taken from the railway bridge, and a more distant one from Sidcot or Hale.

Though our village is without a public-house or assembly-room of any kind, except the parish church, and the whole parish is without either lawyer, doctor or dissenting minister, the central hamlet of Woodborough has an Inn, a Congregational Chapel, a Board School, a Lecture and Temperance Hall, and the Post Office. The shops are also here, and more than one deserving widow has opened what some call a coffee tavern, others a toffee cavern.

The Post Office is at the principal shop. "Man wants but little here below:" let us see how much of that little can be got at our shop. The first objects that catch the eye, here, as at similar shops the wide world over, are those variously decorated cubical cases, which prove not only the universal taste for biscuits, but the fertility of

* See the frontispiece.

invention in their manufacture and nomenclature. Next
to the twice-baked form of the staff of life, in conspicuous
importance are the Postmaster-General's announcements
which, when spelt by th' unlettered muse, teach the
rustic customer on what days mails are made up for
such places as Kilwakivinje, Half Jack, Black Point,
Samsoun, Oil Rivers, and Mosquito Shore. Here, of course,
may be purchased, at all prices, from a halfpenny upwards, those variously tinted portraits of the Sovereign,
which transport anything they stick to from Woodborough
to the ends of the earth. Next is the counter for
stationery and drapery, and on a shelf opposite the door
is a display of crockery, chiefly for facilitating that which
some unknown author, often wrongly supposed to be
biblical, declared to be "next to godliness." As the
body is next to the soul, bodily cleanliness may be fairly
put next to spiritual purity: it would be well if they
were always companions. The shelf below is more
attractive to the young. Sweetmeats allure the tender
mind, and, if nursery morals be sound, spoil the teeth;
but here are other bottles to counteract the ill effect of
lollies and bullseyes; the bane and antidote are both
before us, as in the days of Cato and Shakespear. The
other end of the shop is devoted to grocery and the
provision trade; while over your head hang boots and
shoes with formidable hob nails and iron heels, intermingled with spades and shovels, brushes and brooms,
baskets and buckets, candles and curry-combs; in short,
an inventory of all the articles the shop can supply would
contain something for every letter in the alphabet: let us
try. Arrowroot, Boots and butter, Corduroy and com-
forters, Dips and dust-shovels, Eatables without end,
Frills and frying-pans, Geese and gridirons, Hams and

halters, Ink and irons, Knives and ketchup, Lemons and lollypops, Medicines and Nutmegs, Oatmeal and Pitch-forks, Quills and Ribbons, Soap and Treacle, Umbrellas and Vinegar, Wax and Xylographs, Youths' clothing, and Zoedone, with other articles too numerous to men-tion; which, if not always in stock, can, no doubt, be got to order.

Our shopkeeper is active and industrious, not grasping or greedy. As a farmer he can take the rough with the smooth, without complaining. If the weather does not suit one crop, he thinks it is just right for another. He welcomes alike "good drying weather," and what he calls "a lovely rain." A just, as well as a pious man, he can trust in the good providence of God, and with *the oiled feather* of charity so anoint the wheels of life, that they run smoothly and quietly, and if at any time they get out of gear, he thinks and feels with Dr. Syntax—

> That man, I trow, is doubly blest,
> Who of the worst doth make the best.

[Since the foregoing was written, the worthy postmaster has departed this life, and is worthily succeeded by his widow and family.]

VIII.—WINSCOMBE FOLK.

Let not ambition mock their useful toil,
Their homely joys and destiny obscure ;
Nor grandeur hear with a disdainful smile,
The short and simple annals of the poor.

HE small and needy yeoman,
without either capital or science
to compete with modern agri-
culture, has but a hard life of it.
Unhappily for himself, he has seldom the thrift to lay by in good
years for the short-comings of bad
ones. As with his cider orchards, so
with other crops; in times of plenty
there is waste, in times of scarcity,
want. There may, however, still be seen
here and there one of the old style of yeomen
in the picturesque costume,

Who, serving Ceres, tills with his own team
His own free land left by his sires to him.

But these are becoming scarce.
The tenant farmer as often as not has an absent landlord, who takes no interest in the place beyond getting

his rent. The tenant, of course, has no inducement to
improve another man's land. As Adam Smith said, " It
is against all reason and probability to suppose that a
yearly tenant will improve the soil." Thus the farm remains impoverished rather than improved, to the manifest
loss of the community. The useful spade is confined to
the gardens, and seldom goes deep even there. When I
came to Winscombe and worked in my garden, I was
cautioned against turning up the sub-soil : " It is of a cold,
stiff natur," said the old gardener, " better let it 'bide."
He told me, too, that it was no good sowing peas in this
ground: "They turn off yellow, and dry up before they get
into flower." I rejected the old man's advice, dug up the
cold clammy sub-soil, and got plenty of peas. With the
help of the domestic slops, I also grew broccoli 32 inches
round, which fairly " astonished the natives."

The plough disturbs the sub-soil as little as the spade.
A few inches of the surface are turned over year after
year, but the virgin earth beneath is never brought to the
sunshine, nor breathes the restoring air. The meadows
are as little drained as the plough-ground, and even more
neglected. A small estate changed hands a few years
ago, which used to yield a scanty feed for a horse and
cow. The new owner ploughed up tons of couch and
other weeds, grubbed up the ragged and useless hedges,
and sowed sweet meadow-grass and clover. The land is
now alive with fine cattle ; I have counted a hundred
sheep upon it at one time.

The industrious *moles* do more than most farmers to
drain and top-dress the land ; but the fresh and fertile mould they throw up is too often left, with the
droppings of the cattle, to lie in lumps, to the disfigure-
ment of the pasture, instead of being spread over the

ground to level and enrich it. Darwin teaches the enor-
mous value of *worms* in fertilizing the earth. Gilbert White
had taught the same lesson a century before.* An added
value is in the support they give to the moles. They are
thus useful alike in life and death; but the ignorant farmer
regards both worms and moles as nuisances; just as he
does the rooks, till dear-bought experience teaches him
he cannot do without them. Thistles, nettles, and other
weeds are allowed to ripen their seeds, and spread them
over the neighbourhood, for want of minding the proverb,
" A stitch in time saves nine," and the advice of the old
quaker poet, Scott of Amwell :

> Wield oft thy scythe along thy grassy layes,
> E'er the rude thistle its light down displays ;
> Else that light down upon the breeze will fly,
> And a new store of noxious plants supply.

Thistles might be cut down, if not grubbed up, and
mole-hills might be spread over the grass-land, without
cost to the farmer, if he would use his own eyes and
hands and spare moments, as every good gardener and
successful manufacturer must do. Two hundred years
ago, we read,† " the husbandman is always up and drest
with the morning, whose dawning light, at the same
instant of time, breaks over all the fields, and chaseth
away the darkness from every valley." And again,‡

> When now the cock, the ploughman's horn,
> Calls for the lily-wristed morn,
> Then to thy cornfields thou dost go,
> Which, though well-soiled, yet thou dost know
> That the best compost for the lands
> Is the wise master's feet and hands.

---

* Letter LXXVII, 1777.   † Vaughan, 1651.
       ‡ Herrick's Country Life.

Some of the old folk may still act on Poor Richard's
maxim,

Plough deep, while sluggards sleep,
And you shall have crops to sell and to keep,

and again—

He that by the plough would thiive,
Himself must either hold or drive.

But the march of intellect has driven old sayings out,
with old superstitions, old-fashioned farmers and farmer's
wives, and old-fashioned servants. The cock still crows
in the morn as when he woke the priest all shaven and
shorn, but neither priest nor people now listen to his
shrill clarion. Old farmers' wives find increasing difficulty
in getting servants for dairy work. The country girl of
the period does not like being disturbed in her morning
meditations ; she prefers improving her mind at night.
Cows must be milked punctually and in all weathers, and
dairy vessels must be always and thoroughly cleaned, and
thorough work is as hard to get as well-made butter and
pure wheaten bread. Farmers and other employers of
labour are apt, when they pay the school rates, to think
that the schooling they pay for, shortens the supply of
good servants, and to wonder how farms and other affairs
are to be worked, if all labourers become clerks, and all
maid-servants, governesses. These difficulties will, no
doubt, be got over in time, and everybody will, as before,
find a relative and proper place; but it is certainly one of
the vulgar errors of the day, and one which has kept pace
with the triumphant march of intellect, to imagine, as the
author of the *Dorsetshire Poems* puts it, "that every change
from the plough to the desk, or from the desk towards
the couch of empty-handed idleness, is an onward step
towards happiness and intellectual and moral excellence."

One of the first truths to be implanted at school and at home ought to be the dignity, as well as the necessity, of useful labour and service. The Great Teacher was himself a carpenter. He said, " My Father *worketh* hitherto, and I *work* ; I am with you as he that *serveth*." The Heir Apparent to the greatest earthly crown has for his motto, *Ich dien*—I serve. " A nation of servants," says Emerson, " is better than a nation of served." The kingdom of heaven is composed of the servants of the King of kings. Willingly or slavishly, all must serve, and none can be really free or happy, here or hereafter, who do not love serving. The soldier glories in the service of his country, and thinks it an honour to wear the badges of his service. There is just as much honour in any other service done for the public good. What is the difference between uniform and livery ? Livery is the uniform of a liberated or free man, distinguished from a slave or bond-man. Is any uniform a badge of greater freedom ? Is it anything but the livery of one who serves in the army, or navy, or other public service? The old salutation, " Your servant, sir," still lingers among the gramfers of the old school, and our neighbourhood can boast of several examples of the old style of servants, the old faithful ones, who have become the honoured friends of the families with whom they have spent their lives.* If increased schooling be inconsistent with such service, the change will be deplorable indeed. The lesson all want is, not to do uncommon things, but to do common things well. It is not common to get

---

* A beautiful example of this mutual love and esteem is given in the life of Archbishop Tait, whose old nurse died with her hand in his as he sat by her bedside.

anything really well done.   There is a sad lack of the
spirit of the old rhyme,

> If I were a cobbler, I'd make it my pride
> The best of all cobblers to be.
> If I were a tinker, no tinker beside
> Should mend an old kettle like me.

Our notions of education are too much under the
influence of school men; as if books were the only means
of mental training and nourishment.   A good husbandman, or gardener, or mechanic ; a good cook, or house-
maid, or nurse, will be all the better for knowing how to
read and write and cipher ; but it is absurd to call the
reading and writing and ciphering, education, and the
knowledge gained by observation and experience, something inferior.   I often stand to admire the sower, the
ploughman, the hedger and ditcher, and other men, who
know how to do work of any kind, and as often I think, this
man, if he has read but few books, or none but the Bible,
may be no more ignorant than myself ; he can do what I
cannot. Yesterday, I saw a young boy holding by a halter
a horse he had just caught, and brought out of the field.
The horse was plunging, and would not let the boy
mount, but the little fellow gradually got his hand on
the horse's nose, and was quietly stroking him as I
passed by.   In another minute I heard a rapid trot, and
up came the horse with my little friend triumphant on
his back, rushing by without saddle or bridle, with
nothing but the halter to guide and control a creature so
much stronger than himself.   The boy goes to school,
but another schoolmaster taught him to ride and catch
horses.

There is seldom, if ever, any want of work here.   In
mowing and harvest time, there is sometimes a scarcity

of labourers. Mowing and reaping machines come round, as well as steam thrashing and winnowing machines, but the scythe and sickle are in common use, and the flail is still to be heard on wet wintry mornings.

Still the flail echoes through the frosty air.

We still keep up the picturesque English custom of letting the cows and other cattle graze in the pastures ; but these pleasant pictures are, perhaps, too wasteful to be continued. There is no such waste in Germany and Switzerland; the grass is carefully and continually mown, and brought to the cattle in stalls ; the manure, liquid and solid, being as carefully preserved, and spread on the land. The grass and clover on English way-sides and lanes would keep many a Swiss cow.

Formerly, teasels were grown here for the woollen-cloth manufacturers, some of them going as far as the Yorkshire mills ; but that crop seems to be nearly discontinued, though the soil of the valley suits it well.

Best on stiff loam rough teasels rear their heads.

Poultry, a source of vast profit in France, is supposed to be unprofitable in England ; though eggs and chicken fetch half as much again as they did years ago, and poultry food is as much cheaper. Kept as they are in the haphazard way of picking up what they can in the homestead, laying abroad, and growing too old to lay at all, they may be unprofitable ; but our farmers have seldom the means of knowing. Fowls may not pay to be kept at the cost of extra rent and wages, but that need not be the case in a farm. They are supposed to injure the neighbouring corn crops ; but a practical farmer, writing on thin sowing, says, " I have just threshed and sold a crop of wheat seven and a half quarters per acre, from a field open to an adjoining fowl-house, from which emerge every morning 150 head of poultry, and they have been free to roam at large from the time it was sown to the day of carting the crop ; and this is not the first, second, or third instance of the kind : for however shabby and scratched the plants may appear in their early growth, their ultimate development is grand, and the thickest part of the crop is always that nearest the fowl-house."

Few of our farmers have learned a fact noticed by Gilbert White, that trees contribute much to pools and streams. " This I know," says White, " that deciduous trees entwined with much ivy seem to distil the greatest quantity of water. These facts," he continues, " may furnish the intelligent with hints concerning what sorts of trees they should plant round small ponds that they would wish to be perennial. In dry summers the pools surrounded with ivy-covered pollards are always well supplied, while those without the drip, and exposed to the sun, are dried up."

The neighbourly spirit of our farmers is shown in many ways. They are kind and hospitable in their houses, welcome you to sit and rest, and refresh you with delicious bread and butter, and cider, or milk if you prefer it. Perhaps they are sometimes too free—unkindly kind— with their cider ; for if a cup were taken at several neighbouring houses, the effect might be anything but kindly. In apple time, no boy need be tempted to rob an orchard ; if he will but wait till the fruit is ripe, the farmer will freely give him a pocket-full. A naturalist in search of flowers or other specimens will not be deterred by threats of prosecution with the utmost rigour of the law; if he avoid damaging fences and growing crops, he may go where he likes. We have no game-keepers to breed poachers and ill blood.

The tradesmen, too, are obliging beyond mere catch-penny civility. They will come early in the morning to repair a kitchen grate or oven, and are always ready and willing to suit the convenience of the family and servants. There is, moreover, a great improvement in punctuality since the railway came : it has opened the valley to foreign competition, and the result is a general increase of active life. When sobriety and industry are combined with skill, there is no lack of prosperity. Even in this purely rural valley, we have thriving tradesmen, especially in the primitive trades of the baker, the carpenter, the shoemaker, and smith. There has also been, of late years, full employment for the builder, as the changes in many parts of the parish show.

When the mining works here and at Shipham were carried on, the " grovers " were a " rough lot," and some-times guilty of depredations in the valley. One of their more innocent amusements was playing fives at the tower of Winscombe church. The vicar and churchwardens hav-ing objected to the practice, the Woodborough publican built a fives tower on the green by the inn, where it stood for many years after it ceased to be used.* When new, it, no doubt, drew the players from the churchyard to the tavern, possibly without loss to the church. But the question is worth considering, whether the church might not gain if its services were more connected with healthy life and recreation, and less with death and dismality. Mistaken piety has much to answer for in demoralising

---

* It now forms part of the wall of a barn.

the people by separating religion and worship from the
common duties and pleasures of life. The sabbath was
made for man and not man for the sabbath. The
Lord's Day should not be a day for a man to afflict his
soul. It should be a day of rest from his own devices,
a day of religious instruction, of thanksgiving, and prayer,
and praise ; and if the priest and people were to continue the *Cantate Domine* after church, " Sing unto the
Lord a new song—and praise His name in the dance,"
the publican might miss some of his customers, and come
and join in the dance too. Even the saddest of the prophets foretells the establishment of the true church in
these cheerful words, " Again I will build thee, and thou
shalt be built, O virgin of Israel : thou shalt again be
adorned with thy tabrets, and shalt go forth in the dances
of them that make merry*." That may not mean the
bodily.dancing of priests and people ; but it must mean
the joyous spirit and harmonious action which the dance
so delightfully figures ; and if the inward and spiritual
grace be enjoyed, why not the outward and visible sign ?
The difficulty in allowing these external pleasures in connection with religion, is the risk of the connection ceasing,
and the outward and visible sign remaining, without the
inward and spiritual grace ; but this is true of all outward
symbols, even those of ordinary religious worship.

There is no longer any of the barbarism of the mining
days—those " good old times," when the Mores could
find scarcely a Bible in the country round, and were
abused and persecuted by parsons and squires for attempting to lift the poor out of the pit of ignorance, and
the miry clay of mere animal life. Hannah More and

---

* Jeremiah xxxi. 4.

her sisters were succeeded by other benevolent women, and their good influence is still felt. Mary Tanner, of Sidcot, was known to Hannah More, and her name is affectionately cherished by the poor of this parish. Her loving spirit and wise counsel are often mentioned by our cottagers :

> Sage words of earnest counsel, kind and cheery,
> For life's young warrior starting from the door ;
> Mild tones of comfort for the worn and weary,
> And solace for the poor.*

They will relate with tearful eyes how often good Mrs. Tanner and her family would visit them and sit and work with them, and talk to them as friends and neighbours, and how, instead of scolding them for their bad management, Mrs. Tanner would say she only wondered how they could manage as well as they did, and bring up families on their scanty means. Her mantle has been taken up by her successors. Perhaps a double portion of her spirit has come upon them, for they labour for the intellectual as well as the moral elevation of the people. Those who visit the cottages often meet with as much good sense and moral worth, as much delicacy of feeling and true gentleness of mind and manners, as they find in a round of calls among more fashionable folk. Their practical trust in Divine care for their daily bread, and their lighter hold upon the vanities of this world, often give their conversation a higher tone than that of the gossip of the day, whether social, political, or religious. Though the blessing of the poor is chiefly to the poor in spirit, there is a blessing in earthly poverty too, when it helps the laying up of treasure in heaven. A few years

* Benjamin Gouch's *Life Thoughts, etc.*

ago, a worthy couple who had lost all their children but one, were brought to want by the long illness of the husband and remaining son. The poor woman had to nurse them and earn what she could, and when the boy died, she lived for months on dry bread, that she might be able to get better food for her sick husband. The poor man would weep, and say he could not bear to eat and see her without a share. Hard lot! Yet how rich in self-denying love. The Father's care permitted the temporal want to secure everlasting abundance. "Certainly," says Lord Bacon, " Virtue is like precious odours, most fragrant when they are incensed or crushed ; for Prosperity doth best discover Vice, but Adversity doth best discover Virtue." When the right time came, the distress was relieved, for the deserving poor are not without friends in our valley.

Poverty has its trials and temptations, so has wealth. Men may be good and happy without riches, and nations may be great ; but they rarely last long in luxury.

> Ill fares the land to hastening ills a prey,
> Where wealth accumulates, and men decay.

The author* of " Egypt of the Pharaohs and of the Khedive " compares the Egyptian with the English rural labourer, and gives a lively description of " Achmed, the child of the sun," with his quick step and eye, and wit, and tongue, and frequent holiday festivals, with sunshine and cucumbers, as well as onions and tobacco,— and poor English Hodge, up to his ankles in mud, eating his bread and cheese, if he can get it, sheltered under a tree from the wind and rain of an English summer ; with

---

* F. Barham Zincke, Chaplain to the Queen.

a large family, a sick baby, his hard-working wife just confined with another, and himself bad with the rheumatism ; and what makes their hard lot still harder, is the fact that they are the only workers who never have a fête or a holiday. But there is another side to the picture. The dark cloud has a silver lining. The author goes on to praise the good qualities of both Achmed and Hodge. He likes the lively Egyptian well, but has more respect for Hodge. " Nowhere else on the earth's surface can a harder worked couple be found than Hodge and his wife. If they have their failings, they have their virtues too. They are not afraid of any kind or any amount of work. They don't see much use in complaining. They let other folks alone. They are self-reliant within their narrow sphere. They think there must be a better world than this has been to them. In the meantime they are thankful that they can work and earn their bread.

" And here we have the true nursery of the nation. The schooling is hard, but without it we should not be what we are. It forms the stuff out of which Englishmen are made. It is the stuff that has made America and Australia, and is giving to our language and race predominance in the world."

The caricatures of Hodge in *Punch* and elsewhere are out of date. They may be characteristic of the antediluvian clod-poll, before the flood of elementary education ; but the rural labourer of the present day is not the gaping simpleton of the caricaturists. He has as much common sense as the factory hand, and his employments being more varied, require more resource and a greater variety of knowledge and skill. A man who can mow, reap, plash a hedge, load a hay-wagon, milk, and look

G

after cattle of different kinds, is not the ignorant block-
head city people like to picture him.

Drunkenness is, no doubt, a too common vice in the
country where amusements are scarce ; but is it less
prevalent in towns where amusements abound ?

Winscombe wives rarely speak ill of their husbands ;
though some of them have had, from time to time,
good excuses for doing so. If the man has had a
drunken bout, you will not hear of it from his wife.
She will bear her burden patiently, and it is sometimes
a hard one to bear. But she has her reward. The
wretch who abused or even beat her when mad with
drink, will declare, when he has again become a rational
being, that no man ever had a better wife.

Some of our cottager's wives, as well as widows,
are patterns of virtuous women bravely struggling with
poverty ; hard-working, thrifty, unrepining, honest ;
bringing up their children with exemplary discretion, to
become, in their turn, good servants, or otherwise useful
members of society. But it must be confessed that
all are not of this exemplary pattern. The proverbial
wastefulness of the poor is but two frequent ; the want of
methodical habits to keep things in their right places and
to their proper uses ; the propensity to throw away
everything " done with," as if it were incapable of further
service ; the neglect of the divine injunction to gather up
the fragments that nothing be lost,—these defects of
right training are a common complaint against domestic
servants. Masters and mistresses will preserve the paper
and string of parcels, but you may see servants throw
both away. I lately observed a poor woman, in a third-
class railway carriage, open a paper parcel done up in a
large clean sheet of paper, and tied with strong new

string, such as would have gladdened the heart of the thrifty boy in *Waste not, want not**, but both paper and string were left on the floor of the carriage, and trodden under foot as the woman and her child got out.

We often learn how kindly some of our poor people help one another in times of need, sometimes making sacrifices seldom offered by the rich. They are kind and forbearing to the children, too; and to other people's children as well as their own. " When I see the children peeping over the hedge at my ripe apples," said a poor labouring man, " I can't find it in my heart not to give 'em a lot." " Children be children," said a poor mother blessed with plenty of them. " I don't believe in beating them. I speak them fair, and I don't have much trouble with mine." It is easy for people with nurses and governesses to find fault with the behaviour of poor people's children ; but rich people's are often quite as ill-behaved, with less excuse; often betraying a lack of the only true politeness—consideration of the feelings and comfort of others.

A good-natured farmer may sometimes be seen picking up the little ones as they trudge through the mud, and giving them a lift in his cart. When almost as full of the merry urchins as it will hold, room will be found for yet another : " Just that little mess of a chap ! " And away they all go, as happy as kings and queens, if crowned heads are ever so free from care.

Of course we have our " mischievous boys." What neighbourhood is free from them, where there are any boys at all ? Their mischief is not vice ; it is at worst

---

* Miss Edgeworth's *Parents' Assistant*, " Waste not, want not; or, Two Strings to one's bow." .

misdirected energy. Healthy life must flow into action.
The propensity to exert the growing powers is inherent in
life itself. There is delight in doing, long before there
is any end in view, and longer still before there is any
wish for wages. What boy does not want a knife and a
hammer and nails before he wants to do anything particular with them? The enjoyment is in cutting and
hammering, as many a piece of furniture bears testimony.
As the muscles of the arm grow stronger, exercise is found
with sticks, and in stone-throwing ; the pleasure being
heightened by achievement. Something is hit, or at
least aimed at—a bird, or a cat. Then there is the propensity to scribble, with chalk or pencil, on walls and
doors—a sad nuisance, as the chief attraction is always
to new paint and clean whitewash. But the propensity
is inveterate. Perhaps the best remedy would be the
erection of a parish hoarding, with a light surface for
pencils and a dark one for chalk. Native talent might
thus be developed, and private walls and doors kept
free from superfluous decoration. Such a convenience
for the exercise of idle hands, with football for the
feet, and cricket for both, would be a real public
benefit.

The children of the poor, brought up to face hardship
and hard work, are often better prepared for the battle of
life, which all have to fight in one service or another, than
the children of the rich, whose only preservation from the
weakening effects of luxury at home, is the rougher discipline of the public school. Our village children are for
the most part well-behaved, and turn out well. It is
pleasant to see them going to school, not like Shakespear's
" whining schoolboy, creeping like snail unwillingly," but
walking or running merrily, with clear, bright morning

faces, and the girls with pinafores glistening in the sun, like the garments of the shining ones.

For many years we had two village schools, the Church or "National" School, and the "British" or undenomina-tional; but as there were neither pupils nor subscribers enough to support two efficient schools, they were amal-gamated under a joint committee, who found all the supposed "religious" difficulties melt away. We have now a parliamentary school board, which has enlarged the schoolhouse at Woodborough, and built a new one at Sandford. The rising generation should rise far above the setting one, if secular schooling be as elevating as it is supposed to be. But is it?

There are Sunday schools at Winscombe, Woodborough, and Sandford; the first and last under clerical control, the other, which is the largest, "on the principles of the British and Foreign School Society"—Scriptural teaching without any formal creed or doctrinal catechism.

Old forms of speech linger in rural places. Somerset, as well as Dorset, is noted for a stagnant population, little affected by imigration or novelty of any kind. Rail-way intercourse and schooling have done something of late years to modify the provincial dialect; but we retain many of the words and phrases made poetical by the poems of the Dorset Burns; who justly observes that the pithy sentences of village patriarchs are often weakened as well as expanded by modern wordiness.

Local names abide long in these obscure valleys, and Scripture names are numerous and persistent. Most of the patriarchs are represented here, or have been within living memory. We have had Adam, Abel, Seth, Enoch, Abraham, Lot, Isaac, Esau and Jacob, Moses, and Aaron, Joshua, Eliab, Jesse, David and Solomon;

the prophets Isaiah, Jeremiah, Ezekiel, Daniel, Amos, Joel, Zacchariah ; Shadrach, the four Evangelists, with Peter, James, Philip, Paul, and Timothy.   We have gone as far as Ephesus or Thessalonica for Aristarchus ; but, unfortunately, his name is commonly taken as the provincial pronunciation of Harry Storks.   When names of saints and prophets have failed, resort has been had to angels.   Michael and Gabriel have been seen in the same garden.   Enoch, still in the flesh, succeeded Isaiah in another.

Old fashions, as well as old names and old folk, are apt to linger where progress lags.   The active in mind

and body move away ; the old stay in their old haunts. But the population is healthy and increasing, with an unfailing supply of children.   Both old folk and young are seen here daily, who might be the very originals of those rustic figures which Bewick and Pyne and others have immortalized.*   Maria Edgeworth's *Lucy* would have

* *Vide* Bewick's Birds, 1797, 1804, and Pyne's Rustic Figures, 1822.

seen plenty of "Bewick's" here.* The ploughman, the
hedger, the woodman, the shepherd, the sower, the reaper,
the old man breaking stones, and the old woman with
scarlet cloak ; rough farm labourers, milkmaids, hay-
makers, village children, rustic horses and rusty harness,
old-fashioned cows and pigs and poultry, all are as primitive and picturesque as Bewick and Pyne, David Cox,
William Hunt and Birket Foster could draw them.

Rustic beauties and village belles have never been
wanting in our valley. If May-day were kept as it
should be, there might be some difficulty in choosing the
Queen of the May. Lest any of our village maids should
look into our sketches, and fancy they see in them reflections of themselves, the mirror shall be held up to the
face of nature as it looked a generation ago.

Here is a young damsel tripping along with graceful
step and figure, bright dark eyes, but modest and gentle
ones, and rich flowing raven tresses. It is pretty little
Polly, who began life, after leaving the village school,
with cleaning knives and shoes in a gentleman's house,
and being soon promoted to a higher post, captivated
the heart of a young tradesman, who married her before
she was eighteen, and they became as happy and industrious a couple as you will see anywhere. While he works
at his trade, she goes round with the cart. You may see
them together, harnessing the horse for the daily round,
and a pleasant sight it is. And here is another village
belle, bringing up the cows to be milked. Fine Grecian
features, rosy cheeks, long black hair and eyelashes,
and form of youthful beauty, Lucy might be a model
for a painter. Being an orphan, she lives with her

---

* *Harry and Lucy* concluded ; Vol. I, page 275—9 ; 1825.

grandparents ; milks the cows, helps in the dairy, scrubs
the floor, washes the tea-things, teaches in the Sunday
School, and finds time to read all the books in the
village library. She has a number of sturdy little brothers,
much at home on the backs of great plough-horses, and
very well able to prove the superior power of human
intelligence, even when trained no higher than the third
standard of an elementary public school.   To catch and
mount and ride a big horse requires training, as well as
to catch the meaning of a school question, and mount
and ride a schoolmaster's hobby.   It is a real treat
to watch some of our village mites, and the mutual fun
they and the horses enjoy, tearing about the field, till
the game ends in the great carrying the small to the
homestead.   One day, two little chaps were seen going
by in a cart at full speed, having apparently lost the
control of the horse, which soon after stumbled and fell,
throwing the boys out.   A lady, observing the accident,
went to them and asked if she should get assistance, but
the urchins replied with a grin that they didn't want any
help.   They soon got the horse up and climbed into
the cart again, and away they went as if nothing had
happened.

Many a poet's fancy portrait may be found in the
flesh in our valley.   We have no " organ boy," but lots of

> Great brown eyes, thick plumes of hair,
> Old corduroys, the worse for wear.

Whittier, too, might find here his rustic beauty, who

> On a summer day,
> Raked the meadows sweet with hay.
> Beneath her torn hat glowed the wealth
> Of simple beauty and rustic health.

We have thought our *Brook* might be the original of Tennyson's, and so our children may be the embodiment of those childish charms which true poets, and they alone, can see everywhere. Here we have many

> A merry little maiden,
> With her tangled golden tresses,
> Standing barefoot there all laden
> With a wealth of emerald cresses.

Farmer William's pretty daughter, too, whose graceful figure and pleasant modest looks would charm a poet or painter anywhere. On Sunday you cannot help noticing her sweet happy face, and simple becoming dress as she comes into church. Yesterday, she was just as happy on her knees scrubbing the farm-house floor. *Laborare est orare.* God is best served by doing the work He has ordained, in His love, and in goodwill to all the world. But Gertrude's worth has been found out by a worthy partner, and olive plants already grace their table. And there is Bessy who never misses either day school or Sunday school, and Mary who was top of the school and is now a respectable servant bidding fair to do well, if not spoilt, as some are, by the bad and silly ones who are ever changing their places, and never stay long enough, or even try, to win the respect and confidence of their employers.

But who are these young rustics? Why, they are Mary Howitt's old young friends, "Jack and Harry."* Five-and-thirty years have made no difference. Here they are still, "near neighbours to us all." "Everybody knows Jack and Harry." But we have no such wretch as Timothy Peppercorn. There is not a man in our valley

---

* See Mary Howitt's *Picture Book for the Young*, 1856.

who would run over a dog, as he did, and care nothing
about it.   There are very few, even, who do not pull up,
in muddy weather, to avoid splashing a foot-passenger ;
though we must confess all are not so civil, and some,
mostly strangers, seem to think the roads are made only
for drivers and riders.

Dick's friend, Celestine, is sometimes here at Farmer
Gilliflower's, for the sake of country air and rural life ;
for Winscombe, though not in the postal guide, has been
discovered by some of the doctors, and recommended
as a salubrious and delightful place for rustication.
Celestine learns to milk and churn, and gains health
among the cowslips and buttercups.

Among our rural characters we have had a born
genius, and, what is not so rare perhaps, a born simpleton.
The former was a rough-looking lad, who worked in a
stone-quarry on the hill-side, and supported his old
mother, who lived in a cottage of her own hard by.   His
craving for knowledge was incessant.   He learnt Algebra,
Astronomy Botany, Chemistry, Drawing, Geology, Latin
and Greek ; he read every book he could get hold of,
and wrote a very neat hand, and what is still more to his
credit, he stuck by his old mother, till her death set him
free to seek more fertile fields of science.

> So through the impediment of rural cares,
> In him revealed a scholar's genius shone. *

Our village fool has gone to a better world ; where,
sometimes, perhaps, the wise and fools change places.

---

* He brought me one day the "developement of a curve," beautifully
drawn on purely mathematical principles.   It was to form the base of a
cone upon the side of a larger one.   The fact was, his tin coffee-pot had
lost its spout, and he wanted to fit on a new one, as a problem in conic
sections.   He is now a University graduate.

" Silly Nich'las " was a true "innocent ; " harmless and simple as a little child, though in years an elderly man ; kind and affectionate, he was a lover of children, and pleased as a child to be sent on an errand, or set to work in any way within his capacity. Though not much better than an idiot in understanding, he was faithful and honest, and had a good memory. Whenever he earned a trifle, he would run off to the shop to buy sweets for the children, and tobacco for himself, for old Nick loved the Stygian fumes. The late William Tanner, of blessed memory, once gave him a good cloth coat, which pleased him mightily. Having put it on, he looked on one side, then on the other, and, at last, with tears in his eyes, exclaimed, " Thank God ! " The benevolent donor was more pleased with this expression of gratitude than silly Nich'las was with the gift. He thought it came from a better Wisdom than his own. " Out of the mouth of babes and sucklings Thou hast perfected praise."

Coleridge wrote, "I honour a virtuous and wise man, whether in the person of a laurelled bard, or in that of an old pedlar." We have in our neighbourhood an old pedlar, who is also a peripatetic philosopher ; a kind-hearted, pious man, who deals in rags and bones, and other left-off things ; making, as he says, useless things useful, and thus serving the community by preventing waste. And while he thus gathers up the fragments, that nothing be lost, he helps to dispense the Bread of Life by the inscription on his cart : *God is Love.*

On the rise of the hill, above the vicarage, just where the road turns to Shutshelf, is a cottage in a garden, always kept in good order and repair, and evidently the abode of a thrifty and thriving tenant. It is, in fact, the dwelling of one of our most industrious and skilful tradesmen—

the boot and shoe maker—the very reverse of Watts's sluggard, for,

> You pass through his garden and see no wild briar,
> Though leather and wages grow higher and higher ;
> Old boots don't hang on him, nor thinks he of rags,
> For his bus'ness still waxes, and trade never flags.

One of our departed worthies has been commemorated in the pages of the *British Workman,** under the name of *Farmer Giles.* His real name was Giles Williams. Before the railway came to our valley, coals had to be hauled from Weston over Banwell Hill, which is very steep. It is a hard pull and a long pull up the hill, even for a strong horse, and a load of coals behind a donkey is a heavy job. Giles is figured with the rope's end over his own shoulder, pulling alongside of his donkey. An old neighbour of his, who had known him for many years, said he had known Giles in great straits to get along, but he never knew him complain of his lot, or find fault with other people : he bore his own burden and tried to do his duty. He might have been the original of Jane Taylor's " Contented John."

> For this he was constantly heard to declare,
> What he could not prevent, he would cheerfully bear :
> And thus honest John, though his station was humble,
> Passed through this sad world without even a grumble.

Faith and honesty are often tried by the tax-gatherer. Giles paid his share of the public burdens without grudging. He said we ought to be thankful for the blessings we enjoy in this favoured land, and pay our taxes gladly. He was a just and a loyal man. Whether his party colours were blue or yellow I do not know. He

* January, 1862. *Farmer Giles.*

never looked blue, nor saw things with a jaundiced eye.
Perhaps his green goggles agreed with his love of harmony,
blending the blue and the yellow, and neutralising the
fiery red.

Old Nancy, another of our village characters, has also
departed this life since these sketches were first published.
Her well-known stout figure, with no useless length of
skirt, and with a cap and bonnet meant for use rather
than adornment, is no longer to be seen, trudging to
and from the shop with her small basket ; as she did
when long past eighty. She died in the cottage where
she was born, and where she had dwelt all her long life.
When her husband was near his end, she surprised some
of her less enlightened neighbours by telling him not to
trouble about her, as she would be quite comfortable and
have all she wanted; and during her widowhood, though
she lived quite alone, she said she never felt lonely. Just
before the old man died, he bade her bring him his boots,
for he was "going on a journey." His boots and hat were
put on, and he immediately departed. Neighbours
urged her to have some one to live with her, but she said
she wanted no one " to make a talking and fuss." She
liked to have some work to do, and did not like to be
waited on. She liked to sit and think of what she had
heard at church, and what had been read and said to her
at home. She was a devout church-woman, and kept
the feasts and fasts religiously, helped by a kind neighbour who sent her dainties and salt-fish, to which she
was partial. During her latter days, she often lay awake
at night, but she said the time passed pleasantly. " I
ben't alone." Some one suggested that at her great age
it was not safe for her to live quite alone ; " something
might happen "—she might die. " Well," said she, " so

I may, but my neighbour would see there was no smoke in the chimney in the morning, and she would come in. I ben't afraid of dying." She lived, however, to be too helpless to do without a care-taker. The infirmities of old age became burdensome, and her release from the mortal coil was a relief to others as well as herself.

The site of Nancy's cottage is now covered by a pair of newly-built tenements; an instance among others of "the duties of property" rightly fulfilled in providing better habitations for the poor.

Sometimes in summer time, when reading or working out of doors, I have been moved by the soft strains of vocal prayer and praise coming from a neighbour's garden, where an old blind patriarch, leaning upon his staff at his cottage door, with upturned face and subdued voice, offered the sacrifice of thanksgiving for mercies experienced for ninety years.

One morning, instead of the quiet prayer, was heard a stronger voice, but still a sacred strain. No one could be seen; the sound seemed to come from my neighbour's chimney, but was distinctly audible in the infant's hymn,

> Jesus, Saviour, Son of God,
>   Who for me life's pathway trod,
>   Who for me became a Child,
>   Make me humble, meek, and mild.
>
> I Thy little lamb would be,
>   Jesus, I would follow Thee ;
> Samuel was Thy child of old,
>   Take me, too, within Thy fold.

The hymn ceased, and was followed by a loud cry from above, shouting, "All up! all up! all up!" On looking up, a black figure was seen on the chimney top, making a polite bow and doffing a cap, with no small effusion of soot. It was our merrily pious chimney sweeper, who announces his useful calling and attention to its duties, by a signboard on his house to say:

The sweep lives here, who attends to orders far and near,
With brush and scraper, or machine, he'll sweep your chimneys well
    and clean.

Where the road to Cross and Axbridge divides, on a neck of ground between road and railway, is a lone cottage, which a benighted traveller might pass " in fear and dread," as the possible abode of a foot-pad or high-wayman. It is, however, the dwelling of an honest wood-man and his family, with whom the traveller might find safe refuge and kindly welcome. He is the guardian of the

wood above, and of the board threatening trespassers with the terrors of the law ; but if you ask if you may go in and gather flowers, he answers with a smile, that the notice " is not meant for such as you."

There are, no doubt, too many with whom the selfish spirit of the world prevails; who think first what they can *get*, rather than what they can *do*, and grudge spending either time or money in the service of others. But there are among us more noble men and women, who willingly help their neighbours in the spirit of the charity that seeks no return. It is pleasant to talk to a hard working man of this rank, who was at one time a too free drinker, but who has for many years paid into a provident club, without ever drawing a shilling for sick pay, and who says he is thankful he has not needed it, and is happy to think that his payments have helped less fortunate neighbours. Some members of such clubs talk as if they had been injured by not being ill, and who grudge the delay in the payment of their funeral money. Our neighbour is willing to keep his health rather than his bed, and is in no hurry for his funeral.

One of the most important characters in a rural district is the postman.

> He comes—the herald of a noisy world—
> News from all nations lumbering at his back.

Twenty years ago the rural postman was, like the London hackney-coach horse, one who had seen his best days. Youth has since taken the place of old age. The first postman we remember here was a tall old man clothed in a long drab coat reaching to his ankles, and carrying a long staff; the leathern letter-bag hanging at his side by a strap across his shoulder. His deliberate tramp and knock at the door contrasted, like country and town, with the familiar double rap and hurried step of the London postman. Our ancient has long since gone his last round upon earth, and departed to a sphere where communication is quicker than by mail or telegraph.

The Cutlers Cottage.

More than one successor has followed him. Among them a genial soul, whose friendly interest in his neighbours was shown by his free use of the new post-cards, as means for the diffusion of knowledge.

Poor Sepfel, as he was called in our family, had a more than wholesome dread of coming to want. He denied himself sufficient food and raiment for the *day*, for fear of having none for the *morrow*. The overdoing proved the undoing, as it has done, and continually does, in other walks of life. Sepfel laid up great store, but died before he dared to begin to eat, drink and be merry. In fact, he starved himself for fear of starvation. He was lame, and looked incapable of his long daily walk ; but he chose the whole work and wages, rather than divide both. Our house was the last in his round, and he often stopped and took a cup of tea, if the breakfast things were in the kitchen. His kindly voice talking to the servants, whom he addressed by name, often remarking on the handwriting he knew, and the postcards (which I believe entertained him on his round) sounded pleasanter than the machine-like, speechless noises of the over-worked city postman, telling, like his load of newspapers, of

the madding crowd's ignoble strife.

Hardly less important than the postman is the village carrier. Fortunately for us, the railway has made business for itself without running the errand-cart off the road. On the contrary, it now plies twice a week, instead of once. Calling for orders and delivering goods at the different houses here, as well as at villages off the line of rails, the carrier renders services which the railway people do not. He fulfils the useful service of the

H

German and Swiss postman, who brings the goods
ordered through the post, and takes the cost and postage.*
Our carrier executes all kinds of commissions in Bristol
for his country customers.   He takes our watches to be
cleaned, our knives and razors to be set, our furniture to
be repaired, and brings back all parcelable things.   " It
is always a pleasure to see his honest, country face," said
a lady at Clifton ; and it was a true saying.

His dwelling is as rural as himself and his calling.   On
a bank by the road-side stands his ancient ivy-clad cot,
dated 1628.   It is one of the few remaining thatched roofs,
with thick over-hanging curved eaves, and a rustic porch
which shelters the door and the wicker cage of a blackbird.
The little garden is gay with flowers, especially when tulips
are in season, and in autumn the roof is aglow with the
scarlet Virginia creeper.

Before the abolition of toll-bars, our carrier used to
start late in the evening, so as to arrive at the first gate
after mid-night, and return within the same day.   He is
now emancipated from that bondage, but still makes his
outward-bound or up journey at night, returning the
following afternoon.   In warm summer weather, the trip
must be pleasant enough, along a good road, and through
fine hilly country; now along shady lanes by gentlemen's
seats, and farms, and villages, and now over high open
ground, with views extending far and wide, from the Mendip hills to the distant Welsh mountains.   On a moonlight
night, though the views are limited, the scenery is still
beautiful ; indeed, a midsummer night, from sunset to
sunrise is one of the most enjoyable parts of the day.

---

* While living at Darmstadt, we had our tea from Bonn brought by the
post, 6lbs. at a time, and paid for on delivery.

But our carrier is familiar with the road, and, happily for his customers, thinks more of his errands than of Midsummer Night's Dreams.

The carrier's *Night Thoughts*, however, may follow those of the poet, though in reversed order ; for, starting where the poet ends, when

> Midnight, universal midnight reigns,
>
> He, like the world, his ready visit pays
> Where fortune smiles.

to wit, to the wealthy city of Bristol.   And then return-ing next evening,

> As when a traveller, a long day past
> In painful search of what he cannot find—

a rare case with our carrier—

> At night's approach, content with his own cot,

he finds his " consolation " in the poet's opening line,

> Tired nature's sweet restorer, balmy sleep !

Most likely our carrier's meditations wander but little from his "useful toil " in helping his neighbours to supply their various wants.   Honoured be his ministry !   If, as he jogs along behind his faithful White-foot, and smokes his solitary pipe, his thoughts run more upon parcels than poetry, useful work than the philosophy of usefulness, he may nevertheless be in the inward enjoy-ment of the reward of honest service ; because in all such service, according to the providence of God, HE is present, with those peace-bestowing "ministers of His, that do His pleasure."* Who is not happy when usefully

* Psalm ciii. 21.

employed, with his hands and heart together? The happy influence is not confined to what is called religious or Christian work ; it attends all work done in the fear of the Lord, in neighbourly love, and the honest fulfilment of duty. All such work is religious and Christian ; .the carrier's as much as the missionary's.

In dark and stormy nights in winter, the carrier's ,journey over the bleak lonely hill called Broadfield Down must try his fortitude and courage. When the snow lies deep, and the nights are dark, he sometimes starts earlier in the day to reach Bristol before nightfall ; but this is seldom, and more for his horse's sake than his own. Content to take the rough with the smooth, he starts on his midnight journey all the year round, and returns in safety with his varied load, welcomed by all who expect a parcel.

A parcel ! I know not how it may be now, for "the old order changeth ;" but seventy years ago the arrival of a parcel was an event to stir the childish heart. To a child for the first time at school, a parcel from home made the heart beat quick and the eyes overflow. Home and school were farther apart in every way than they are now. The old *half* was longer than the modern *term ;* and time as well as coaches went slower. The mail might come daily, but a "parcel per mail " was a costly affair : the errand cart twice a week, or the slow stage wagon, were the parcels-delivery institutions of those days. A parcel from home came, perhaps, only once in the half. Eagerly and lovingly were its sacred seals broken, its cord unloosed, and all its varied contents handled tenderly. A mother's love, home, and its blessed influences, breathed from that parcel. More frequent intercourse is an undoubted blessing, but neither the more frequent small parcels, nor the hasty notes of these hurrying days, can stir the soul like the angel visits of the big hamper, and the red-sealed quarto letter of old.

And then the Christmas parcels ! School parcels, at least in the old times, partook of the pathetic ; a parcel at home in the Christmas holidays was a feast spread by mirth itself. Painters have seized the happy moment when a young mother, surrounded by her eager little ones, draws forth the various treasures of the deep from granny's well-filled hamper; or when an emigrant family, in mingled smiles aud tears, open the parcel from the old folks at home, the far-off home they will " ne'er see again." Scenes like these are dear to English artists and English hearts, and are more wholesome as well as more pleasing to healthy minds than the sanguinary horrors too prevalent in foreign galleries.

Since the foregoing was written, the worthy old carrier has taken his last journey, and is, I doubt not, where the weary are at rest. We miss his useful services and his useful knowledge of Bristol shops. His picturesque cottage remains, but shows the wear and tear of more than two and a half centuries.

Several others of our most picturesque cottages and rustic buildings have decayed and disappeared in the last twenty years, owners and occupiers alike unable to keep them in repair. There is something very charming in the poet's ideal cottage :

> I knew by the smoke that so gracefully curled
> Above the green elms, that a cottage was near,
> And I said : "If there's peace to be found in the world,
> A heart that is humble might hope for it here."

And if humility were always united with temperance, industry and thrift, the cottage would indeed be the

abode of peace ; for there can be no genuine humility
without religion.   But the cottage homes of England are
not always so happy as they look.   Their roofs do not
always keep out the rain and snow, and the smoke instead
of curling gracefully above the green elms, sometimes
fails to go up the chimney.   The cottager is too often
more at home in the public-house than in his own cottage, and the cottage then soon ceases to be his own.   It
is bought for a trifle by a neighbour or left to decay.
The author of *The Deserted Village* tells us that

> A time there was ere England's griefs began,
> When every rood of ground maintained its man.

But he gives us no date !   There is more truth in what
follows :

> But times are altered ; trade's unfeeling train
> Usurp the land and dispossess the swain.
>
> .   .   .   .   .   .
>
> These, far departing, seek a kinder shore,
> And rural mirth and manners are no more.

The decreasing population of the rural districts, and
the over-crowding of the towns, is a subject which forces
itself upon the attention of politicians and philanthropists,
who are at their wits' end for a remedy.   The poet's rood
of ground, even multiplied by twelve, with a cow added,
will not preserve

> A bold peasantry, their country's pride,

unless the bold peasant improves in sobriety and thrift,
and advances with the times in the science and art of his
calling.

> How small of all that human hearts endure,
> That part which laws or kings can cause or cure ;
> Still to ourselves in every place consigned,
> Our own felicity we make or find.

IX.—THE SIDCOT CONJURER.

There are more things in heaven and earth, Horatio,
Than are dreamt of in your philosophy.

HAMLET.

A secluded valley, where labourers and small farmers dwell from generation to generation, old superstitions are apt to linger. Instances have been noticed with us; but I incline to think they are held rather as old traditions, than as facts. There may linger, here and there, some vague belief in omens, such as the flight of magpies, or in the consequences of sleeping under the cross-beams of a ceiling, or in the efficacy of a horse-shoe on the door or well-bucket. Our late vicar told me he had met with an instance of the cross-beam superstition. An old person had been for some days apparently dying, and the relations who watched around could not account for the delay of departure till they observed the position of the bed. This was no sooner shifted than the dying occupant "went off quite comfortable." The explanation of this remarkable circumstance is not more simple than that of the effect of the horse-shoe in securing a full bucket. Wishing to learn how far the charm was believed in, I asked one of our cottagers why the horse-shoe was fixed to the bucket, and received the simple reply, " 'Tis to tilt the bucket when he do go down the well."

The dowsing rod is generally included in the class of old superstitions by persons who have not seen it in use. It is used here as a means of finding springs, and the most incredulous admit the fact of the rod's unexplained motion, whatever may be its cause. One of the most noted practitioners with the divining rod was a man in this neighbourhood, Charles Adams of Rowberrow, who was employed by Mr. Marshall of Leeds. Adams considered that the moving of the rod is not due to the mere presence of water or metal, but to some vein or vault in which these matters lie, and from which there is some unexplained force or influence that affects the nerves of the holder of the rod, giving him what he called "a sort of turn," the rod at the same time turning round. " Now," continues Mr. Marshall, " Reichenbach, in his researches, gives some remarkable instances where slow chemical changes going on at some distance underground, were distinctly perceptible by persons susceptible of mesmeric influence."*

About a hundred years ago, there lived in a cottage, still standing, nearly opposite the old Friends' meeting-house

---

* See a Narrative of Practical Experiments, etc., by F. Phippen, 1853.

at Sidcot, a real Conjurer of the old school. His name was Beecham, and he had a wife whose name was Joan. He had the reputation of being a great "medicine man;" had a magic staff and books, wore a red cap, and was consulted as conjurer, or cow-doctor, whenever dryness in pump or cow, or loss of appetite in sow, disturbed the farmer's peace of mind. The time came at last for the wizard's staff to be broken, and his books to be wound-up. In view of the grave, he insisted on being buried under a certain tree in his own garden; telling his wife, if his directions were not complied with, "I'll trouble 'ee." The mortal clay, however, when vacated by the conjurer, was decently buried in the churchyard; and the widow, diligent, not disconsolate, remained in the old cottage, earning her bread by making cakes and sweets for other people. Thus she lived till she died, no one ever finding her cakes bewitched, or her sweets turning supernaturally sour. She lived and died with the character of a plain, honest body—a good old soul.

But now for the marvellous part of the story. On the anniversary of the old conjurer's death, or burial, tradition has forgotten which, one Wednesday morning, when the Friends were sitting in solemn silence in their usual week-day meeting for worship, their meditations were interrupted by the sudden appearance—not of Beecham's ghost—but of the woman who lodged with his widow, and who took care of the meeting-house. Pale with fright, she cried, "Oh Friends, do'e come out; there's all Joan Beecham's things a vallen' about the 'vloor." Two Friends, one a Minister, the other an Elder, solemnly rose and left the room, probably thinking more of preventing further disturbance of the meeting than of meddling with disturbance elsewhere. However, they followed the doorkeeper to widow Beecham's, and there witnessed a kind of disturbance they had never seen or heard of before.   As they entered, a heavy, old-fashioned chair came to meet them ; pots and pans were flung violently about ; old Joan's heavy pastry pan rocked up and down as if moved by invisible hands.   The Friends were shrewd experienced men, with a full share of the sobriety and worldly wisdom, if not spiritual discernment, with which their Society has always been credited.   They were not likely to be taken in by the trickery of two old women ; but they could discover no imposition ; nor could they ever explain or account for what they had witnessed.   The facts are undeniable. The report of the occurrence spread in the neighbour-hood, and many persons visited the spot to inquire into the circumstances.   Amongst others came Hannah More; but neither her superior sense and learning, nor the sagacity of commoner people could unravel the mystery. The conjuror never troubled the widow again, and the occurrence gradually subsided into the general collection of ghost-stories.   And so it might have remained, had not later experience caused some re-action from the general contempt for alleged supernatural occurences. Cases very similar to that at Beecham's cottage are said to be not unfrequently witnessed in " table-turning " circles ; and though such reports are sneered at by those who have not witnessed them, their sneers are in turn smiled at by those who have.   Sneers, however, prove nothing one way or the other.   The facts are attested by too many respectable witnesses to be disposed of in that way.   They are admitted by many scientific men, and various theories have been started to explain them.

These theories, however, are little more than a classifica-
tion and nomenclature of the phenomena. Mesmerism,
which was decried as imposture fifty years ago, is now,
under the more scientific name of hypnotism, deemed
worthy of some examination. We now hear of *animal
magnetism, psychic force, unconscious cerebration, levitation,*
and so on ; but how the *psychic force* and *unconscious cerebration* of the widow Beecham could have caused the
levitation of her kneading-trough, and her late husband's
heavy armchair, remains as much a mystery as ever. A
less scientific theory has been offered in this particular instance. It is suggested, as the conjurer had threatened
his wife to "trouble" her on the return of the day of
his decease, or burial, that possibly his conjuring crew
—for it is assumed that he was in league with others—
might for the credit of magic in general, and their late
confederate in particular, have planned a scheme for ful-
filling his threat. But this supposition leaves the mystery
as great as ever ; for if the movements of the pans and
chattels were effected by mechanical means, no uncommon sight and shrewdness could be needed to discover them. It is said that professional jugglers do more
wonderful tricks. Perhaps so. But who was the juggler
here? Where was he concealed? And where was his
apparatus? Where were the wires, and who were the
wire-pullers? A little stone-floored cottage can hardly
be compared with a theatre expressly arranged with
stage and machinery for organised and avowed deception.
The fact is, we live in an age of Sadduceeism. Scientific
men avow it, and glory in it ; religious men to a great
extent accept it tacitly. Creed is one thing, belief is
another. We will not "*say*" that there is no resurrection

neither angel, nor spirit ;* but we have no real belief in
either. When we hear of any alleged supernatural
occurence, we do not trouble ourselves to inquire into it ;
we say at once it is incredible, and we laugh at the
credulity of those who think it may possibly be true. Dr.
Johnson was laughed at for his credulity in joining a
committee to investigate the case of the " Cock-lane
ghost ;" though he seems to have been very easily satisfied
that it was a deception. His biographer justly observes,
" The fact was, Johnson had a very philosophical mind,
and such a rational respect for testimony, as to make him
submit his understanding to whatever was authentically
proved, though he could not comprehend why it was so.
Being thus disposed, he was willing to inquire into the
truth of any relation of supernatural agency, a general
belief of which has prevailed in all nations and ages.
But so far was he from being the dupe of implicit
faith that he examined the matter with a jealous attention, and no man was more ready to refute its falsehood
when he had discovered it."† The Cock-lane ghost may
have been a hoax, though the philosophers failed to de-
tect the imposition. The promised phenomena were not
fulfilled in their presence, and they concluded " that the
child had some art of making or counterfeiting a particular
noise, and that there was no agency of any higher
cause,"‡—a rather lame conclusion, though it might be
the next best to a simple " not proven."

The march of intellect during the present century is
supposed to have laid all the ghosts, and settled the

* Acts xxiii. 8.
† Boswell's Life of Johnson.
‡ Idem, Note.

question of the supernatural in the negative. Philosophy is still on the march, but its conquests, as yet, have not gone beyond physics. All its "forces" are physical; even its *psychic* forces are marshalled amongst the rest of the material *corps.*

The Scribes and Sadducees scoff at the Pharisees and Doctors of the Law. The Scripture accounts of the Magicians of Egypt, the Witch of Endor, and similar stories, together with the Jewish laws against witchcraft and necromancy, and the Gospel cases of demoniacal possessions, are taken as illustrations of the popular superstitions of the time ; in which even Christ himself is supposed to have shared.

Many who would repudiate Sadducecism reject modern ghost stories on the ground of their useless and frivolous character.

Nec Deus intersit, nisi dignus vindice nodus
Inciderit.

But is it necessary to assume Divine interposition in all cases of intercourse with the inhabitants of the spiritual world ? Admitting the possibility'of such intercourse, it would probably be between congenial spirits, whether good or bad, wise or foolish.

If a late cynical philosopher's estimate be a true one, the visible world is chiefly peopled by fools and knaves, and there is no reason to suppose that they become wise and honest by merely casting off their bodily sloughs. We might, therefore, reasonably expect that a large proportion of the intercourse between the congenial spirits of the two worlds would be of a frivolous nature. Those in the spirit-world would be chiefly such as yearned after the flesh pots of Egypt, and their friends in the

natural world would be of the like genius; and, accordingly, we find the craving after necromancy and
spirit news is chiefly amongst people who are satisfied
with neither physical science nor the Word of God. The
silliness of spirit-rapping, and the falsehood of many of
the spirit sayings, are quite consistent with the reality of
spirit intercourse; which may be now permitted as a
means of counteracting the prevailing disposition to deny
the existence of a spiritual state of being.

Beecham, the conjurer, in casting off his earthly body,
would not cast off his turn for magic. He would remain
the same man, wizard or rogue, he was before. Admitting
the possibility of his communicating with his wife, and
through her, with the material world, the knocking about
of her familiar chattels would not be an unlikely way
for him to "trouble" her. On the other hand, it may
be reasonably objected that, even admitting the possibility of a departed spirit "troubling" a near connection still in the flesh, would not the "trouble" be purely
a mental disturbance, or, at most, a bodily suffering re-
sulting therefrom? How, it may be asked, could a spirit
without earthly organs move earthly chairs and pans?
Here, perhaps, we may be allowed to call in an element
acknowledged by our Sadducee philosophers—*psychic
force.* Their old opponent, in his epistle to the Corinthians, says there is not only psychic force, but a *psychic
body.** "There is a psychic body as well as a spiritual
body." Our English translators have turned the *psychic*
body into a *natural* body; but *psychic* cannot mean
the mortal flesh and blood. It is *psychic* (soulish) Ἔστι
σῶμα ψυχικὸν, καὶ ἔστι σῶμα πνευματικόν. Now if this

* 1 Corinthians xv. 44, 45.

psychic or "natural" body be the *soul-ish* body of the
"*natural man,*" as distinct from the spirit of the
"*inner*" or spiritual man, have we not some clue to
the mystery? Is it not possible that this *psychic* body
may in peculiar circumstances be capable of assuming,
temporarily, some mundane element such as electricity,
and thus communicating with the material system? This
would account for the magnetic force sometimes so
wonderfully displayed, as well as for the occasional appearance of a hand and arm, in electric light, as attested
by many trustworthy witnesses. If there be any truth
in this theory, the *psychic force* displayed in the Sidcot
conjuror's cottage may have been the action of the *psychic
body* of the Sidcot conjuror himself.

At any rate, these things cannot be disposed of by
begging the question, or by what Canon Wilberforce
called " the ecclesiastical pooh-pooh."

Since the fore-going was written, a *Psychical Research
Society* has been sifting the truth out of the confused
heap of ghost-stories ; and, more recently, the Editor of
the *Review of Reviews* has been reviewing the views of
other reviewers, with peculiar views of his own. We can,
at least, agree to the following sentiments of our reviewer:
" Either these things exist, or they do not. If they do
not exist, then obviously there can be no harm in a
searching examination of the delusion, which possessed the
mind of almost every worthy of the Old Testament, and
which was constantly affirmed by the authors of the New.
If, on the other hand, they do exist, and are perceptible
under certain conditions to our senses, it will be difficult
to affirm the impiety of endeavouring to ascertain what
is their nature, and what light they are able to throw
upon the kingdom of the Unseen."

But suppose the *certain conditions* are disorderly, and only exist in disorderly states of the mind or body, is the kingdom of the Unseen likely to be revealed in any clearer light than in the Old and New Testament? " If they believe not Moses and the Prophets, neither will they be persuaded though one rose from the dead."

Old Sidcot Meeting-house and cottage.

X.—THE WILD BEASTS.

Birds and beasts,
And the mute fish that glances in the stream,
And harmless reptile coiling in the sun.
WORDSWORTH.

IN a country so long and thickly peopled as England, there can be but few wild beasts, except the too prolific species called vermin, which man has tried in vain to exterminate. The ancient inhabitants of this valley and the country round in pre-historic ages, have all passed away, and are now only known by their remains in the bone-caverns and other subterranean sepulchres.

I

These remains, however, prove that in a recent geological period the district was inhabited by the Mammoth, the Elephant, the Woolly Rhinoceros, the Urus and Bison, the great Elk and Rein-deer, and a small kind of Horse; with the great cave Lion and Bear, the Hyæna, and more recent Wolf; this last remaining into modern historical times.

The oldest species now surviving in this country is the ancient British Ox, preserved in Chillingham Park in Northumberland, and a Caledonian breed at Taymouth in Perthshire. Those formerly kept at Wollaton, Notts, at Gisburne in Craven, Yorkshire, at Chartley in Staffordshire, and at Lyme Hall Park in Cheshire, are now extinct; the last survivor of the small herd at Lyme Park having been shot in November, 1885.

The Red Deer, more widely spread in North Britain, and still, I believe, sometimes sighted in Martindale forest in Cumberland, remain in considerable numbers among the wooded hills of this county and the borders of Devonshire. But none of these noble beasts are now left in the Mendip combes, or in the scanty remains of the Selwood and Cheddar forests; from which the bishop, in the reign of Henry III., stocked his park at Wells.

The bravest wild beast now left is the Badger, or Brock, from which Brockley combe takes it name. He inhabits also the caves in Burrington and other combes, and is sometimes met with in the rocky ground between Sidcot and Shipham.

Foxes are not numerous, as this is not a hunting country. Sometimes, however, we hear the hounds, and see them in full cry across the valley: a sight which even the most humane cannot view without pleasurable excitement. The love of the chace is inherent in human nature, and its uses cannot be denied. But if fox-hunting—

Which rural gentlemen call sport divine—

be a "manly sport," the same can hardly be said of harrying a poor timid hare.

Poor is the triumph o'er the timid hare.

Some years ago an old fox was killed after a long chace, and was found to have run all the way on three feet; having apparently escaped from a trap with the loss of a fore-foot. Another old fox was brought here on the shoulder of a labouring man, or a poacher, who asked for "a shilling for killing this stinking varmint : he'd a' had all your fowls." Asked if he did not get more kicks than shillings for his pains, he replied, "Ah! they do swear at I, some on 'em." The natural death of a fox is, no doubt, by the teeth of hounds, not by those of a trap, still less by the snare or shot of a poacher. The huntsman professes to believe that the fox, as well as the horses and dogs, enjoys the chace. Possibly he may, as long as he feels he can out-run, or out-wit, his pursuers. Being himself addicted to sport it is more to his credit to fall in the field than to be out-witted by one sharper than himself : a fate peculiarly galling to a fox.

We are not much troubled with Hares in this valley ; but they have sometimes visited our garden and paddock, where an amusing scene occurred one evening. A Hare and a Magpie were observed at play together, jumping about as hares and magpies do, when the pie suddenly took wing. The bewildered look of the hare as she raised her head, and looked round for her companion, would have made a picture for Joseph Wolf or Stacey Marks.

Rabbits are fairly, and not intolerably, abundant on Blackdown, Dolbury-warren and other hills.

Otters are found sparingly in some of the water-courses of the turf moors, but the scanty fishing in our valley does not tempt them hither.

Squirrels frequent the apple-orchards and the few remaining woods, and build conspicuous nests in the fir trees of the Winterhead Avenue at Sidcot. One winter's day, while watching a flock of Fieldfares and Redwings searching among the fallen leaves of an orchard, I observed a squirrel descend an old tree and run across the ground, probably to some savings bank where the thrifty creature had a deposit-account. In the autumn before, I had noticed one leaping from branch to branch of an ivy-grown oak, with a small red apple in his mouth : a picture worth all the cider the little creature could forestall; though I fear the farmers generally prefer the cider. Since then, the oak, the squirrel, and the flowery coppice, have all disappeared : the ground has been cleared for potatoes, which are more substantial fare than pictures of squirrels and woodland scenes. Yet one cannot but regret the disappearance of the woods and coppices, where we could say with Rogers—

> The ring-dove builds and murmurs there,
> The squirrel leaps from tree to tree,
> And shells his nuts at liberty.

The pretty little mischievous, but sometimes useful, Weasel may often be seen crossing the road. The Polecat is, fortunately, not common here. The royal Ermine, in the vulgar form of the Stoat, has been observed playing in the fields, but never detected preying upon the poultry. If ermine is worn by Royalty and Justice as a symbol of unflinching courage, the symbol must be limited to that virtue of the stoat. The rest of his character can hardly be considered worthy of either the throne or the judgment-seat.

Rats and mice may be taken to symbolize the base and thievish propensities which lurk as in drains, and creep in the dark. They are, unhappily, too common wherever men dwell, and as hard as human vices to get rid of. A writer in an American paper, some years ago, says— "the human intellect rarely appears at so great a disadvantage as when devising remedies for rats; except when placing faith in those remedies." After exposing the inefficiency of all others, he concludes with this only effective one: "If you tear down your house, plough arsenic into the foundation, and build upon its site a strong enclosure filled with large and hungry cats, the rats may desert it. The remedy is a costly one, and has its inconveniences, but so far it is the only cure which can be tried with any reasonable hope that it will be effective." But rats and mice, as well as cockroaches, crocodiles and flies, are useful scavengers, and, like other evil beasts, and evil things, may prevent worse. Too many mice are a nuisance ; but you may hear the same said of Nightingales and other musicians, where they abound and disturb the rest of the weary, or the meditations of those who consume the midnight oil.

The country bachelor, in the nursery song, who, by the rats and mice, "was forced to go to London to buy himself a wife," must have allowed them to increase and multiply unduly, in spite of his own example. Perhaps he lived before Whittington, when cats were scarce and dear.

The *Long-tailed Field Mouse* is rather a pretty creature "Wee, sleekit, cow'rin, tim'rous beastie!" Who can read Burns's lines without sympathy?

> I doubt na, whyles, but thou may thieve,
> What then? poor beastie, thou maun live !
> A *daimen-icker** in a thrave
>   's a sma' request ;
> I'll get a blessin' wi' the lave,
>   And never miss't !

But the wee sleekit beastie of the field is as great a nuisance as the domestic beastie, if left to multiply unchecked by hawks and owls and other "vermin." The hoards which this thrifty creature stores underground are said to attract other less thrifty creatures to grub for them. Pennant believed the damage done by the swine in forest districts is partly due to their mooting after the stores laid up by the field-mice : thus

> ......proving foresight may be vain ;

and that—

> The best laid schemes o' mice an' men
>   Gang aft agley.

Beside these familiar animals, a much rarer mouse is occasionally found in this neighbourhood,—the Harvest Mouse, first discovered by White of Selborne; who writes to Mr. Pennant, 22nd January, 1768. "As to the small mice I mentioned, I have further to remark that, though they hang their nests for breeding amidst the straws of the standing corn, above the ground, yet I find that, in the winter, they burrow deep in the earth, and make warm beds of grass; but their grand rendezvous

---

* A grain now and then, out of two shocks of corn.

seems to be in corn ricks, into which they are carried at harvest. A neighbour housed an oat-rick lately, under the thatch of which were assembled near a hundred. Two of them, in a scale, weighed down just one copper halfpenny."

The harmless Water Vole, commonly called the Water Rat, is more pleasing both in appearance and in manners, than his distant relation the land rat. "There be land-rats, and water rats," as Shylock said: "Water thieves and land thieves." But our Water Vole, though it has a thievish name, is a comparatively innocent creature, a vegetarian, and related to the respectable Beaver family. Mr. Wood describes one "sitting upon a water-lily leaf, and engaged in eating the green seeds"—a picture it seems strange that such a gentle lover of Nature, and so clever a delineator of animal life, should have destroyed, instead of preserving it in his sketch-book ; but he says it happened in his earlier life.

Allied to the Water Vole is the Campagnol or Short-tailed Field Mouse, or Field Vole. It is not a very pretty little animal, and is very mischievous, burrowing into the ground and eating the sown wheat. The young trees in the New Forest and the Forest of Dean were nearly des-troyed by swarms of these little creatures. After trying cats and stoats and other means in vain, the foresters sank pits all over the forests, and in that way caught many thousands. There were long-tailed mice among these depredators, but the bulk of them were the Cam-pagnol or Field Vole.

The Shrew is remarkable for being seen oftener dead than alive ; a circumstance not fully explained, though partly accounted for by the singular fact that only the owl will eat the shrew alive or dead.

The Water Shrew, an elegant swimmer, is to be seen
in some of our water-courses, and the pretty Dormouse,
more squirrel than mouse, is sometimes caught by our
village boys, who call it a "seven sleeper."

The "little gentleman in velveteen," who gives the
farmers such practical lessons in draining and sub-soil
plowing, is found, not only in damp meadows, but, contrary to a common belief, on the hills and far from water.
He is called here the Wont, and the heaps of mould he
throws up in making his *wriggle* are called *wont-heaves.*

Hedge-hogs are common here, and sometimes destroy
young chicken. Broods hatched in stray nests in the
hedges often fall victims to the prickly urchin. But his
attacks are sometimes less excusable. About bed-time
one night there was a great outcry from a hen-coop near
the house. Search was made, but no marauder could be
discovered. In the morning three chicks were found
dead, with their breasts devoured ; a mode of destruction
different from that practiced by rats and other vermin.
Another instance occurring inside the hen-house, a trap
was set, baited with a dead chick. Next morning who
should be found in the trap but the audacious Mr.
Prickles! To do him justice, however, he is a nice
household pet; devoted to cockroaches, and apt to become familiar, if not stroked the wrong way. He is a
veritable pin-cushion, each particular hair of his back
being a solid-headed pin, stuck through his skin point
uppermost. A hedge-hog kept in a London kitchen was
found one morning inside a large pat of butter, into which
he had burrowed as into his native bank. White of Selborne says the urchin is useful in biting off the roots of
plantain, a troublesome plant in lawns; but he never rendered any such service here to pay for his chicken

suppers. For all that, I like him as one of the few rustics left.

Another common object of the country, should, according to systematic zoology, have had precedence of all others—the Bat, one of the four-handed creatures allied to monkeys, mice, and men. There are several different kinds : a large and a small one are often seen in the summer evening air, where they look best, as all do, when doing what they can do well. On the ground and hanging in caves, bats are ugly things; but they are fearfully and wonderfully made, and are useful in destroying myriads of creatures, perhaps as innocent as themselves, but unbearable in excess. The Bat and Mole are among the queer couples of society, like the cat and mouse, and robin and wren. Moles and bats, though the one lives in the air and the other under-ground, agree in disliking day-light : " Blind as a bat," " blind as a mole," " lynx-eyed in darkness."

Children are sometimes taught that nothing in nature is ugly, but fallen human nature. The sentiment is more pious than true. If nature in man is fallen, so is nature around him. The earth is no longer a Garden of Eden ; it brings forth thorns and thistles, poisonous plants and evil beasts, which would not have existed if everything had continued " very good." Sacred Scripture does not confirm the notion that nature, as it now exists, is as it was designed by the Creator. To teach a child that all the creatures in a natural history book are beautiful, is spoiling its ideas of beauty. Some of the reptiles, and insects and others, are " ugly as sin," being corresponding images of the deformities of fallen humanity, or what the Americans call " inherent cussedness."

Mary Howitt, in her *Picture Book for the Young*, already referred to in our account of Winscombe Folk,* tells us about a fight between two village boys, who were parted by the good Celestine, while Farmer Gilliflower put a stop to a similar difference between two feathered cockerels. Peace being restored, Celestine addresses the boy Dick on the inherent cussedness of human and feathered creatures. " Of course, I do not know of a certainty," she says, " but I sometimes think that if human beings—boys and girls as well as men and women—would be good, and kind, and helpful to one another, and try to get rid of the evil that is in them, that then, perhaps, the cruelty and the savage passions in animals would cease too, and the world would be very lovely, would it not, Dick, if it were full of love?"

It was the belief of the ancients that " all things in heaven are also in the earth in an earthly form, and all things in the earth are in heaven in a heavenly form.†" And again, that man is a *microcosm*, or little world, containing the essential realities which are represented visibly in the *macrocosm* or physical world. Hence, Kirby, in his famous *Introduction to the Study of Entomology*, says : " To the most ancient people, the creation was a book of symbols, a sacred language, of which they possessed the key, and which it was their delight to study and decipher."

This sacred language of the book of Nature is abundantly used in the Sacred Scriptures or Books of Revelation, and was applied in their interpretation both by St. Paul and the early Fathers of the Christian

* Page 89   † Hermes Trismegistus.

Church.* The same idea has impressed thoughtful minds
in all ages. Thus Milton :

> What if earth
> Be but the shadow of heaven, and things therein,
> Each to other like, more than on earth is thought.

And Wordsworth :

> Trust me that for the instructed, time will come
> When they shall meet no object but may teach
> Some acceptable lesson to their minds.

Charles Kingsley found his belief becoming every day
stronger, "that all symmetrical natural objects—aye, and
perhaps all forms, colors, and scents—which show organi-
zation and arrangement, are types of some spiritual truth
or existence ; that everything I see has a meaning, if I
could but understand it."† Professor Agassiz writes :
" There will be no scientific evidence of God's working in
nature, until naturalists have shown that the whole creation is the expression of thought, and not the product of
physical agents merely." And again, " Let naturalists
look at the world under such impressions, and evidence
will pour in upon us, that all creatures are expressions of
Him whom we know, love and adore, unseen." " Man is
the end to which all the animal creation has tended, from
the first appearance of the first palæozoic fishes."

Henry Drummond writes, " It is clear that a remarkable harmony exists between the organic world

---

* See *Tracts for the Times, No. 89 ;* and for a more complete view of the
subject, the *Arcana Cœlestia, Apocalypsis Revelata* and *Doctrine concerning
the Sacred Scriptures* by Emanuel Swedenborg.

† Letter from Eversleigh Rectory, July 16th, 1842.

as arranged by Science, and the spiritual world as arranged by Scripture." And he quotes Professor Shairp:
" This seeing of spiritual truths mirrored in the face of
Nature rests not on any fancied, but in a real analogy
between the natural and spiritual worlds. They are, in
some sense which science has not ascertained, but which
the vital and religious imagination can perceive, counter-
parts one of the other."* How can it be otherwise, if the
organic world and the spiritual are from the same Source?
If the books of nature and of revelation are by the same
Divine Author, must they not, each in its way, show
that Author's mind—*the Divine goodness and wisdom ?*

But the Creator's thoughts and intentions have been
marred by man's abuse of the God-like faculties bestowed
upon him. He is no longer an image and likeness of
God, but has to be made so by becoming "a new
creature."† In the mean while, "the whole creation
groaneth and travaileth in pain together."‡ Both *macrocosm* and *microcosm* are in disorder ; the world without
shows the deformities of the world within.

It may be said that ugly and ravenous creatures existed before the creation of man. If that be an ascertained
fact, may not such creatures be regarded as forms corresponding rather to the incomplete, than the deformed
state of man, before the *cosmos* was evolved out of *chaos* ?

Moral deformity, or evil, is nothing but the misplace-
ment or abuse of what, in its right place and use, is good.
Self-love and the love of the world, even the sensual and
animal appetites, which, when in disorder and excess,
sink man below the level of the beast, are, in their right

* *Natural Law in the Spiritual World.*
† 2 Corinthians v. 17.   ‡ Romans viii. 22.

places and proportions, as innocent as they are useful and necessary. There was a serpent in the Garden of Eden, wise in its generation, subtle; but not necessarily venomous. And the heel, which the serpent bruises, though the lowest part of the body, and in closest contact with the earth, is as necessary to the perfect man, as the unruly member in his mouth. Better be speechless than given to lying and slander; better limp on the road to heaven than walk with ease in the counsel of the ungodly: yet a dumb man lacks one of the chiefest gifts of humanity, and a lame man is but "'a limping Christian," even with the help of Baxter's " High-heeled shoe."*

Most people find, with the author of *Trivia*, how hard it is

> Through winter streets to steer their course aright,
> How to walk clean by day, and safe by night.

Yet few would refuse to walk for fear of going astray, or walk only on clean-swept paths for fear of soiling their feet. Better go wherever duty calls, and if the feet are soiled by the dirtiness of the world's ways, submit to have them washed by the Divine Truth, that the disciple may be " clean every whit."†

The old serpent may then be left in the garden, and will be as harmless as the dove.‡ " The wolf also shall dwell with the lamb, and the leopard lie down with the kid, and the calf, and the young lion, and the fatling together ; and a little child shall lead them."§

---

* *A High-heeled Shoe for a Limping Christian*, by Richard Baxter (?)
† John xiii. 8—10.   ‡ Matt. x. 16.   § Isaiah xi. 6.

XI.—THE BIRDS.

Come, all ye feathery people of mid-air,
Who sleep 'midst rocks, or on the mountain's summit,
Lie down with the wild winds, and ye who build
Your homes amidst green leaves by grottos cold.

A DISTRICT so varied in surface, including hill and dale, moor and rock, with coppice, orchard, garden, meadow, ploughed land, and marsh, might be expected to harbour a great variety of birds; and accordingly, if we take in the turf moors outside the valley, and the neighbouring sea shore, our list will include a large proportion of the British species. Our neighbourhood has also been rather specially favoured by distinguished visitors, as will be seen in the following pages.

The *Egyptian Vulture* is included in modern books of British Birds on account of a visit paid by a pair to this county in 1825. One of them was shot at Kilve, near Alfoxden, and their flight would probably be seen from these hills. A much nearer view, however, was enjoyed of another great bird of prey in the winter of 1860 ; when a fine *Erne* or *White-tailed Eagle* honoured our humble abode with a visit. The first notice of the distinguished visitor was given by the poultry in the yard, who were seen flying for refuge to a covered barton, followed by the sheep and an ass from the adjoining paddock. On looking up, the cause of their instinctive fright was discovered, with out-spread wings and open bill, and so near that its sparkling eyes were distinctly seen. Balked of its prey the Eagle flew across the valley, over the hills and far away, and was shot on the other side of the channel. Colonel Montagu mentions one shot on the Mendip hills in 1802, and the Quantocks were visited by another in 1889, which carried off several lambs, and what was even more lamentable, a lady's dog. There is a fine specimen of the *Sea Eagle* in the Taunton Museum, shot at Stolford in November, 1856, and a younger one taken more recently at Brean Down.

The same collection contains a good example of the *Osprey*, which is included in the birds of Somersetshire ; though this part of the county offers little attraction to a Fish Hawk.

The *Peregrine Falcon*, seldom seen in our valley, has long been a resident on the Steep Holm and at Brean

Down, where it is called the Great Falcon. It bred for many years in the Cheddar cliffs, where it was called the Hunting Hawk, and might be seen in the morning and evening:—

> A pair of falcons wheeling on the wing,
> In clamorous agitation, round the crest
> 'Of a tall rock, their airy citadel.

They would chase the rock-doves and daws, but were not often seen in the middle of the day. The young were taken every year, for sale, at the great hazard of life. One of the old women who lived among the cliffs used to tell of her son's brave and fatal exploit in descending the face of the rock to get the young hawks, and how "his foot slipped, and he was dashed all to atoms." Time had worn out the mother's anguish and horror, but not her sense of her boy's courage. Nevertheless, in descending high perpendicular cliffs, discretion is the better part of valour, especially when the venture is not, like that so well described by the poet, for the Heaven-blessed purpose of restoring an infant to its mother, but to rob a a mother of her own.

The *Hobby*, which might be called the Lesser Peregrine, figures in many collections in this county, and is said to have been seen here ; but that is very seldom. The still rarer *Orange-legged Hobby* or *Red-footed Hawk* has been taken at Cheddar, and there are local specimens in the collections of Mr. Tanner of Sidcot, and Mr. Byne of Bath. The *Merlin* is also among our occasional visitors, and has been seen quite lately at Woodborough.

The *Kestrel* builds among the rocks of Wavering Down and Barton. Useful as a destroyer of mice and cock-chafers, the Windhover is tolerated, even by game-keepers, in spite of its occasional poaching. It is, therefore, the commonest of English hawks, though not so common as it was.

The *Sparrow Hawk* is not so indulgently treated ; yet it can hardly be called rare in this neighbourhood. Not long ago, one was observed sitting quietly on a walnut-tree branch within a few yards of our kitchen door. In the evening it came into an outhouse, where it roosted several nights, undisturbed by curious interviewers. It seemed to be incapable of vigorous flight, as if it had been wounded ; but after a few days it disappeared. Not long afterwards a similar hawk sat upon the same branch, and while servants were looking on, dashed at a brood of chicken, and carried one off. Before the excitement and laughter at this expedition were over, another chick disappeared in the same way. Some years ago a Sparrow-hawk was caught in the Sidcot Toll-house, having dashed in after a sparrow. The boldness of this bird is wonderful. Mr. Edwards of Wrington has a specimen, which was captured in his dining room, after killing a canary in a cage hanging in the window. The hawk is preserved with the canary in its talons.

It has been observed that small birds appear to be stupefied by the descent of a hawk, as they are said to be fascinated by the gaze of a serpent. They will make no effort to escape, when they could easily do so by dropping into the hedge. Whatever this benumbing or mesmerising influence may be, if it remove the *apprehension* of death, it robs death of its sting, and may at the same time remove the *corporal sufferance.*

> The sense of death is most in apprehension,
> And the poor beetle that we tread upon
> In corporal sufferance finds a pang as great
> As when a giant dies.

K

We may hope that the pang is not so great to either giant or beetle as is commonly imagined. Dr. Livingstone felt quite easy in the lion's mouth, and there is true philosophy in this as in other passages in *Adam Bede* : "What little child ever refused to be comforted by that glorious sense of being seized strongly and swung upwards? I don't believe Gannymede cried when the eagle carried him away, and perhaps deposited him on Jove's shoulder at the end."

The *Kite* or *Glede* has been occasionally seen here. Mr. Byne of Bath has a fine specimen, trapped in 1865. One was shot not long since near Street, and there are others in the county collections ; but so conspicuous and rapacious a bird, which has long ceased to be common, must become more and more rare. Bad as the Kite's character is among gamekeepers and henwives, it is not so black as it is painted. With a decided taste for poultry and game, it has quite as much relish for rats and snakes, and other vermin, including moles, of which nearly two dozen have been found in a single nest. Moles are among the farmer's friends ; but there may be too many of them for his good or their own. Kind Nature, ever unfailing in its resources, provides a remedy, if not prevented by man's foolish selfishness. To save the moles from starvation, the kite takes the part of farmer's friend, and in the philosophical spirit of Malthus, prevents the underground population from pressing unduly upon the means of subsistence. Let the farmer put a just value upon each of his numerous friends. If his royal friend *Milvus regalis* be without mate or family, one such may be better than none, though probably better than more.

The *Buzzard* is commoner on the Quantock Hills than with us. It is, however, to be met with on the Mendips.

The *Rough-legged Buzzard* has been observed in Burnham
and other places ; but no instance is known, I think, of
the *Honey Buzzard's* appearance in this county. The
Marsh Harrier, or *Moor Buzzard*, has been taken at
Brean Down and elsewhere ; the *Hen Harrier*, with its
mate the *Ring-tail*, and the *Ash-coloured* or *Montagu's
Harrier*, in other parts of the county. Mr. Cecil Smith
considered the last to have been always the commoner
species, though they are both now very scarce. One was
trapt at Brean Down in June, 1864.

The *Harriers*, in their habits, and approach to a facial
disc, connect the Falcons with the *Owls ;* the nearest
relation, perhaps, being the *Hawk Owl.* A specimen of
this bird was shot in August, 1847, while hawking, in the
middle of the day, on Backwell Hill, between Nailsea and
Yatton. The only British specimen previously known
was taken, in an exhausted state, off the coast of Cornwall,
in March, 1830. Since 1847, there have been four recorded visits in Scotland and one in Yorkshire,* but none,
as far as I am aware, in the South of England. Another
variety of the owl family has, however, shed a ray of
ornithological glory upon our own obscure valley, as the
following record will prove:—" *Tengmalm's Owl,* Winscombe, Somersetshire, winter, 1859-60 : Gould's Birds of
Great Britain."† A pair were observed on the side of
Winscombe hill : one escaped, the other is in the
collection of Charles Edwards, Esq., of Wrington.
Several other specimens have been recorded, but almost
all in the northern and eastern counties. Both these
species inhabit the northern regions of the globe, and are
described in the celebrated work of Richardson and

* Harting's Handbook, 1872.   † Idem.

Swainson, the *Fauna Boreali Americana.* How they found their way to Brockley and Winscombe is more easily asked than answered.

The little *Scops Eared Owl,* an inhabitant of central Europe and Asia, has also wandered as far as Somerset-shire, and left its remains in a glass case at Bath.

Of the proper English Owls we have in this neighbour-hood occasionally both the *Long-eared* and the *Short-eared Owl,* the latter sometimes appearing in numbers. The common *Barn Owl,* called here the *White Owl,* is not so common as it was before some old elms were cut down, "wur the girt white owl did 'bide." We miss its silent evening flight across the home-paddock, like a great moth. The *Tawny, Brown* or *Wood Owl* is our commonest species. If not oftener seen, it is much oftener heard. When we first came from London we took its *hooting* for the shouting of boys at a distance, till we discovered our feathered friend up in an elm close by, and heard him and his wife chattering together in their peculiarly owlish way.

Farmers, who are apt to treat their feathered friends ungratefully, cannot deny the value of the nocturnal labours of the owls. If the gamekeepers complain that a young leveret and sundry young rabbits may now and then be traced to the owl's abode, the farmer will not be much disturbed by that, nor object to be deprived of some of his moles as well as his rats and mice. Yet, the old stupid ignorance still prevails in some districts. Quite lately a Norfolk bird stuffer received no less than 40 Barn Owls slain in one season.* Is it any wonder that mice swarm ?

* *Field Club,* March, 1892.

The *Great Butcher Bird* is said to have been seen several times at Sidcot ; but some doubt has been thrown upon the observation, the bird not having been very distinctly seen. The *Woodchat* has been shot in Cheddar Wood ; the *Red-backed Shrike*, one of our prettiest birds, is quite common. These birds destroy numberless chafers, beetles, and mice, and probably do little or no harm to any one else.

Ravens formerly frequented Crooks Peak, and still build on Brean Down and Cheddar Cliffs, but not now in our valley. Mr. Knight gives me an amusing instance of the superstition still lingering about these birds,

"Of death and dolour telling."

An old man at Cheddar being asked to get some raven's eggs, as well as hawk's, from the cliffs, had no hesitation in letting himself down by a rope to get at the hawk's nest; but as to the raven's—"No, I wouldn't touch one o' they for five pound. John Vowles—he said he didn't care, and he took the eggs,—and he died. And poor Mr. Arthur, I saw him shoot two, and when we got down, there was but one ! and poor Mr. Arthur, he was took ill, and he died. And, you med smile, but I wouldn't touch they for five pound."

The *Carrion Crow* has here a " local habitation and a name"—as a nimmer of chicken and ducklings before they are fairly carrion. The thievish *Magpie, la Gazza Ladra*, has the like ill-fame, as well as a reputation for filching things of more value to their owners and of none to herself. But let us give the black creatures their due. They are useful scavengers, and probably weed out the sickly chickens, which would " eat their own heads off ;" and as to other valuables, the gravity of the story of *the*

Maid and the Magpie was the loss, not of " trash," but of a " good name."

> Who steals my purse steals trash ;—
> But he that filches from me my good name
> Robs me of that which not enriches him,
> And makes me poor indeed.

We sympathize with the maid, and rejoice in the vindication of her good name ; a word, too, for the magpie. One killed as a mischievous depredator was examined for proof of guilt, after execution, and when the pie was opened the truth began to sing; for the crop was found to contain nothing more precious than " seven grains of poisoned wheat, nine wire-worms, and a table-spoonful of beetles and larvæ*."

The *Hooded, Royston or Grey Crow* is not often seen in Somersetshire, but Mr. Edwards has a specimen killed at Rowberrow warren, where his gamekeeper says he has seen several others.   Professor Newton, in the last edition of Yarrell's Birds, identifies the Grey with the Black Carrion Crow ; but his arguments are inconclusive. Though the black and grey Crows may mingle, there is no evidence that the progeny are fertile, and the pairing seems to be only casual.   Mr. Borrer in his *Birds of Sussex* says he has never known an instance.   The habits of the two species also differ.   The Roystoners are migratory, arriving in October, and leaving in March, while the black Crows remain to breed.

The *Rook* is no less familiar in our valley than in other parts of the country.   There is a rookery at Bartòn, the western hamlet of Winscombe, and another at Loxton, on the opposite side of the stream.   Also one at Cross, on

---

* *Zoologist*, 1864.

the south side of the hills. There are, therefore, plenty of coloured labourers to clean the land for our farmers, and save the crops, which but for them would have but little chance. Like other coloured labourers, however, they are rather tolerated than cherished ; being expected to work on the terms that virtue is its own reward, or at best, that wire-worms should be the wages in full for rooks, the grain they have saved being reserved for the crops of the farmers. Such is the way of this selfish world ; but the farmers should bear in mind the expostulation urged on behalf of the *Birds of Killingworth*,

> You call them thieves and pillagers ; but know
> They are the winged warders of your farms,
> Who from the cornfields drive the insidious foe,
> And from your harvest keep a hundred harms.

The *Jackdaw*—what is the wife's name ?—may generally be seen, here as elsewhere, in company with Parson Rook ; but he is not here " a great frequenter of the church," either for perch or dormitory. The gay laughing *Jay* is not so common as the *Magpie*. His partiality for garden stuff, and his pretty wing feathers, expose him to the shot of the fowler. He is fond of peas and cherries as well as eggs ; but he is also a great gatherer of chafers and their larvæ, snails and slugs, and other kinds of grub ; while the acorns and berries he eats are no loss where no other use is made of them.

Among the stuffed birds in the hall of Sidcot School there used to be a specimen of the *Cornish Chough* or *Red-legged Crow*. Mr. Tanner's collection included another, and Mr. Edwards's of Wrington a very fine one. These were local examples, and the species is still to be found on the coast of Dorsetshire,* unless destroyed within the

---

* *Birds of Dorsetshire*, by Mansell—Pleydell.

last five years ; but it is no longer an inhabitant of the
Mendip hills, and is rarely seen even in Cornwall, where
it was formerly common.

The name of *Chough* is certainly not confined to the
Reg-legged Crow. The Inn sign of the *Three Choughs* is
not peculiar to the old house at Yeovil, where the Cornish
Chough might probably be known; it is a sign found in
other counties, where it most likely means the Jackdaw.
Commentators take him to be the Chough meant by
Shakespear in his fine description of the cliff that bears
his name, at Dover—

> The Crows and Choughs, that wing the midway air ;
> Show scarce so gross as beetles. *

What he says, too, of "Chough's language, gabble enough,"
agrees with the "chattering daws," and when he speaks of
" russet-pated choughs, many in sort," we may, perhaps,
take the russet as a figure of speech, answering to the
" sere and yellow leaf," and referring to the grey head of
the daw, and the grizzly beak of the rook, rather than
the vermilion bill of the Cornish Chough.

In the fine old glee of the *Chough and Crow*, the birds
alluded to are most likely the Daw and Rook, whose
going to roost would be more familiar than the red-legged
and carrion crows. Although a " Rookery" is a familiar
scene, Rooks are, as often as not, called " crows"; as in
"The Cotter's Saturday Night "—

> November's chill blaws loud wi' angry sough ;
> The short'ning winter day is near a close ;
> The miry beasts retreating 'frae the pleugh ;
> The black'ning trains o' craws to their repose.

* KING LEAR, IV. 6.

The Crow family is considered by some Ornithologists as the type of perfection of Birds. At home alike in the air and the tree tops, on the ground and on the sea-shore ; lofty and powerful in flight, perchers, and yet good walkers, they have every birdish accomplishment, but that of swimming; and the head of the family, the Raven, is the first of the few birds mentioned in Holy Writ.

Before parting from the family we must remember the visit to Bridgwater in 1805, of the *Nutcracker*, mentioned by Colonel Montagu. Since that date about twenty visits have been recorded ; five in Devonshire and Cornwall, and one at North Petherton in this county. It is therefore quite possible that this interesting bird may some day be seen in our Valley, or in the more wooded country farther west, as we have seen it in the forest lands of Bavaria and Tyrol, hammering a nut or acorn on the branch of an oak, or perched on the top of a lofty pine, calling to its mate, and when answered, flying into the depths of the forest.

Starlings, an old inhabitant says, were never seen in Winscombe valley when he was young. Of late years they have been among our commonest birds. The young Starling is so different from the adult as to have been described by Montagu and figured by Bewick and others as a different species, namely the *Brown Starling* or *Solitary Thrush.* Of this Mr. Edwards has a specimen with the brown plumage varied with white. Starlings are useful birds, and do little or no harm ; feeding almost wholly on wire-worms, grubs, beetles, and such creatures as the farmer and gardener wish to be rid of. A writer, quoted in the *Birds of Somersetshire*, says that during a very dry summer a flock of starlings had collected in a field of vetches, when an old labourer remarked, "Them starns are getting no end o' they tares." On shooting one, however, and opening its crop, it was found to be crammed with insects, beetles, and a mass of green aphis. The tares were covered with the green fly, and it was these, and not the tares, that the starlings were clearing off.

In pairing time these amusing and handsome birds build in our roofs, and entertain us with their quaint ways. The male has a sweet melodious warble, and is often a capital mimic, if not a ventriloquist. One fine old bird, who built for several years in our stable roof, had a remarkably rich gift for both minstrelsy and imitation. Standing on the gable, sunning his glossy plumage, he would warble his proper song, then suddenly break off, and whistle to the dogs, mimic the poultry, crow, and bark, and appear to enjoy his entertainment, as the Mocking Bird and other mimics do. The talking power of the Starling was familiar to Shakespear—" I will have a Starling taught to say *Mortimer.*"

A rare and elegant bird, allied to the Starlings, is the *Rose-coloured Pastor ;* a bird of the East, so named from its frequenting sheep-walks, where its useful services protect it from destruction. It frequents also the Mediterranean countries, both Northern Africa and the European peninsulas, coming to Spain and England, and returning, if happy enough to escape with life, " out of England into France, out of France into Spain," as that good man, Dr. Faustus, taught his geographical class. The Pastor, or *Rose Ouzel*, is usually figured as on the ground ; but, like the Starling, it is also a tree-percher. A specimen in the collection of Mr. Edwards, was shot in a mulberry tree in a garden at Axbridge. There are other Somersetshire specimens in the museums at Bath and Taunton, as well as in private collections.

Another rare and beautiful bird, allied to the Starlings and Thrushes, the *Golden Oriole*, has been twice found within the limits of our view, and might be a regular summer ornament of our English gardens, if the organs of destructiveness and acquisitiveness could be controlled for a few years. But when a man can write to a newspaper, and have his letter inserted without rebuke, that of a flock of Orioles, he " succeeded in bagging all but one," there can be no hope of our often seeing these beautiful birds alive in England, and hearing their singularly sweet whistle, as in the woods of South Germany, and the vineyards of France. The same may be said of the beautiful *Hoopoe*, a bird often seen in the Rhine countries, and not a very rare visitant of Devonshire and Cornwall. It is included in Mr. Smith's *Birds of Somersetshire*, having once been observed near Taunton, and there are specimens in most of the local collections.

The brilliant *Bee-eater* does not seem to have visited Somersetshire, but we are informed that no less than "twelve were *procured* in one day at Helston !" Another equally beautiful bird that might occasionally adorn our country, the *Roller*, has once visited this county, and, of course, paid the penalty. It was "taken" in an orchard near Taunton, and its skin is said to be preserved : which is certainly better than wearing out in some lady's hat.

The *Waxwing* or *Chatterer* has been several times found in this district, and figures in local collections ; where alone rare beauties can be seen, except by the lucky chance of anticipating the gunner.

Even the *Kingfisher* is now comparatively scarce, and
if the fashion of wearing birds' skins as hat decoration
last much longer, it will outlast the birds whose beauty is
thus abused.   Feathers, such as ostrich's and peacock's,
are things of beauty not suggestive of destruction ; but a
pair of wings with a glass-eyed head between them is
offensive to good taste.   A local museum of Natural
History is a desirable institution for every county, and
no one can object to collections being also made by
private individuals for the like use.   That is quite distinct from the wanton destruction caused by mere cupidity,
and the propensity to shoot any rare or conspicuous object, and then boast of the deed in the newspapers.   The
love of collecting is at best too apt to sink into mere
greed, where the scientific and æsthetic interest is degraded into the miserly one of possessing specimens
of money value.

·The Kingfisher, Bee-eater, Roller, and Oriole vie in
brilliancy of plumage with tropical birds ; but the Oriole
is the only one of the gay company that has any pre-
tension to the musical gift that distinguishes so many
British Birds :

> Merry it is in the good greenwood,
> When the mavis and merle are singing.

Sir Walter Scott is right in making them sing together.
A duet between them is indeed a treat, when both are in
full song on a warm evening in Spring :

> The Throstle with shrill sharps—
> Upon his dulcet pipe the Merle.

The song of the Throstle is perhaps generally preferred
to that of the Blackbird.   It is more varied and lively,

but inferior in mellowness to that of the Merle, to which
the name of the " Mellow Mavis" would seem to be most
appropriate ;

> When the grey dawn
> He hails ; or when with parting light, concludes
> His melody.

> The Merle's note,
> Mellifluous, rich, deep-toned, fills all the vale,
> And charms the ravished ear.

Another fine singer and constant resident in our apple
orchards, is the *Missel Thrush;* preferred by Montagu and
others to the Throstle.   In spring, while the female is
sitting, the rich loud note of the Missel Thrush from his
perch on a tall elm may be more striking than that of the
Throstle ; but perhaps in such cases "comparisons are
odious."   It is certainly strange that an ornithologist
should deny this fine songster any other note than the
" loud   untuneful   voice "   heard   before   a   storm,   and
which has given it the name of Storm-cock.   It is the
largest of our singing birds, and when seen with out-
spread wings and tail, fluttering about a yew or other tree
in search of berries, is a beautiful object, worthy the
pencil of Audubon.   It is a familiar bird, building in apple-
trees near houses, and not disturbed by cautious visitors.
Built before the leaves are expanded, and often in a
fork but six or seven feet from the ground, the nest is
easily seen and inspected.   This is consistent with the
bold character of the birds, for they will drive away the
Magpie, and other intruders, and seem to confide in
those who visit them in peace.   A pair built for several
years in an apple-tree branch overhanging a garden walk,
where they were daily visited, and appeared well satisfied

with their abode. Farmers and gardeners have no reason
to dislike the Missel Thrush; as it lives upon berries and
insects, worms, slugs and grasshoppers, and not on garden
fruit. The Throstle and Blackbird certainly take their
share of ripe currants, raspberries, and cherries ; but for
at least nine months out of twelve, they are the gardener's
helpers, clearing out snails innumerable, and keeping
down the worms in the lawns. A fair share of the
smaller fruits the gardener may afford to give for nine
months' labour in snail-picking, and three of delicious
music ; to say nothing of valuable lessons in early-rising:
for the damage done in the garden is " while men sleep,"
and birds are " up and doing."

There is a little confusion in the use of the familiar
names *Merle* and *Mavis*. The former is certainly the
name of the Blackbird, *Turdus merula*, but he is sometimes called the Mellow Mavis, the latter name being
usually given to the Song Thrush or Throstle. Spenser,
however, writes :

> The Thrush replyes ; the Mavis descant playes ;

and Skelton, in his *Philip Sparrow*, writes:

> The Threstill with her warblynge,
> The Mavis with her whistell.

The author of *The Folk-lore of British Birds* thinks Spen-
ser's Thrush and Skelton's Mavis both mean the Missel
Thrush, which is called in East Lothian, the Big Mavis.
It would therefore seem that *Mavis* is a general name in
the Thrush family ; the Storm-cock being the Big
Mavis, the Redwing the Redwinged Mavis, and the

Blackbird the Mellow Mavis. The Blackbird is also called the Black Ouzel, or Ouzel-cock.

> A black Ouzel, cousin Shallow.
> HENRY IV., III., 2.

> The Ouzel cock, so black of hue,
> With orange tawny bill.
> MIDSUMMER NIGHT'S DREAM, III. I.

Fieldfares and *Redwings*, known here as Winter Thrushes, may be seen in flocks searching among the dead leaves in the orchards. Where a hawthorn or mountain ash attracts them to the garden, they soon clear off the berries; their varied attitudes and flutterings making many a pretty group, as they gather their appointed food, and give us, in return, a feast of beauty.

The *Ring-Ouzel* is not uncommon on our hills in its spring and autumn migration. More than twenty have been seen together; but they seldom stay with us during the breeding season. Some have been observed in Burrington combe at that time, but no nests have been found. They prefer the more remote ravines of the north and far west ; passing by the wooded Quantocks, and frequenting the wilder combes of Exmoor and Dartmoor. They are not uncommon in the hills around Dulverton.

A member of the Thrush family, seldom seen in this country, has found its way, like other distinguished foreigners, to these hills and vales. *White's Thrush*, so named because its first known visit was paid to the county of Gilbert White of Selborne, has been twice found in Somersetshire ; the first in January 1870, at Hestercombe in the Quantocks ; the second in the January following at Langford, in this neighbourhood—shot while feeding on hawthorn berries. Another was taken at Pocklington, in Yorkshire, in January, 1882. Between this date and the first record in January, 1828, fifty-four years, fourteen instances are on record, half of them occurring in January, and all in the winter half of the year. The species is the *Turdus varius* of the German naturalist, Pallas, and is a native of Siberia, China, and Japan.

The *Water Ouzel*, or *Dipper*, is not, I think, to be found in the small watercourses of our valley, though it has been seen at Cheddar, and probably elsewhere in the neighbourhood, and is common in the Quantock streams. This singularly interesting bird, like too many others, is sacrificed to the idol of sport. It is suspected of feeding on fish and the spawn of salmon and trout ; the real fact being that it feeds on their foes; " destroying," as Mr. Buckland says, " vast numbers of the water insects and larvæ which prey upon the ova." Macgillivray, one of the best of observers, says the same. It appears from the evidence of forty martyrs to science, sacrificed to save the lives of fish, that " of all these birds, the stomach of only one contained a single fish's egg, and that was a diseased one." If, therefore, a Dipper should ever appear in our brook, it is to be hoped these facts will save its life, and help to save, also, the rising generation of trout.

It is strange that such an observer, and frequenter of mountain streams as John Ruskin, should acknowledge, as he does in *Love's Meinie*, that he had never seen a Water Ouzel alive. A very interesting account of this bird will be found in *Science or Romance? The Game of Speculation*, by Rev. John Gerard, S. J., of Stonyhurst.

It is scarcely necessary to name all the familiar summer Warblers that come more or less regularly to our valley or its surroundings. The Fauvette or Garden Warbler, *Curruca hortensis,* can hardly be called common. Though a fruit eater, it feeds also on insects, and is one of the few birds that is fond of the caterpillars of the cabbage butterfly. For this merit, and for its song, which rivals that of the Nightingale, this modest little bird ought to be spared by gardeners, both amateur and professional.

We have both the White-throats, *Curruca cinerea* and *Sylviella*; the former comparatively common, in spite of the antipathy of gardeners, who regard Peggy White-throat and her family as among the worst of fruit thieves. But if they are among the autumn claimants for a share of Nature's gifts, and are not mindful enough of the gardener's superior claims, he ought not to forget that Mr. and Mrs. White-throat, as well as himself, have worked from dawn to dewy eve long before any fruit could be gathered, feeding their family entirely on insects that would have left the gardener no fruit to gather or protect. Cecil Smith says the crop of a White-throat he shot in July "was perfectly crammed with the remains of various insects."

The Wood Warbler, or Wood Wren, *Sylvia sylvicola*, and the Willow Wren, *Sylvia trochilus*, are insect-eaters, and the gardener's friends ; but he seldom knows enough of birds to distinguish between his friends and his enemies.

John Burroughs, who writes so delightfully of American birds and forest scenes, thinks the Willow-Wren, " the only British Warbler that exhibits the best qualities of American songsters." He thinks the European birds a more hardy and pugnacious race than the Americans, the songsters more vivacious and powerful, but less melodious and plaintive.

L

The *Chiff-chaff* is here sometimes at the earliest date given by White of Selborne, namely, the 19th of March. It is usually the first of the summer warblers, though sometimes preceded by the Cuckoo's mate, the Wryneck, which has been seen as early as March 10th (1878). The The *Black-cap* is three or four weeks later.   Seldom before the middle of April is its fine clear note heard, a welcome sign of established spring.

Nightingales, though common further west, in the neighbourhood of Taunton and Bridgewater, do not much affect our valley.   For many years, they forsook us altogether, but since 1865 they have again visited us ; not, however, in sufficient force to answer Coleridge's description, when

> far and near,
> In wood and thicket, over the wide grove,
> They answer and provoke each other's song.

The midnight minstrelsy of a number of rival singers as they are often heard in the home counties, is very different from the fitful and disappointing notes of a lonely one.   We sometimes take an evening stroll to hear the Philomel, and after waiting, deluded again and again by a few detached though unmistakeable sounds, return disappointed.   I cannot say with Portia that

> I think
> The Nightingale, if she should sing all day
> When every Goose is cackling, would be thought
> No better a musician than the Wren ;

but there can be no question that the effect is greatly heightened by the still solemnity of night :

> Soft stillness, and the night,
> Become the touches of sweet harmony.

And when the soft stillness is only broken by the fitful strains of a solo singer, the impression of sadness may perhaps be the natural one. Shakespear elsewhere speaks of the Nightingale's "complaining notes," and Spenser says :

> Philomele her song with tears doth steep.

Not to mention the well-known lines of doubtful authorship,* about her "doleful'st ditty."

Michael Drayton, describing the "mirthful quires" of Warwickshire, says :

> In the lower brake, the Nightingale hard by,
> In such lamenting strains the joyful hours doth ply.

And Milton :

> Where the love-lorn Nightingale
> Nightly to thee her sad song mourneth well.

and again in the familiar lines :

> Sweet bird that shun'st the noise of folly,
> Most musical, most melancholy !
> Thee, chantress of the woods among,
> I woo, to hear thy evening song.

On which Coleridge exclaims :

> A melancholy bird ! O idle thought !
> .   .   .   .   .
>   It is the merry Nightingale,
> That crows and hurries and precipitates,
> With fast, thick warble his delicious notes,
> As he were fearful that an April night
> Would be too short for him to utter forth
> His love-chant, and disburthen his full soul,
>   Of all its music !

---

* Sometimes attributed to Spenser, sometimes to Shakespear, and again to a less-known poet.

Wordsworth has the same lively impression of Milton's
melancholy bird :

> Those notes of thine, they pierce and pierce,
> Tumultuous harmony and fierce.

Keats begins his Ode to a Nightingale with almost
envy of its happy lot :

> But being too happy in thy happiness,
>   That thou, light-winged Dryad of the trees,
>   In some melodious plot
> Of beechen green, and shadows numberless,
>   Singest of summer in full-throated ease.

But after all he concludes his ode to the "immortal bird"
by referring to its " plaintive anthem " :

> Adieu ! adieu ! thy plaintiff anthem fades
>   Past the near meadows, over the hill-stream,
>   Up the hill-side ; and now 'tis buried deep
>   In the next valley's glades.
> Was it a vision, or a waking dream ?
> Fled is that music—do I wake or sleep ?

The older poets, who associate melancholy with the
Nightingale, speak of the bird as female, preferring my-
thology to ornithology. *Philomela* might well sing sadly,
if she could sing at all; but the feathered Nightingale that
sings is the male, and *his* song is not found melancholy.
Thomson says—

> *She* sings
> Her sorrows through the night, and on the bough
> Sole sitting, still at every dying fall,
> Takes up again her lamentable strain.

While Cowper,* in his *Nightingale and Glow-worm* tells us:

> A Nightingale, that all day long
> Had cheer'd the village with *his* song,
> Nor yet at eve his note suspended,
> Nor yet when eventide was ended.

The Glow-worm, whose light, indeed, is none of the brightest, appeals to the singer to satisfy his hunger upon some less luminous subject :

> That you with mnsic, I with light,
> May beautify and cheer the night.

It is pleasant to read that

> The songster heard his short oration,
> And warbling out his approbation,
> Released him, as my story tells,
> And found a supper somewhere else.

Perhaps no poet has bettered the prose of the pious angler, who—speaking of the Nightingale—says : " He, that at mid-night when the weary labourer sleeps serenely should hear, as I have very often, the clear airs, the sweet descants, the natural rising and falling, the doubling and redoubling of her voice, might well be lifted above the earth, and say : ' Lord, what music hast Thou provided for the saints in heaven, when Thou affordest bad men such music on earth?' "

Among the inferior minstrels may be noticed the lively *Redstart*, which is one of our familiar summer birds. A brood was hatched in a hollow stump on our lawn, where the young birds could be seen, till a strange cat found them out, and left nothing but a wing on the

---

* Cowper must surely have been mistaken in supposing he heard
  " A Nightingale on New Year's Day, 1792." !

ground.   The *Black   Redstart* is occasionally seen
here, and is said to be a nearly regular autumn visitor at
Weston-super-mare ; probably on its return from more
northerly latitudes.   In South Germany it is commoner
than either the common Redstart or the Redbreast :
another member of the same family.

Tlie *Bluebreast* has been more than once met with in
Devonshire, and is exhibited in some of our collections.
A specimen at Exeter is said to have been killed in
Somersetshire ; but this rare and beautiful species cannot
be fairly included in our list of local birds.   The same
may be said of the *Dartford Warbler*, which was a resident
in Dorsetshire until the rigorous winter of 1881.*   Our
own county and neighbourhood can boast of a visit from
the *Alpine Accentor*, which occured no further off than the
deanery garden at Wells, in 1833.

On the hills we have the *Wheatear*, the *Whinchat*,
and the *Stonechat*, the last the commonest.   The Whinchat is certainly not common here, and appears to
be as rare on the Quantocks, where the Stonechat is
as numerous as it is here.   Nor is the Wheatear at all
abundant in this part of the Mendips.   So conspicuous
a bird could hardly escape observation where present.
We see it sometimes on the hillside between Shutshelf
and Axbridge, but not nearly so often as the Stonechat,
which may generally be seen there ; especially in its gay
summer suit, when it is one of our prettiest birds.

We cannot truly say of our familiar friends, that—

> The Robin-redbreast and the Wren
> Are God Almighty's cock and hen.

If that ancient belief still hold anywhere out of the

---

* *Birds of Dorset* by Mansel-Pleydel.

nursery, it is probably due to the similarity of plumage in the sexes; every Redbreast being taken for a *Cock-robin*, and needing as a help-meet a *Jenny-wren*, that every Jenny may have her Jockie. Another point of connection is that both sing in winter:

> Besides the Redbreast's note, one other strain,
> One summer strain, in wintry days is heard,
> Amid the leafless thorn—the merry Wren.

The *Gold-crest* is almost as common here as the Wren. Some years ago, a pair hung their mossy cradle in the ivy of a tree close to the house, and not eight feet from the ground. Here, undisturbed by human and feline curiosity, the little pair reared their tiny brood, and we trust the family are still among our feathered friends.

The *Grey Fly-catcher* is another familiar garden acquaintance; building in the trellis over the window; the male perch-on the back of a garden chair, while the other is sitting. Wishing to take his likeness, I stuck a walking-stick into the ground a few yards from the window; an arrangement that seemed to please him very well. There he perched all day, and every day, watching for insects; every now and then darting after a butterfly or other winged prey, which he sometimes carried to the nest, and sometimes devoured himself. It was amusing to watch the movements of his head, and his bright eyes ever on

the watch for game.   There seemed, also, a good understanding between him and the cat ; for it was nothing
unusual on a sunny day to see him on the top of the
stick wide awake, while the cat slept at the bottom.
It is a Somersetshire superstition that

> If you scare the Fly-catcher away,
> No good luck will with you stay.

The *Pied Fly-catcher* is a rare visitor to this county.
It has been shot near Taunton, and some years ago, a
pair built in a wall plum-tree in Mr. Clothier's garden,
near Street.   Being a true bird-lover, he gave strict
orders that the birds should be protected, and had the
pleasure of seeing them bring out their brood.   A specimen was seen at Hale Well in April, 1889.   Its song
resembled the Redstart's, its manners those of the Grey
Fly-catcher.

Of the Tits we have all the common British species.
The *Long-tailed Tit* is abundant in our orchards and
gardens, and its bottle nest often spied in our hedges.
There seem to be two varieties of this bird, one " having
a white head."   The Whiteheads claim to be the senior
branch of the family, inhabiting Scandinavia, and bearing
the title *caudatus* conferred on them by Linnæus ; the
English branch is, therefore, asked to give up the title
caudatus and take that of *rosea*.   As, however, Whiteheads are occasionally found in our southern climate—
one in Somersetshire in 1872—perhaps it might be well
to defer altering an appropriate name till we are quite
sure of a distinction of species.   The rosy tint is peculiarly delicate ; but is the English bird more rosy than the
Scandinavian ?   Both the *Marsh Tit* and *Cole Tit* are
now divided into two or more species.

The *Bearded Tit*, one of the loveliest of birds, figures, as far as skin and wires and glass eyes can represent it, in various local collections, and has been seen alive in Devonshire and Cornwall, but not, I believe, in this county. The Norfolk Broads are its last resort, and even there it is in danger of speedy extermination. No British bird loses more with the loss of life than this most delicate little creature. The exquisite bloom of its pearly-grey head and white throat, its shining black moustache and rich chestnut plumage, with its bright orange bill and brilliant eyes, are dimmed by death, while the grace of its form and attitudes cannot be restored by any skill of bird-stuffers. Its movements are those of the liveliest Tits with added charms of its own. But the species seems likely to be lost to the list of British Birds, before its right place in the list is settled. Whether *Parus*, or *Panurus*, or *Calamophilus*, Bearded Tit, Reed Pheasant, or Least Butcher-bird,—let them call it what they like, if they will let it live and multiply, and delight those who can enjoy its grace and beauty, without being troubled about its place in a cabinet or catalogue.

The *Pied Wagtail* or *Dish-washer* remains with us all the year, though we seldom see more than one or a pair in the depth of winter. In the deep snow of January, 1865, we had the agreeable company of a Wagtail and a Robin together in the house. Peggy Wash-dish made herself at home in the scullery and kitchen, helping to clean the dishes, while Robin as naturally came into the dining-room and stood behind a chair—or sat on its back. Their portraits were taken, Peggy with her winter white throat; but whether, when the spring came round, the smart Wagtail in the black stock might be a follower, or Peggy herself, was never known.

The *Grey Wagtail* is also a permanent resident, though scarce compared with the former. As it goes northward in summer, it is sometimes called the *Winter Wagtail,* as in Rennie's edition of Montagu. The *Yellow Wagtail* on the same ground he calls the *Spring Wagtail,* as it arrives in England from the south in spring. It is, in fact, a summer bird here.

Scientific naturalists usually quote the Latin or Greek names of species to make identification more certain. I had done so throughout this chapter of birds, but found more confusion in the learned names than in the vulgar. This is particularly the case with the Wagtail tribe. No one can need a more descriptive name than that of the *Pied Wagtail;* but who would recognize our old familiar friend as *yarrelli?* So with the *Yellow Wagtail,* the name is a true name; it describes the thing signified; but this is set aside for the unmeaning one of *raii**—with a small *r,* though the name of a great naturalist! If the Linnæan name of *alba* be misapplied to our Pied Wagtail, the name suggested by Rennie, *Lotor,†* would be appropriate, and agree with the provincial *Dishwasher,* and the Frenchman's still more descriptive *Lavandiere.* If the bird called by Linnæus *flava* be the *Blue-headed* and not the *Yellow Wagtail,* and the name be considered equally descriptive of both, our Yellow Wagtail might be called *Citrinella* like the Yellow Bunting. *Lotor* and *Citrinella* are true as well as pretty names; *raii* and *yarelli* are neither. The latest fashion in nomenclature appears to be as follows:—the lively Pied Wagtail is to have the cheerful name of *lugubris;* the White is to be properly

---

* Ibis List by Ornithologists' Union, 1883.

† *Montagu's Dictionary,* Second Edition, 1831.

alba ; the Grey to be *sulphurea* ; and the Blue-headed *flava*—a curious mixture of English and Latin colours. The Yellow or Summer Wagtail, formerly called *flava*, is to be distinguished(?) by "a name ever to be revered by the wise and good," that of John Ray ;* a name so intimately connected with that of Willoughby, that we might be inclined to prefer "Willoughby's Wagtail," to *Motacilla raii* with a small *r*. But it is pleasant in these days of atheistic science, to remember a Fellow of the Royal Society, who wrote on the *Wisdom of God in the Works of the Creation.*

Of Larks and Pipits we have, besides the familiar *Sky-lark*, the *Meadow Pipit* or *Tit-lark*, the *Tree Pipit*, and occasionally the *Wood-lark*. The *Rock Pipit* is a common bird at Weston-super-Mare.

Familiar as the Sky-lark is to English people, and known by name and fame wherever English poetry is read, no one with any music in his soul, can watch unmoved "the rising of the lark"—"the herald of the morn."

> Hark ! Hark ! the lark at heaven's gate sings,
> And Phœbus 'gins arise ;
> His steeds to water at those springs
> On chaliced flowers that lies.

We could almost envy the feelings of an American landing on our shores, and witnessing for the first time what he had often read of, as we do of the Mocking Bird and Humming Bird of America—the "Bird of the

* John Ray or Wray, F.R.S. 1628—1705.

Wilderness" so often sung by poets in strains set to
heavenly music :

> O'er fell and fountain sheen,
> O'er moor and mountain green,
> O'er the red streamer that heralds the day,
> Over the cloudlet dim,
> Over the rainbow's rim,
> Musical cherub soar, singing away !

So sang one of Nature's true poets ; and thus sings
another, of this inspiring minstrel of the sky :

> Higher still, and higher,
> From the earth thou springest,
> Like a cloud of fire ;
> The blue deep thou wingest,
> And singing thou dost soar, and soaring ever singest.

It is a creature that symbolises the thoughts that rise
from the low cares of earth to the sweet charities of
heaven : " Blithesome and cumberless, emblem of
happiness ;" viewing the world from above, but not
despising it ; returning to the lowly duties of life, refreshed by higher contemplations :

> Type of the wise who soar, but never roam—
> True to the kindred points of heaven and home.

Our small enclosures, rampant hedgerows, orchards,
and open ground, with abundance of wild plants, called,
when in their wrong places, weeds, attract a full share
of feathered company. *Buntings* are not so common
as *Yellow Ammers.** The scarcer *Cirl Bunting*, first
observed by Col. Montagu at Kingsbridge in Devonshire,
and next between Bridgewater and Glastonbury in this

---

* *Ammer* is correct, being the German name for Bunting.   Yarrell had
it so, but his recent editor has gone back to Hammer.

county, cannot be called common here, but is hardly
scarce enough, or showy enough, to be in danger of extermination. The handsome *Reed Bunting*, which is said
to be "common by all the brooks and rivers in the
county,"* is not often seen in our valley, though not un-
frequent along the waters below Banwell. The *Snow
Bunting* has been seen near Weston, and in other parts
of the County. In its winter dress as the *Tawny
Bunting*, it may be commoner than is generally supposed.

The Finch family is numerous here, especially that of
Philip Sparrow. He has been much criticised of late,
and with some heat and severity, especially in corn growing districts where game is preserved. Where sparrow-
hawks are exterminated sparrows multiply, and sporting
Man claims all for himself. But the sparrows feed their
young on caterpillars, and consume immense quantities
of aphides, flies, and other matters, and only when the
harvest is ripe or gathered, do they "put in their little
bills." Farmers complain that the services rendered are
not worth the cost, and this may be the case in the corn
lands, and where game is preserved. The "little bills"
ought to be accepted by the sportsmen in whose interest
the hawks are destroyed. But where the balance of
Nature has been upset in the interests of Sport, it may
fairly be restored in the interests of Industry and Use.
No lover of birds or apologist of sparrows will complain
of farmers doing duty for the hawks, and keeping the
sparrow family within reasonable bounds.

The poets differ as much as the naturalists in their
opinions of Philip Sparrow. William Howitt is very

* *Birds of Somersetshire.*

severe upon him, but Barry Cornwall is more·charitable.
What Howitt calls impudence, the gentler poet calls
fidelity :

His familiar voice,
His look of love, his sure fidelity
Bids us be gentle with so small a friend,
And much we learn from acts of gentleness.

·Opinions of birds, as of politicians, are seldom un-
prejudiced. The Sparrow suffers by an odious comparison
with the Robin.   From our early childhood, our sym-
pathies are moved toward the kind attendants on the
Babes in the Wood, and, again, toward the unfortunate
victim of the Sparrow's archery ; on whom the verdict is
wilful murder against the Sparrow, though Ruficide, or
accidental death, would seem to be equally consistent
with the evidence.   The prejudice against the accused is
further shown by the uncharitable reflections made upon
his frank avowal of the deed.   Instead of giving him
credit for his brave and honest confession, it is condemned as a piece of heartless effrontery.   Had he been
conscious of any evil intent, there was nothing to prevent
his absconding, like one formerly ; but he owned up like a
brave and noble-hearted fellow, and trusted to the fairness
of a jury of his peers.

The *Chaffinch* is exposed to almost as much unfriendly
criticism as the Sparrow, and' still more from gardeners;
and he can hardly claim as much right to put in his little
bill for services rendered.   He is a much handsomer
bird, and is not without other merits.   He helps to keep
down the groundsel and other weeds that lazy gardeners
and slovenly farmers leave to ripen their seeds.   The gay
Chaffinch would be much missed among the " common
·objects of the country," and so would its beautiful nest as

a specimen of the " Architecture of Birds."*   John Burroughs calls the Chaffinch " the prettiest of English Song
Birds," and gives it credit for two-thirds of the music
of an English spring.   We may not agree in either
estimate, but are grateful for our American friend's appreciation, as well as for his charming books on American
rural life.   His appreciation of the Chaffinch as a song
bird is shared by many in Germany, but by few in
England.

The elegant *Goldfinch* labours in the same sphere of
usefulness as the gay *Chaffinch*, besides helping the
Linnet and *Redpole* with the thistledown,

> The Goldfinch on a thistle head,
> Stood scattering seedlets while she fed.

Goldfinches were more abundant here when teasles were
grown ; they are now comparatively scarce.   The bird-
catchers also found out the neighbourhood, and we feel
their evil deeds.

Siskins are sometimes numerous here in winter, feeding on various hedge seeds, and particularly on those of
the alder and birch, hanging like Tits from the pendant
sprays.   Mr. Byne's collection contains, among other
rarities, a female specimen of the *Serin Finch*.   It was
captured in a garden in the town of Taunton, in February,
1866.   As the Serin is a native of the Mediterranean
countries, its appearance in winter, and in a town garden,
is suggestive of an escaped cage bird ; and Mr. Cecil Smith
included it with some hesitation in his Birds of Somersetshire.   Several specimens have been observed on the

---

* *The Architecture of Birds* by James Rennie, one of the early volumes
of the *Library of Entertaining Knowledge :* a valuable series of the
Society for the Diffusion of Useful Knowledge, sixty years ago.

south coast, chiefly in Sussex, but in the summer half of the year from April to October.

The *Brambling* or *Mountain Finch* appears here occasionally.   A small flock remained at Weston some weeks in the hard winter of 1890—91.   *Greenfinches* and *Bullfinches* are both common birds here; the former building in an evergreen oak in our garden, and the latter frequenting a cherry tree close by, where I have seen from the window three pairs at one time, enjoying the buds as we do Brussels sprouts.   There can hardly be a prettier bird-picture, unless it be that of the same birds in a bed of Alpine forget-me-nots, where they come to feed on the seeds close to the window.   The Bullfinch fulfils no vulgar uses, and is, perhaps, rather an expensive æsthetic luxury ; but the thinning out of fruit buds is not always a loss, while the beautiful bird would be sadly missed in our country lanes.

The *Hawfinch*, though called *vulgaris*, is no common bird ; but it has been seen several winters in a garden at Sidcot and has been captured on Winscombe hill.

Crossbills are among our occasional visitors, sometimes in considerable numbers, though never in such flocks as are recorded in certain great "Crossbill years."   The first of these on record was in 1254, and another in the reign of Queen Elizabeth.   " The yeare 1593 was a greate and exceeding yeare of apples, and there was greate plenty of strange birds . . . . having a bill with one beake wry-thinge over the other . . . . The cocke a very glorious bird, in a manner all red on the brest, backe, and head . . . . They came when the apples were rype, and went away when the apples were cleane fallen."*   Another great

---

* Quoted by Yarrell and Morris.

flock appeared near Bath in 1791, when one birdcatcher took a hundred pairs in the months of June and July. Again in the summer of 1821, Selby mentions a large flock composed of females and young birds, frequenting the fir plantations, and moving northward. The years 1836-7-8 and -9 are mentioned as Crossbill years, and again in 1866, " people were killing them in their gardens in great numbers."* Very characteristic of "people," whose first idea of a beautiful bird is of something to be killed ; and the second, of something to be stuffed with tow, or seasoning. The late Mr. Thring of Uppingham had Crossbills in his aviary, so tame as to take seeds from his fingers.

Woodpeckers are familiar birds here. The *Lesser Spotted* or *Barred Woodpecker* is not unfrequently seen on a walnut tree near the house ; as often as not on a horizontal mossy branch, or on a twig, like a perching bird, sometimes with wings outspread, as figured in Gould's Birds of Europe. It has been observed at work on oak-galls, grasping the branch with one foot and the stalk of the gall with the other, hammering the galls with its bill, and breaking the shell to get at the grub inside. It is fond also of frequenting elms, which are our common hedge timber. The *Greater Spotted Woodpecker* has been seen here at Kingwood and at Rickford combe, but is rare. The *Great Black Woodpecker* is said to have oc- curred in the county, and several times in Dorset, Hants, and Devon; but this is contradicted by recent authorities, who exclude the species from the list of British birds. The common *Green Woodpecker*, called here the *Rainpie* and *Yokel*, frequents our elms and orchards, and is often

* Cecil Smith.

M

seen on the ground searching among the " emmet-
butts." Its laughing cry is oftenest heard in its un-
dulating flight across a field.   In this apple district the
orchards are the usual nurseries for young Woodpeckers.
Some of the old apple-trees are well-known both to
the yokels and the local ornithologists ; but the Woodpecker's wonderful carpentry is not confined to these; it
chooses also the elm, chestnut, sycamore, willow, ash,
beech, and lime : rarely, if ever, the resinous fir tribe, and
probably never the hard-wooded yew.   " The Woodpecker tapping the hollow beech tree " is, no doubt, a
familiar rural sight and sound ; but the hole for nesting
is cut in solid wood, and a marvellous piece of work it
is: a labour of love, evidently, and not the "slavish
misery" absurdly imagined by the French naturalist; who
seems to have considered labour a curse, and to have had
no conception of the joys of forest life, or the pleasures of
preparing a home for expected progeny.

      Mr. Knight, who has long been familiar with the Rain-
pie family, has noticed a fact not mentioned in any book
I have referred to, " that when the Woodpecker aims a
blow the eyelids close by a sort of sympathetic action,
evidently to shield the eyes from the flying chips, and
this happens even when the beak does not actually strike
the wood.   The chips are often removed out of sight ; a
habit noticed by Wilson in the Downy Woodpecker of
America, and by Montagu in the Marsh Tit.

      Nuthatches are common in our orchards, and in winter
familiar enough to come with the Sparrows and Chaf-
finches to the kitchen-door.   One year a pair built in a
hollow branch of an apple-tree, so near the ground that
a boy took the young birds when fledged, and brought
them to the house.   They sat on the table while their

portraits were taken, and were then restored to the nest. A pair of old birds entertained us for some weeks last winter by their frequent visits to an Irish yew on the lawn. Their characteristic attitudes, with the head downwards and stretching outwards, as figured by Gould and others, with the contrast of colour, the dark olive yew setting off the delicate grey back and reddish sides, and the rose-coloured yew-berry in the bill as the bird flew away with it, composed quite a pretty picture; which was repeated every few minutes for days and weeks, till the birds had cleared the tree of its rosy fruit.

The Nuthatch is, perhaps, the only bird, unless it be the Wren, which runs downwards as well as upwards. The *Tree-creeper*, like the Woodpecker, climbs and flies down to begin the ascent again. The Creeper, *Certhia familiaris*, is as "familiar" here as in other places wherever there are trees for it to creep on.

The *Wryneck* has been heard here as early as the 10th of March, a week or more before the usual time. It may often be seen perched in a hedge, or on the low branch of a tree, uttering its kestrel-like cry, and twisting its head in the peculiar way which has suggested its familiar names of Wryneck and Snake-bird : the latter agreeing also with the snake-like hiss the bird sometimes makes. "Cuckoo's mate" is another familiar name of the Wryneck, its cry being generally soon followed by that of the Cuckoo.

It is well known that the Wryneck, which cannot be called a climber, has the toes two and two like the Woodpeckers ; while the Creeper, the nimblest climber of all, has them three in front and one behind, like perching birds. My dear old friend the late Dr. Kaup of the Darmstadt

Museum, an eminent zoologist,* told me that the Grey-
green Woodpecker (*Picus canus*) common in the German
forests, climbs with three toes in front; but the re-
versible hind-toe of our Woodpeckers seems to be
incapable of more than an angular position; which may,
perhaps, appear forward when seen from below.

The *Cuckoo*, "that wakes the world anew," is far from
being the invisible creature of the poets; though Barry
Cornwall says :

> Thou, Cuckoo bird,
> Who art the ghost of sound, having no shape
> Material, but dost wander far and near,
> Like untouched Echo, whom the woods deny
> Sight of her love.

and Wordsworth :

> Even yet thou art to me
> No bird, but an invisible thing,
> A voice, a mystery.
>
> .   .   .   .   .   .
>
> And thou wert still a hope, a love,
> Still longed for, never seen.

It is seen here often enough in material shape, and not
unfrequently in pairs.   It will sit long and patiently on
a bare branch, singing or shouting, bowing its head and
moving its tail as regularly as a toy, until a mate comes
in sight, when a chuckling note is heard, and presently
the pair are seen flying across the field.   Sometimes it
will perch on the railings near the house, bowing and
spreading its fine fan-tail, and what is more remarkable,

---

* He established the genus *Dinotherium*, and wrote the catalogues of
Fish in the British Museum, a Monograph of the Owls, and many other
treatises on scientific zoology.   He was much esteemed by Professor Owen,
Dr. Gray and others, including Joseph Wolf, the animal painter.

several are sometimes seen together on the same fence. An old grey cuckoo with wings and tail spread is a beautiful bird. When a boy, I bought a young one at Leadenhall Market, and kept it in a cage till November, when it was seized with migration-on-the-brain, and fluttered itself to death.* Perhaps they do not leave this country so early as is supposed. I once saw a fine old bird in a garden near London in September, feeding on caterpillars in a lime tree. They probably remain as long as they find a supply of food.

The *Nightjar* or *Fern Owl* is not uncommon here. Flying past in the dusk of the evening, its beauty cannot be seen. It is a striking object when seen by daylight, as it may be, sitting with wings depressed, upon a low horizontal branch ; not crossways, as usual with most birds, but more generally in the direction of the branch. When disturbed, it utters a kind of chuc-chuc, and flies round rather wildly ; a picturesque sylvan object. The absurd name of *Goatsucker* is still retained in *Caprimulgus.* Rennie's suggestion of *Nyctichelidon* is better.

Allied to the Nightjar is the *Swift*, a bird until lately considered a kind of Swallow, but now separated from that genus, and regarded as nearer allied to the Humming Birds! Though there may be some reasons for this new arrangement, it is hard to believe them of greater weight than those on the other side. To the common observer,

---

* A shoemaker near Wigan purchased a young Cuckoo from a boatman, who had taken it from a Tit-lark's nest, and being a lover of birds, he by unremitting care, managed to rear it. The bird has several times repeated its well-known cry, and enabled many people to boast that they have heard the Cuckoo in November. Amongst a purely working-class population, in the heart of the colliery district, there are many men who take a deep interest in the works of nature, and not a few who can classify both birds and flowers.

the Swift is a kind of Swallow, similar in appearance, habits, and flight, and with very little resemblance to the brilliant, flower-seeking, long-billed, and tubular-tongued Humming Birds.

Swifts, Swallows, and *Martins* are all common birds in our valley.

Sand-martins affect the railway cutting at Uphill and elsewhere, but I have not observed them in the banks of our rocky valley. An *Alpine Swift* is reported in the list of foreign visitors at Weston.

Summer birds are commonly called *visitors* and *guests,* as by Shakespear :

> This *guest* of summer,
> The temple-haunting Martlet.

But the Martlets and other birds of summer are native Britons.   They go abroad for the winter, like other people of delicate lungs, and homeward fly in the spring. They probably return to their own particular homes, for you may observe individuals and parties on their first arrival, passing by the old nests, while others come directly to the eaves, seeming to recognize with a pleasant greeting the place of their nativity.

The migration of birds is still a mysterious subject. The facts are no longer doubted, as they were by that candid and careful observer, Gilbert White, a century ago.   The actual passing of birds of passage has been frequently witnessed, and is seen every season by light-house keepers and sailors ; but the gathering together and flight by night of multitudes of birds, not usually living in flocks, is a very curious and interesting phenomenon, still waiting explanation.   Spring and fall are the migratory seasons ; change of temperature and

failure of food being the proximate causes of the move-
ment ; but they do not explain the mid-night flight, and
the separation of the sexes, and of old and young, in the
flocks successively crossing the seas. The theory of an
hereditary tendency to follow the tracks of their ancestors
does not explain the phenomenon. Atheistical science
is pleased with anything that ignores Divine Providence.
It fancies itself far in advance of the old philosophy ; but
it has yet to explain the nature of instinct.   " The instinct," says Sir Humphrey Davy, "which teaches the
Swallows always when and where to move, may be regarded as flowing from a Divine Source, and speaks
in an intelligible language of a present Deity."

> Power divine,
> Supremest Wisdom and primeval love,
> The God of Nature is your secret guide.

Thus wrote Gilbert White in 1769 : has modern science
any better explanation ?
Of the Pigeon tribe we have in the neighbourhood all
the British species.   The *Wood Pigeon* or *Ring-Dove*
builds in our woods, and sometimes in an old elm near
the house, which being out of the way of gunners, is the
resort of many welcome birds.   The Cushat Dove coos
there in summer time ; the Brown Owl hoots there on a
moonlight night ; the Rooks sun their shining purple on
the top ; the Cuckoo sings and bows on a bare branch,
where he can be both heard and seen ; the Woodpecker
climbs and taps, and flies laughing away ; the little
Creeper creeps round and round the trunk, and Magpies
and Jays make merry among the leafy boughs.
The *Stock-Dove*, though called by Bewick and White
the Common Wild-pigeon, is not so common here as the

Wood-pigeon. White says it is a bird of passage in the
south of England, coming towards the end of November,
and leaving early in Spring. He says, writing in 1773,
that before the beechen woods were much destroyed,
Selbourne was visited by " myriads of them, reaching in
strings a mile together, as they went out in a morning to
feed." Mr. Cecil Smith says the Stock-Dove is resident
in Somersetshire throughout the year, and seems to increase more than the Wood-pigeon.

The *Rock-Dove* breeds in this valley at the Barton and
Callow Rocks, as well as at Burrington and Cheddar.
This has been questioned by the late Cecil Smith, and by
the editor of the last edition of Yarrell ; who would re-
strict the Rock-dove's breeding to rocks on the sea
coast. The birds seen here and at Cheddar, might
possibly be descendants of tame pigeons ; but I see no
good reason for this opinion. They do not appear to
differ from the typical form and colour, and they have the
habits of the purely wild species. Mr. Knight saw one
fly into the cliff at Callow on March 26th last, and has
no doubt it had a nest there.

The common opinion that this species, and not the
Stock-Dove, is the origin of the domestic Pigeon, is confirmed by the preference of tame pigeons for buildings
rather than trees. They very seldom perch upon trees,
but seem to have an instinctive preference for the firm
basis of buildings, which answer to their ancestral rocks ;
avoiding the more or less covered and swaying hold of
branches. Pigeons are familiarly seen on roofs and
elevated buildings, as on the house-tops in Spitalfields, as
well as on country churches. The Royal Exchange and
the Guildhall in the heart of the City of London, and the
buildings round St. Mark's at Venice, are well-known

favorite haunts of tame Pigeons ; but not the trees in Kensington Gardens and the Parks.

The *Turtle Dove*, one of the most elegant of birds, with a voice and manners most winsome and gentle, a type of simplicity and faith, is a summer visitant to some parts of the county, and is sometimes seen in this district. Mr. Tanner's specimen was taken in Cheddar wood.

Our valley cannot boast of many of the birds sacred to " sport," but we sometimes hear

> The roosting *Pheasant's* short but frequent crow,

both in Banwell wood and on the south side of the hills.

We have also a few of both the *Grey* and *Red-legged Partridge.* The latter are the scanty progeny of some French birds, turned out seventy years ago on Cheddar moors by the Rev. J. C. Cobley, the vicar of Wins-combe, whose father was then vicar of Cheddar. The French having driven away the English, the vicar tried to get rid of them; and Mr. Smith of Max, who gives me these particulars, has seen none for many years. Mr. Edwards, of Wrington, however, shot some French birds on our hill in 1880, and a young one on the 10th of September, 1884, which is the latest news I have heard of them.

Black Grouse, after many years' absence, appeared again on Blackdown a few years ago, in the shape of half-a-dozen Grey Hens. Some pains were taken, in vain, to procure a male bird ; but after a while, the keeper reported that a fine Black-cock had joined the hens. They are now established on the Down ; and on the hills further west, the Quantocks, Brendon Hill and Dunkery Beacon, they are abundant.

Red Grouse can only be included in the list of our local birds as visitors. Some years ago, a north-country friend

of ours said he heard the peculiar cry of the male bird on
Shutshelf Hill, and several were taken near Weston about
the same time, having probably come across the Channel
from Wales.   A pack was reported on Wavering Down
in 1881, and several brace were shot ; but they are now
believed to have been Heath Poults or Grey Hens.   But
Mr. Edwards informs me that he shot an unmistakable
Red Grouse on Blackdown on September 24th, 1884.

Quails are seldom met with in this neighbourhood ;
which may be partly because they are not very easily
seen except in flocks.   A nest of thirteen eggs was
found at Sidcot not many years ago.

A much nobler fowl is reported to have been seen
within the view from our hills—the *Great Bustard.* This
almost extinct relic of the ancient inhabitants of the
Wiltshire downs and Norfolk plains still lingers, in spite
of the persistent efforts to number it with the Dodo
and Great Auk as an extinct species.   It is still occasionally met with in the neighbouring counties of Wilts and
Devon, but had never been seen in Somersetshire till
the autumn of 1870.   On the 27th September in that
year, Mr. Harting says he saw from the railway, near
Shapwick, a bird which crouched at the approach of the
train.   It was then at some distance, and he at first took
it for a Pheasant ; but recollecting that an open turf-
moor, with no wood or coppice near, was an unlikely
haunt for Pheasants, he kept his eye on the bird as the
train approached, and saw it jump up and run swiftly
away, " exhibiting the long legs and white flanks of a
Bustard."*   The fact of a pair being shot at Braunton, in
North Devon, a few months later, helps to support
Mr. Harting's authority.   Two pairs of Bustards were

---

* *Field* newspaper, 14th January, 1871.

taken on Salisbury Plain the following year, and another in 1880. There is a magnificent pair in the museum at Devizes, as well as an inferior one. In Norfolk, a more generous and scientific spirit has prevailed over the acquisitiveness of collectors. A Bustard found there in 1876, was carefully protected and provided with a mate, in the hope that the species may be preserved from total destruction.* It is greatly to be desired that the example of Norfolk may be followed in Wiltshire and elsewhere, so that the Great Bustard may be preserved as a British bird. Though carriages may now be seen at Stonehenge, there is yet room for a few Bustards on

> The spacious plain
> Of Sarum, spread like ocean's boundless round,
> Where solitary Stonehenge, grey with moss,
> Ruin of ages, nods.

The Bustards would soon multiply, and be oftener seen, if pilgrims of Salisbury Plain would use field glasses instead of guns, and be content with seeing the living birds, instead of coveting their skins—and, perhaps, the glory of a newspaper paragraph announcing the acquisition.

An almost equally rare and remarkable bird is reported to have occurred on our hills in 1881,† the *Pratincole*, (*Glareola pratincola*) a bird seldom seen in this country, but included in the list of British birds as "a rare straggler from Southern Europe and Asia." The first visit on record was in 1807, since which date ten others have been mentioned.

The *Cream-coloured Courser* has not, I believe, been seen nearer than the neighbourhood of Christchurch in

---

* *Field*, 8th of April, 1876.
† Yarrell, vol. 3, page 234, and *Zoologist*, 1881, page 309.

Hampshire; but a *Sand Grouse*, the *Tetrao paradoxa* of Pallas, a bird which seems to be a link between the Grouse and the Pigeons, was seen by Mr. Knight a few years ago at Worle.

The *Plovers* are represented in this immediate neighbourhood by the *Peewit* or *Lapwing*, which is pretty numerous, both on Blackdown, Callow, and in the valley ; where it breeds in the meadows about Max and Slough Pits. It is a charming ornament on a lawn.

The *Great Plover* or *Stone Curlew* is sometimes seen on Callow Hill.

The *Golden Plover* is found among the hills further west, but not, I believe, on the Mendips. The *Dotterell* is, however, an inhabitant of our hills, though a rare one. The *Ring Dotterell* is common on the shore between Burnham and Watchet. Mr. Cecil Smith contradicts Meyer's statement that these birds are not seen on muddy or marshy shores. The shores of Somersetshire along the Bristol Channel are not distinguished for freedom from mud.

The *Grey Plover* is one of our shore birds, and, if we take in the coast seen from our hills as far as Minehead, we may find sometimes the *Turnstone* and the handsome *Oyster-catcher*, whose black and white plumage and red bill make it a conspicuous object of the sea-shore.

Next to these birds, we might be disposed to place the Crakes, Rails, and Snipes ; but systematic writers interpose the Cranes.

The common *Heron* is called a Crane here ; but some of our folk say they have seen much larger Cranes flying overhead. And this is not incredible, as the great *Cran e* occasionally visits the extensive marshes and turf-moors in this county. One was shot in 1865 near Burnham, another in 1889 at Stolford on the Quantocks, where another was seen in 1890. We may hope that others may come and go without being shot. It is, however, much more than a century since this fine bird ceased to be "the *common* Crane " in England.

There is a carefully preserved *Heronry* at Brockley combe: The birds are often seen flying across this valley, and not unfrequently descend and fish in our small stream and pools at Max, East Well, and Fuller's Pond. Their foot-prints are often seen on the sandy banks and shallows of the brook below Max Mill.

The *Squacco Heron* has been shot at Bridgwater Bay, as well as in the adjoining counties of Wilts and Devon. It may, therefore, sometimes fly over these hills.

A *Night Heron* was shot near Glastonbury in the summer of 1881, and brought to Mr. Clothier. The range of this bird extends round the world, from Japan to America. It is common in Hungary and found in Norway and Portugal. Birds of such powerful flight as the Heron tribe may be occasionally seen wherever their natural food may be had.

Both the *Bittern* and *Little Bittern* are sometimes found in our marshes. The latter is rare, but the former not uncommon. Several were killed last winter near Bridgwater.

Those quondam British birds, the *Spoonbill*, the *Glossy Ibis*, and the *Black Stork* have all been found in this county, within the view from our hills, and the *Avocet* figures in the Bath Museum ; but the *White Stork*, abundant in Holland and Germany, does not seem to have extended its graceful flight to our district, though it has been occasionally seen in Devon and Cornwall, and in Ireland. Possibly the rarity of its visits to England may

be partly due to its being almost a domestic fowl on the
Continent, its return in spring being welcomed like that
of the Swallow in England.   The arrival of the Storks is
an interesting and beautiful sight, announced by distant
voices in the sky, before the flock becomes visible overhead.   Their descent from the heavens in a slow, wheeling, spiral form, with little or no visible motion of the
wings, is a sight often witnessed in spring between Frank-
fort and Heidelberg, and not easily forgotten.

The *Curlew* breeds among the hills of Dunkery
Beacon, and is sometimes seen here.   It frequents our
coast in winter.   The *Wimbrel* appears in its migration
in spring and autumn occasionally, but it is a rare bird
with us.   The *Redshank* is also in our list of local birds,
and the *Green Sandpiper* or *Summer Snipe* is an annual
spring arrival.   The *Ruff* is at most but an occasional
visitor : one was shot at Weston in 1864, but we have no
evidence of its having come over the hills.

Woodcocks and Snipes are not uncommon here in the
season.   The *Solitary* or *Great Snipe* is also occasionally
found in the neighbourhood.   Mr. Edwards has a pair in
his collection which look like *Sabine's Snipe*, a bird
"very like a Woodcock."   He has also a pair of the
little *Jack Snipe*, or *Judcock*, one of which came by its
death in a singular way, its head being impaled on a
thorn !   It is now " set up " as fluttering on the identical
branch with the thorn through its head.

The pretty *Grey Phalarope* is often seen in spring and
autumn near the mouth of the Axe.

The impossibility of limiting the variety of Nature to
one continued chain of connected genera and species is
discovered in attempting such an arrangement of even
our British birds.   The *Crake* kind is an instance.   They

are taken as part of the *Rail* family, and considered as a
link between the Waders and Swimmers ; the *Corn
crake*, an inhabitant of corn and grass fields, and called
the *Landrail*, being placed nearer the water-fowls than
the Cranes and other decidedly water-birds. The
Spotted Crake is, however, a nearer link to the water
birds, and, though the bills are very different, seems otherwise allied to the *Water Rail.* Then come the *Gallinules*
and *Coots ;* but the *Phalaropes*, with lobe feet like the
Coots, are placed by the ornithologists with the Sand-
pipers and Snipes.

The *Corncrake* is, of course, common here as elsewhere.
The rarer *Spotted Crake* was abundant in the summer of
1890 in the north marsh, and the still rarer *Baillon's
Crake* has been found at Weston in 1840 and 1870.

The *Water Rail* is a regular inhabitant at Max, and
so is the *Moor-*   *hen* or *Gallinule*
w h i c h   b r e e d s
along   o u r

brook, where its nest and young may be easily discovered
by the bright red on the little ones' bills. The nest,

among sedges and marsh-marigolds, is a picturesque object.

The *Coot*, though not nearly so common as the Gallinule, is not unfrequently seen in our valley. One was brought here, some years ago, by a man who had caught it on the hill, and came to ask what it was. A *Purple Gallinule* was taken near Badgworth in August, 1875, as stated in *Science Gossip*. The occasional appearance of such unlikely birds for long flights is very remarkable. This species inhabits the south of Europe, and is supposed to be the same as the *Porphyrian* of the ancient Greeks and Romans. Being an ornamental Water-fowl, it may have escaped from some collection. There have been several other instances of its appearance, both in the South and North of England, which may possibly be accounted for in the same way. It is well, however, to take along with us the fact that birds of long and heavy flight are known to migrate and cross wide seas. Wilson mentions this as a curious fact in the habits of the Carolina Rail, a bird which seldom flies more than a hundred yards at a stretch. Yet these birds are often met crossing from the continent of America to the West India Islands. He mentions several coming on board ship three hundred miles off the coast. These birds are not dependent on wing alone : they swim and dive well.

The *Great Crested Grebe* and the *Little Grebe* or *Dab-chick*, may be included in the list of species sometimes to be found within a day's excursion of Winscombe. The Dabchick is not a scarce bird ; but I believe it does not visit Winscombe waters.

A *Great Northern Diver* was shot near Weston in 1884, and a *Red-throated Diver* was found dead near Taunton.

There is a specimen in Mr. Edwards's collection, as well as one in the Bath museum.

Were we to mention all the Water-fowl to be found in winter within the view from our hills, the list would include about sixty species; for even the *Cormorant* and *Gannet* sometimes come within those limits, as well as *Auks, Guillemots,* and *Puffins* from Lundy or Puffin island.

Even that *rara avis in terris,* the *Black Swan* has been seen at Weston. Two were shot there in 1884, which might have come from one of their settlements on the Volga or Danube, or, possibly, from some preserve nearer home. They are mentioned here, as well as some other rarities, not as inhabitants of our valley, but as objects of interest, which, having been seen, may haply be seen again.

The *Wild Swan* or *Whooper,* and probably the smaller *Bewick's Swan,* sometimes appear here in hard winters. Wordsworth speaks of two pairs of Swans on Esthwaite lake in his school-days, as " the old magnificent species, and as superior to the Swans of the Thames as these are to geese;" but this comparison must have been due either to a poet's imagination and recollection, or to the age and condition of the birds—not to any difference of species. They must have been well-preserved specimens of the Mute Swan, not Wild Whoopers, which only come in severe winters.

Wild Geese, believed to be chiefly the *White-fronted* and *Bean* species, are not unfrequently seen on the wing in hard wintry weather, and were very numerous at Uphill in the winter of 1890—91. On January 10th, 1892, a Sunday evening, between four and five o'clock, we were startled by a visit from eight large dark-coloured Geese,

N

which flew past the window, and alighted in the home-
paddock ; where they rested, till alarmed by a shot—
which happily missed—when they flew over the house,
showing light coloured breasts.   They were otherwise
dark, with long necks, *nigroque similima cygno.*   They
walked rather than waddled, and stretched out their necks
as they looked round.   It was too dusk to be sure of the
species, but their size, dark colour, and general appearance gave the impression of the *Canada Goose*, which is
said sometimes to visit the adjoining counties.

Bernicle Geese have been shot at Cheddar, and *Brent
Geese* at Weston.   The *Shieldrake* or *Burrow Duck*
breeds freely in the rabbit holes on Brean Down and the
sandhills at Burnham.   The *Shoveller* is an occasional
visitor at Weston.   Mr. Knight and Mr. Edwards have
each a specimen.

Wild Ducks come to our valley in winter.   One was
found last June in the swampy copse at Max, sitting on
a full clutch of eggs.

The *Redbreasted Merganser* has been killed at Weston-
super-Mare, where also *Sabine's Gull* has occurred on
three recorded occasions.*   The *Little Gull*, the *Ivory
Gull*, the *Glaucus Gull*, and *Richardson's Skua*, are all reported by the Rev. Murray A. Matthew as having been
seen there ; and the same observer says that the *Fulmar*
and *Fork-tailed Petrel* have both been found there.

The little *Storm Petrel* is also sometimes driven to our
shores, having been shot even near Bath.   In the great
gale of October, 1881, and again in 1884, *Wilson's Petrel*,
an American species, but occasionally found on the
European side of the Atlantic, was caught at Weston.

---

* *Birds of Somersetshire*, pages 580 and 584.

Besides these rarer birds, our coast is visited by the *Black-backed Gull*, the *Herring Gull*, the *Common Gull*, and the *Kittiwake.* The *Black-headed Gull* is an occasional visitor. The *Common Tern* is not infrequent in spring and autumn ; and the *Arctic, Lesser*, and *Black Tern* are also in the list of species to be seen from time to time along the coast visible from these hills. A *Manx Shearwater* and a *Little Gull* were shot on the Axe in 1890.

It is, perhaps, unreasonable, and would certainly be in vain, to ask collectors to refrain from availing themselves of opportunities for acquiring rarities ; but we may fairly protest against the vulgar butchery, too often reported, to the disgrace of legitimate "sport," and the disgust of all people of common humanity.

If no scarce birds were shot but those intended for public and private museums, there might be a chance of their being oftener seen alive. When the forms and feathers can be examined in detail in museums and books of birds, it would seem to be a much more interesting and agreeable pursuit to go out with a good glass, and observe, or if possible, sketch or photograph, the living birds in their wonderfully graceful attitudes, than to destroy these pleasant pictures, for the sake of the skins or of idle "sport"—

> Like him
> Who throws away his days in idle chase,
> Of the diminutive birds.

Dear old Thomas Bewick told a relation of mine*

---

* Charles Fothergill of York, "an ardent naturalist," mentioned by Yarrell as well as Bewick. See *Nature Notes*, Vol. III, page 14, January, 1892 ; and Yarrell, Vol. I, pages 104 and 108, last edition.

that he " had shot but one bird in all his life, and had re-
gretted that shot ever since."

I have been a lover of birds all my life, and from my
youth till now, have delighted in painting their beautiful
forms and feathers, and have vainly tried to sketch the
inimitable grace of their movements; but I never desired to end their happy lives.   Rather would I, with
Wordsworth,

> Mark how the feathered tenants of the flood,
> With grace of motion that might scarcely seem
> Inferior to angelical, prolong
> Their curious pastime !

and admire, not in water-fowl only, but in all the
feathered tenants of the air, how

> Their jubilant activity evolves
> Hundreds of curves and circlets, to and fro,
> Upward and downward, progress intricate
> Yet unperplexed, as if one spiral swayed
> Their indefatigable flight.

XII.—FISH AND REPTILES.

If the time serve, I will beg your favour
for a further enlargement of some of those
several heads of which I have spoken.
                    THE COMPLETE ANGLER.

HOUGH the Falconer might go further and fare worse, his comrade, Piscator, would be like a fish out of water in our Mendip valley. Nevertheless, our brook is not without its finny inhabitants. Beside the small fry, which an angler regards as fit only for bait, we have Trout both at Max and up the stream, nearly to its source at

East Well. The still nobler Salmon, until ten years ago, ascended the brook as far as the flood-hatch at Max Mill, and tried in vain to leap the water-fall. Mr. Smith tells me that he used to take Salmon, from ten to fourteen pounds weight, every year, until the waters of the Axe were poisoned by the lead works at Charterhouse. As those works are now stopped, we may hope the Salmon will again find their way from the Severn Sea to the Lox Yeo, and come again up Winscombe Brook. That they once abounded may be inferred from the name of the stream at its mouth, which I take to be derived from the Norse or German name of the Salmon—*Lax ;* pronounced, not like wax, but as a north-country man pronounces *sacks,* the *a* sounding like *ask,* and *cask,* and *father,* but not drawled out like the Londoners' *barsket* and *carsle.* Lox Yeo may, therefore, be taken to mean Salmon river, and the village of Loxton, Salmon-town. Perhaps at no distant date, the salmon may return, and a fishery be re-established. Meanwhile, we must protect the first arrivals, and be content with our Fresh-water Flounder and humbler fry, even down to the minute but really beautiful Stickleback, which is well known to be a very interesting creature to keep and watch in an aquarium.

Lampreys are said to be found in the Severn ; here the *Lampern* is the nearest approach to that delicacy, and is so superior to the common Eel as to be in danger of extinction, had not Nature protected it by an uninviting aspect. All Eels are slippery; but the Lampern's sucker-like lips and snake-like wrigglings frighten its captors, and it escapes, while vulgar Eels are caught. Wherever the Lampern is secured, it establishes the fame of an Eel-pie house. " It is pitiful," says a sensible naturalist,* "to see how much nutritious and palatable food is wasted through prejudice and ignorance, and none could confer greater benefits on the country than he who would teach the poor, both by precept and example, how to avail themselves of the food that lies wasting at their feet."

Isaac Walton gives an elaborate receipt for dressing Eels, and then adds, "But now let me tell you, that though the Eel thus dressed be not only excellent good, but more harmless than any other way, yet it is certain that physicians account the Eel dangerous meat. I will advise you, therefore, as Solomon says of honey, 'Hast thou found it, eat no more than is sufficient, lest thou surfeit ; for it is not good to eat much !'"

And while we are in the fisherman's good company, let us leave the slippery fish for a moment to take another hint from *The Complete Angler.* "Concerning your host ; to speak truly, he is not to me a good companion ; for most of his conceits were either Scripture jests, or lascivious jests, for which I count no man witty ; for the devil will help a man that way inclined to the first, and his own corrupt nature, which he always carries with him, to the latter. But a companion that feasts the company with wit and mirth, and leaves out the sin which is usually mixed with them, he is the man ; and, indeed, such a man should have his charges borne : " Sentiments worthy of a Christian fisher of men. And it is worthy of note, that the Fish was a Christian emblem centuries before the adoption of the Cross.

REPTILES are not creatures to be loved, though they have their right or permitted places in creation, as the serpent

---

* The late Rev. J. G. Wood.

had in the Garden of Eden. They are as common, perhaps, in our Mendip Valley as elsewhere, and behave as
they do in other like surroundings. Adders and Snakes
and Blindworms are still common enough ; though my
friend, the *Dominie*, has killed more than a hundred
vipers with his own hand. Frogs you may watch through
their wonderful evolutions, from the spawn by the edge
of the stagnant pool, to the lively tadpole and diminutive
frog, till, in due course, the "Frog, he would a-wooing go,"
with or without maternal sanction. A pond full of croak-
ing frogs in the twilight, is not a pleasant scene ; but
perhaps, the croakers are a less evil than the putrid water
would be without them.

Toads, called "ugly and venomous," are, perhaps, rather
severely handled by the immortal dramatist : "Some say
the lark and *loathed* Toad change eyes." Be that as it
may, they have their sweet uses, like adversity, and wear
yet a precious jewel in their heads, as in the time of
Shakespear. Our Blindworms have no stings, but our
Newts and Lizards would, I presume, give the same ·
flavour to the witches' cauldron, as their northern kin-
dren did in the days of Macbeth.

My young friends at Sidcot School have supplied me
with a list of Land and Fresh-water Shells found in this
district, including more than eighty different sorts of
Snails—a truly fearful list for people fond of gardening !
It includes *Bulimus Montanus*, found on Callow Rocks,
and another remarkable creature, *Testacella Manger*, a
slug with a small external shell, and a great devourer of
earth-worms : a perplexing creature for gardeners and
farmers.

Earthworms have lately received much scientific notice.
A collection of several different species has been

investigated by a Reverend Fellow of the Linnæan Society, who describes them in the *Field Club.** One variety enjoys the peculiar name of *Allolobophora fœtida*, and an equally " peculiar smell," which the investigator likens to the odour of a dunghill, while an angling friend of his finds it more like that of boiled cabbage, and " rather gratifying than otherwise "—an important testimony to the healthiness of angling. Another species is called, in plain English, the Putrid Worm, and there are others equally nasty, living in " fearfully polluted water," and, we may hope, preventing pestilence, while the naturalist makes " an exact investigation of the group, which is certain to throw considerable light on the evolution of species." Leaving such investigations to those who can appreciate the gratifying aroma of boiled cabbage, we will limit our contemplation to species further evolved; though fully acknowledging the wonders discoverable in the lower animals, and the wonderful skill and patience of such men as Darwin, Lubbock and others, whose works we all read with interest and admiration.

* February, 1892.

XIII.—BUTTERFLIES AND FLOWERS.

Thou art, O God ! the life and light
Of all this wondrous world we see.

.   .   .   .

W HEN youthful spring around us breathes,
Thy Spirit warms her fragrant sigh,
And every flower the summer wreathes
Is born beneath Thy kindling eye ;
Where'ere we turn, Thy glories shine,
And all things fair and bright are Thine.

THOMAS MOORE.

WE shall make no invidious comparison
between the relative beauty of Birds,
Butterflies and Flowers. Those who
remember the celebrated gardens and collections of
Loddiges at Hackney, will be neither willing nor able

to decide whether his Flowers, his Humming-birds, or his Butterflies, were the most beautiful of the various treasures which so often called forth his pious ejaculations : " Who knoweth not in all these that the hand of the Lord had wrought this ? In whose hand is the soul of every living thing."*

A complete list has been given in Chapter XI, of the BIRDS, which may be seen, from time to time, in this valley and its surroundings ; but a similar notice of all the Insects and Plants would exceed the bounds of our book and knowledge. We must be content with the mention of those most remarkable for beauty or rarity.

Of BUTTERFLIES, the lively images of Psyche, or the soul—the apotheosis of that which is "first natural and afterwards spiritual"—of man raised from his first imperfect, greedy, crawling state, to soar above the earth, drink nectar from floral cups, feed on ambrosial sweets, and enter into the wedded state, our hills and vales rejoice in most of the British kinds. Red Admirals and Peacocks frequent the gardens, though they are not so common as Garden Whites. Painted Ladies prefer the more elevated regions. The different Fritillaries are sometimes abundant, at other times, scarce. Commas were more common when teazles were grown. Clouded Yellows appear only at intervals, and Marbled and Black-veined Whites are scarce. We have Coppers and Brimstones, Orange-tips, Large and Small Tortoise-shells, Brown Argus and Grayling, Hairstreaks, Black, Brown, Green and Purple ; Bedford, Chalk-hill and Common Blues ; Skippers, Grizzled and Large, Dingy, Chequered and Small.

---

* See *Botanical Cabinet*, No. 1655, and throughout.

Purple Emperors have been found in Brockley combe,
but Admirals of the White are seldom, if ever, seen here
in the apotheosis form; nor do we ever find lepidopterous
Beauties of Camberwell, or Swallow-tails, whether nomin-
ally common or scarce.

On the shady side of these lovers of light are moths
innumerable. The great bat-like Hawkmoth, with mot-
tled wings like an owl's or a night-jar's, and a skull and
cross-bones on its back, is common in the potato grounds.
It sometimes comes into a room in the evening, its large
wings in rapid motion, and its singular squeak giving it
much resemblance to a bat. Its pretty little cousin that
plays so well the part of humming-bird, enjoying the
warm sunshine like a butterfly, ought to be protected and
preserved—not with a pin through its back, which de-
stroys all its beauty with its life ; nor yet as game is
preserved, to be slaughtered in the Fall ; but as Storks
are in the Netherlands, and Vultures in Mexico, and as
Humming-birds ought to be, but unhappily are not, in
Brazil and other tropic lands which abound in these living jewels. We have nothing to approach them here, but
the iridescent feathers of the Ring-dove and the Kingfisher
among birds, and the Rose Beetle and Fire-tail Fly
among insects. These are both brilliant creatures, and
can ill be spared where brilliancy is not over abundant.
The Rose Beetle is said to injure the roses ; but we can
have them both. If a sea-kale plant is allowed to blossom,
the beautiful green and gold beetles will gather to its
honeyed sweets. They come to the tree-peonies too,
which need no such foreign jewelry, though their beauty
is not marred thereby.

Returning to the moths, we see, by daylight, beside the
Humming-bird, the Burnets, Cinnabars, and troublesome

Currant-Moth. The Tiger-Moth is not uncommon, and we have the Emperor, Buff and White Ermines, Lime Hawk-Moth, Oak Eggar, Magpies, Swifts, Gold-tails, Emerald, Swallow-tail, Forester, Lackey, and others of more ominous names: the Dingy Footman, the Drinkers, the Black Arches, the Death's-head, the Ghost, Satin and Brimstone—truly an appalling assemblage!

THE FLORA of the valley and surrounding hills and marshes is as varied as the surface of the country. Among the more noteworthy plants may be mentioned the following :—Alpine Cress or Shepherd's Purse, *Thlaspi alpestre*, abundant at Winterhead ; Spurge-olive, *Daphne Mezereum*, growing wild at Sidcot ; where are also found *Helleborus viridis* and *fœtidus*, though Withering says they are "never truly wild" as British plants. The Autumn Gentian, *Gentiána Amarella*, grows on Sandford and Callow hills, and on Wavering Down and Hutton hill is found the *Pimpinella Dioica*, or *Trinia vulgaris*, as it is called, though really uncommon. The curious little parasite, the Lesser Dodder, *Cuscuta epithymum*, grows among heather and other heath plants, where also we find the Dropwort, *Spirea Filipendula*, and the Hair-bell, *Campanula rotundifolia*, and other common weeds, including numerous thistles. But the Hair-bell Campanula is not so common on our hills as the Harebell Hyacinth is in our valleys ; though neither kind of Bluebell is so abundant here as in many parts of the country, where the woodland floor and parks are sometimes blue with the Wild Hyacinth. Eyebright, *Euphrasia officinalis*, Rest Harrow, *Ononis arvensis*, and Speedwell, *Veronica chamædris*, are all abundant; but worth naming for the sake of their pretty names.

Among the less·common wild flowers are the Rock Rose, *Helianthemum vulgare*, which is plentiful on the high banks of Banwell Roddy. Lower down on the same road-side, among Willow-herbs, Meadow-sweet and other common weeds, is the Narrow-leaved Everlasting Pea, *Lathyrus sylvestris*, climbing in the rampant hedge-row. The Purple, or rather brilliant blue, Gromwell, *Lithospermum purpuro-cæruleum* grows in the woods of Shutshelf and Sandford hills. Columbine, *Aquilegia vulgaris*, I have found not long ago in Kingwood, and have heard that Solomon's Seal, *Convallaria multiflora*, may also be found in the neighbourhood ; but neither of these garden plants are common in our valley.

The Lily of the Valley, *Convallaria Majalis*, grows on Churchill Batch, but does not flower freely till brought into the better soil of a garden, where it spreads and blossoms abundantly.

Daffodils, *Narcissus Pseudo-Narcissus*, abound in the narrow combe between Pattenham and Shipham, as well as at Langford, Rickford, and elsewhere. Both the Pale Narcissus, *Narcissus biflorus*, and the Poet's Narcissus, *Narcissus Poeticus*, are found growing wild in meadows and orchards, though they are not considered indigenous British plants. They were, however, found in England before any notice can be found of Snowdrops.

An abbot of Cirencester, in the thirteenth, century,* left on record his idea of "a Noble Garden," which, he says, " should contain Roses, Lilies, Violets, Sunflowers, Poppies, and Narcissus." But he does not mention

---

* *Vide* Disraeli's *Curiosities of Literature.*

Snowdrops. Nor are they named by any writer in prose or poetry, as far as I can discover, before the middle of the seventeenth century. An observer like Shakespear could not have failed to allude to such a flower had he known it. Bacon does not include it in the flowers of spring, with the Crocus, Anemone and Primrose ; nor is it mentioned in Herrick's *Hesperides*, where so much is said about Lilies and Violets, Primroses and Cherry-blossom, and many more. He could not have failed to mention such a flower had it been known to him. Neither Isaac Walton, nor Sir Henry Wotton, nor " Jo. Davors, Esq.," whom Walton quotes in his *Complete Angler*, printed in 1653, can have seen a Snowdrop. Wotton writes :

> The fields and gardens were beset
> With Tulips, Crocus, Violet :

but the Snowdrop is not named. Davors writes :

> Among the Daisies and the Violets blue,
> Red Hyacinth and yellow Daffodil,
> Purple Narcissus like the morning rays,
> Pale Gander-grass, and azure Culverkeys :

but he sees no Snowdrops.

Culverkeys are the *Aquilegia*, or Columbine ; Gander-grass is, I presume, the *Galium* or Goose-grass ; but what the Purple Narcissus may be, who can tell ?

The earliest notices I find of Snowdrops, are by two writers quoted in Johnson's Dictionary, the Hon. Robert Boyle, who wrote on colours about 1665, and Thomas Tickell, who wrote on the death of Addison, whose secretary he had been in Ireland from 1717 to 1725. When, therefore, he wrote about

> A flower that first in this sweet garden smiled,
> To virgins sacred, and the Snowdrop styled,

he might allude to a garden in Ireland. Boyle speaks of "those purely white flowers that appear about the end of winter *called Snowdrops*," as if they were not then generally known.

Snowdrops grow wild here along the brooklet from the ruined mill; but how and when they came there is not known. In a marshy coppice near Max, we find the Bog-bean as already mentioned, and on the banks of the brook and in the smaller water-courses, the Purple Loose-strife, the Yellow Iris, and the Marsh Marigold are abundant; but the beautiful Water Forget-me-not or Scorpion grass, *Myosotis palustris*, so common in other parts of the country, is not among our water beauties. It grows in the Rhines below Axbridge, but seems to dislike our spring-water, as much as the Fox-glove does our limestone rocks. That handsome plant grows only where the sandstone crops up, as on Sidcot Hill and along the lane below Eagle's crag.

On Blackdown, we find the Yellow Asphodel, the Bog Violet and Pimpernel, and two, if not three, kinds of Sundew. The Marsh Andromeda, or Wild Rosemary, has also been included in the flora of our hills, but I have not met with it nearer than the turf-moors about Street, near Glastonbury. In that neighbourhood may be found also the Arrowhead, *Sagitaria sagitæfolia*, and the Flowering Rush, *Butomus umbellatus*. In the ditches of the North Marsh, along the line of Railway between Sandford and Yatton, as well as nearer Weston, may be seen the pretty little Frog-bit, *Hydrocharis morsus ranæ*.

The numerous *Carices*, or Sedges, to be found in our marshy land, include *C. pseudo cyperis*, which, according to Mr. Worth, grows in a "pond near Winscombe."*

* Tourists' Guide, page 19.

Cotton Grass, *Eriophorum angustifolia*, grows sparingly
in the Max meadows, and more abundantly on Blackdown and the turf moors.

We have in some of our meadows the Dyer's Green-
weed or Woad-waxen, *Genista ·tinctoria*, but not the
handsome Common Broom, *Genista scoparia*, from which
the royal Plantagenets took the name.

The Common Furze, Whin, or Gorse, called here
Vuzzen, is abundant on the hills, though not quite so
resplendent with us as it is on some of the hills further
west, being kept down by occasional burning. The top
of Callow Hill was literally ablaze last March, resembling
a prairie fire, and keeping up the ancient character of the
hill as a bare or callow one.

The Ox-eye Daisy, *Chrysanthemum leucanthemum*,
one of the handsomest of weeds, is very abundant, especially on rocky banks and rough garden walls; but the
splendid Corn Marigold, *C. segetum*, is not common here;
nor is the Goat's-beard, *Tragopogon pratensis*. Wild
Succory, *Cichorium intybus*, is commoner, and still
more common is the Common Comfrey, *Symphytum
officinale*.

The Alkanet, *Anchusa sempervirens*, and the Leopard's
Bane, *Doronicum pardalianches*, appear from time to
time as garden weeds, as also doth the Moth Mullein,
Verbascum Blattaria, both the yellow, and the less
common, but more elegant creamy-white variety, growing
both in gardens and on railway banks. A species
of Salvia *S. Verbenaca* is common on the banks of
some of our lanes. Both these weeds might be improved by cultivation, and the latter might possibly
develope into the beautiful variety so common in Switzerland and Germany.

O

The chequered Tulip or Lily, *Fritillaria Meleagris,* grows near Wells, but not, I think, in our district.

The Musk Mallow, *Malva moschata,* is sometimes found here, but is rare.

The Autumn Crocus or Meadow Saffron, *Colchicum autumnale,* is over-abundant in some of our ill-drained meadows; but we have none of the true Wild Crocus, *Crocus vernus* which William Howitt, in his Book of the Seasons, says is so abundant in the meadows near Nottingham.

The sandy shore near Berrow is adorned with the beautiful Marine Convolvulus or Sea Bindweed, *C. Soldanella,* and the Sea Holly, *Eryngium maritimum,* as well as other sand-loving plants ; and on Brean down, hard by, are the White Rock Rose, *Helianthemum polifolium,* and other rock plants.

The Steep Holm in the Bristol Channel is distinguished as the last refuge of the *Pæonia corallina,* which Withering says "grows on islands in the Severn, but is not truly wild." Care is now taken to preserve it from extinction. I had a small bit of it in my garden, but it has been lost, and the only specimen I know is in the Meeting-house yard at Sidcot ; where I hope it may be left to increase and multiply.

Cheddar is famous for its Pinks and Ferns, and there also is abundance of the Yellow Poppy, *Papaver cambrica,* which, unlike the Peony, when brought into the garden, becomes quite a troublesome weed.

The lovely and fragrant Cheddar pink, *Dianthus cæsius,* still flourishes in inaccessible parts of the Cliffs, and grows freely on rough garden-walls, where it sows itself so abundantly that I have had the pleasure of sending seed and seedlings to correspondents in Scotland, Wales, and elsewhere, including an attempt, which I heartily wish might succeed, to embellish the unsightly heaps of slag in the waste howling wilderness of the Black country. Of the Hawkweeds, we have *Hieracium Schmidtii, H. stenolepsis, vulgatum,* var. *maculatum, murorum, boreali,* and at Ebbor, the rarer *tridentatum.* But the botanical reader should obtain the Monograph by Fred. Janson Hanbury of Plough Court, which is not only a valuable scientific treatise, but an example of accurate delineation and exquisite hand-colouring, rarely, if ever, equalled.*

Ferns are abundant, but not so luxuriant as among the hill combes further west. We have a perennial greenness of Hart's tongue, *Scolopendrium,* and the *Ceterach* is one of the commonest ornaments of our limestone walls, mixed with *Ruta muraria* and *Asplenium Trichomanes. Cystopteris fragilis* is not uncommon. In the combes of Blackdown, the Mountain Fern, *Lastrea Oreopteris,* and the Hard Fern, *Blechnum boreale,* are tolerably plentiful. The Limestone Polypody, *P. calcareum,* is abundant at Burrington and Brockley, and at Cheddar cliffs ; and the Royal Fern, *Osmunda regalis,* in the turf moors. The common Brake adorns the Church knoll, and the Lady Fern grows at Sidcot, but she is now scarce on Winscombe hill. The common Polypody and Male-fern are as common here as elsewhere. *Asplenium Adiantum nigrum* is found at Hale and Sandford, and on the way to Shipham. *A. marinum* grows at several places near Weston-super-mare. Neither the Beech Fern, nor the lovely Oak Fern, can be found, I believe, nearer than the Ebbor Rocks. Moonworts are found on the hills, Ladies' Tresses on the slopes, and Adders' Tongues in the orchards.

* The drawings, and, I believe, the colouring of the plates, are by Miss G. Lister, and are evidently " a labour of love."

Of British species of Orchis, we have in our district the Man, the Bee, the Butterfly, and Bird's-nest, but not the Fly orchis, the most remarkable mimic of all. The commoner kinds are abundant in the damp meadows. The rarer Dwarf Orchis, *Orchis ustulata*, has been found on Wavering Down.

Of the Bee-orchis, or Bee-flower, Langhorne* wrote :

> See on that flow'ret's velvet breast,
> How close the busy vagrant lies !
> His thin-wrought plume, his downy breast,
> The ambrosial gold that swells his thighs.

> Perhaps his fragrant load may bind
> His limbs ;—we'll set the captive free—
> I sought the living bee to find,
> And found the picture of a bee.

Throughout the winter the banks along the lanes are evergreen with ivy, hart's-tongue, violet, primrose, and other hardy vegetation. In frost and snow, when the mavis and throstle, sad and silent, shelter among the brambles, the hedges, though bared of hips and haws and bryony-berries, are still coloured with brown oak and beech leaves, brambles and ferns; while, here and there, a shining holly—not common in our hedges—displays its coral beads; if haply not stript for Christmas decoration. The stone walls are adorned with the emerald cups of the Pennywort, *Cotyledon umbilicus*, with Spleenwort and Ceterach ; soon to be varied by the red stalks and young leaves of the early *Geranium lucidum*, and abundance of rich green moss on every damp stone. And then

> E'er lingering winter wings his flight,
> The gay *Peziza* springs to light.

---

* The critic, and translator of *Plutarch's Lives*, who was rector of Blagdon.

These scarlet fairy-cups are abundant here, though gathered and sent away by hundreds every year. They are generally covered more or less with dead leaves; but when discovered often lie upon rich beds of moss. Very soon the hardy Arum appears above ground, to tell of future "lords and ladies." The less attractive Dogs' Mercury keeps company with the swelling catkins above, and the first warm sunshine spangles the banks with the glossy Celandine. And now, while January has but just opened the door to the new seasons, we see among the remnants of the old, the welcome Snowdrop—

> Wan herald of the coming year,
> We see her pennon fair unfold,
>   While yet the skies are dark and drear,
> And streaming on the wintry gale,
>   We bid her spotless banner hail.

The wild Snowdrops on the sheltered banks of the brook, by the old ruined mill, appear before their garden relatives, often flowering early in January.

Winter Aconite, Hellebore, Coltsfoot, and here and there precocious primroses and violets, with a sprinkling of daisies, answer to the increasing solar force; while in damp coppices and hedge-rows appears the

> Satin-shining palm,
> On sallows in the windy gleams of March.

Lent lilies, too—

> Daffodils,
> That come before the swallow dares, and take
> The winds of March with beauty ; violets dim,
> But sweeter than the lids of Juno's eyes,
> Or Cytherea's breath ; pale primroses—

Shakespear's close observation of nature, as usual, has marked the true succession—daffodils, violets, primroses :

all abundant in our valley ; especially the first, which are gathered by thousands. On the sunny side of Daffodil Valley, among the mossy stones of the hazel copse, they are often in bloom the first week in March, before the village children can make bunches of violets. They are past their prime when

> The rathe primrose decks the mead.

At Langford they grow by the side of a stream, reminding us of Wordsworth's description of those on the banks of Ulleswater :—

> A host of golden daffodils,
> Beside the lake, beneath the trees,
> Fluttering and dancing in the breeze.

Violets, "half hidden from the eye," perfume the air almost unperceived. The perfume of flowers is most grateful when, like the quality of mercy, it "is not strained." It is marred by excess. Bacon likens it to music; "The breath of flowers is far sweeter in the air when it comes and goes like the warbling of music ;*" and Shakespear makes the like comparison—

> That strain again : it had a dying fall :
> O it came o'er my ear like the sweet south,
> That breathes upon a bank of violets,
> Stealing and giving odour.

The Violet was, evidently a favorite of Shakespear—

> To throw a perfume on the violet
> . . . .
> Is wasteful and ridiculous excess.

* Bacon's Essays ; "Of Gardens."

Primroses here deck the banks and coppices, rather than the meads—

> Thee, when young Spring first questioned Winter's sway,
> And dared the sturdy blusterer to the fight ;
> Thee on this bank he threw,
> To mark his victory.

Spring's victory, though certain, is not yet undisputed—

> When well-apparell'd April on the heel
> Of limping Winter treads.

Though the woods are carpeted with primroses, violets, anemones and wood-sorrel, winter is not yet completely conquered. The hardy Butchers'-broom adorns its prickly leaves with tiny blossoms ; but

> Stern winter's reign is not yet past—
> Lo ! while your buds prepare to blow,
> On icy pinions comes the blast,
> And nips your root, and lays you low.

Icy blasts are to come, bringing "blackthorn winter." While the sloe blossom adorns the hedges, and the hawthorn and briar put forth their green leaves, the arctic air comes as the bitter east wind, nipping the tender foliage, and too often blighting the gardener's hopes ; teaching him a lesson, perhaps familiar, but one best learned in the dear school of experience—

> This is the state of man : to-day he puts forth
> The tender leaves of hope, to-morrow blossoms,
> And bears his blushing honours thick upon him ;
> The third day comes a frost, a killing frost.

And such is the state of man in a higher sense than Wolsey, or perhaps even Shakespear, thought of. The change from the wintry state, as the mind begins to turn

\

towards the Sun of Righteousness, is not a sudden jump
from cold and deadness to spiritual warmth and fruitful-
ness ; the tender leaves of hope are too often nipt by
recurring cold, and, though followed to-morrow by flowers
of faith, the fruits of charity are yet to form and ripen :
often through states harsh and sour, before they are
mellowed in the autumn of life Spring, however, comes
on—

> When daisies pied and violets blue,
> And cuckoo buds of yellow hue,
> And Lady-smocks all silver white,
> Do paint the meadows with delight.

Cuckoo-buds must be our familiar Buttercups, and Lady-
smocks are what we call Cuckoo flowers—the *Cardamine
pratensis;* that we connect with the voice of the Cuckoo ;
but which the people in Roman Catholic times associated
with the Blessed Virgin.

Shakespear reminds us of another common plant,
more feared than admired, the common stinging-nettle.
Everywhere spoken against, it is nevertheless worthy of
a better reputation. It is one of those common things
neglected by ignorance, but wholesome and useful if made
use of. It was not without reason that Hotspur said,—

> Out of this nettle, danger, we pluck this flower safety.

I am not aware that any of the cottagers take the trouble
to collect and boil the young shoots ; but they are wholesome greens, and are also said to be capable of gilding
paper. They nourish the larvæ of some of our most
beautiful Butterflies, and furnish the gold from which the
Chrysalis is named.

Our English climate, even in Somersetshire, is too
variable to give spring an undisturbed reign. The ice-king

comes on again and again, and seldom yields his
sceptre till spring has grown into summer. Meanwhile,
in spite of drawbacks, vegetation advances. Sweet violets
give place to their lovely blue woodland cousins.

> The violet in her green-wood bower,
>   Where birchen boughs with hazels mingle,
> May boast itself the fairest flower
>   In glen, or copse, or forest dingle.

The bold oxlip, as Shakespear calls it, succeeds the
primrose ; cowslip-balls and daisy-chains come in.

> Yon tufted knoll with daisies strewn
> Might make proud Oberon a throne.

Then silver daisies yield to golden buttercups, and
another golden flower, despised and vulgar, yet not too
mean for a poet's notice, the irrepressible dandelion—

> Dear common flower, that grows beside the way,
> Fringing the dusty road with harmless gold—
> First pledge of blithesome May.

Now blue-bells mingle with the young fronds of ferns,
Marsh-marigolds bedeck the brooklet banks, and soon
the hedges are gay with rosy crab and spindletree, and
bossy May.

> And in the warm hedge grow lush Eglantine,
>   Green Cow-bind and the morn-lit coloured May,
> And Cherry-blossom, and white cups whose wine
>   Is the bright dew yet drained not by the day ;
> And wild roses, and ivy serpentine,
>   With its dark buds and leaves wandering astray ;
> And flowers azure, black and streaked with gold,
>   Fairer than any wakened eyes behold.

Summer is come,

> And the milk-maid singeth blithe,
> And the mower whets his scythe,
> And every shepherd tells his tale
> Under the hawthorn in the dale.

Summer is come, but it is hardly at home before the longest day is past, and what we call Midsummer is over. Now are our English hedgerows in their prime. Roses and woodbine, bindweed and bryony, and flowering hops, mingle with hawthorn and bramble, guelder rose, buckthorn, privet, and holly ; the traveller's joy overspreads the wayfaring tree, the everlasting pea hangs over a wild luxuriance of willow-herb, meadow-sweet, campion and reeds, while the water-courses are gay with the purple loose-strife and yellow iris.

> And where profuse the wood-vetch clings,
> Round ash and elm in verdant rings,
> Its pale and azure pencilled flower,
> Should canopy Titania's bower.

The nettle-leaved campanula is common in the lanes, and, on the hills, the hair-bell mingles, though sparingly, with the three English heath flowers, of which the *Erica Cinerea* is perhaps the most abundant.

> Flower of the wild ! whose purple glow
> Adorns the dusky mountain's side.

Our corn-fields, as might be supposed, are abundantly adorned with weeds of various kinds. The smaller bindweed, *Convolvulus arvensis*, climbs the corn-stalks ; sun-loving pimpernels, tiny forget-me-nots, and pansies cover the ground. The beautiful corn blue-bottle, *Centauria cyanus*, and the glowing marigold *Chrysanthemum segetum*, so abundant in some places, are scarce with us; but the scarlet poppy is as abundant here as anywhere, and not less splendid for being common.

And then come Autumn's glories,

> Crowned with the sickle and the wheaten sheaf,
> While autumn, nodding o'er the yellow plain,
> Comes jovial on :

less welcome than spring to the young and hopeful ; but full of thankfulness to those who see in it the endless goodness of the Eternal ; the completion of one stage in the journey of life, the beginning of the next ; the harvest of one state, the seed of another.

> ALMIGHTY FATHER—
> ————the rolling year
> Is full of Thee. Forth in the pleasing spring
> Thy beauty walks, Thy tenderness and love.
>
> .   .   .   .   .   .
>
> Thy bounty shines in autumn unconfined,
> And spreads a common feast for all that lives.

The autumn colchicum has taken the place of the cowslips ; the welcomed catkins of the hazel have been followed by the brown nuts,—too often forestalled by impatient gatherers ;

> where— a broken bough
> Droops with its withered leaves, ungracious sign
> Of devastation.

The less molested, but more abused hop has hung its tonic clusters in the hedges ; hips and haws have succeeded the roses and whitethorn, and sour sloes the blackthorn.

The spindle tree is splendid in scarlet leaves and blossom-like fruit ; bright berries glow among the sweet lingering woodbine that still scents the evening air ; autumn leaves are glowing. The apples are gathered, or lie in red and yellow heaps on the orchard green ; the traveller's joy puts on its woolly mantle, and appears as Oldman's Beard ; while the holly and misseltoe prepare for Christmas decorations, and the bryonies hang their coral and ruby chains from spray to spray. Now Flora, Ceres and Pomona rejoice in Nature's banquet ; their lingering gifts surviving till again

Dead nature breathes and stirs.

But nature is never dead. It receives life continually from the Divine Source of all life. There is no cessation, and only in very severe seasons, if ever, is there a total absence even of flowers. The Chrysanthemums are not over when the Christmas roses appear, and the Laurestinus and yellow Jessamine, with, perhaps, a lingering rose or precocious primrose, enliven the garden till snowdrops again proclaim the returning Spring.

THE GEOLOGICAL HISTORY OF THE MENDIP HILLS.

BY PROFESSOR C. LLOYD MORGAN, F.G.S.

THE geological history of the Mendip Hills involves at least six distinct and separate phases. I propose first to give a brief summary of these six phases and then to add some further details with regard to those which seem to be the more important.

When the scene opens, the range of hills, as we know it, has no existence; for we have first to trace the preparatory stages during which their material structure was fashioning in the womb of the Palæozoic sea. The site of the Mendips must be represented in the imagination as a waste of waters, beneath which were accumulating the beds of old red sandstone which form the oldest rocks of the existing range of hills. Land lay not far to the north, while to the south stretched the sea in which were formed the Torquay limestones, with their abundant remains of corals.

The whole of the area which is now Southern England was at this time undergoing slow and gradual depression beneath the waters, and the shores to the north of the Mendips were step by step submerged. The formation of sandstone gave place gradually to the accumulation of limestone. Corals, sea-lilies (crinoids), and shell-fish (brachiopods) with many other forms of marine life, including fishes with strong fin-spines and powerful crushing teeth, by which they were able to crunch up living coral and sea lilies—all these came up from the south, and lived and died in the clear water which now rolled over Mendip. So long did this state of things continue, so great was the accumulation of calcareous matter, that the beds of mountain limestone and associated strata so formed reach a thickness of at least three thousand feet. Then followed a period, one of the most interesting in geological history, when the physical conditions became remarkably different; a period during which beds of sandstone, at first marine (millstone grit), and then probably freshwater or brackish, and associated with beds of clay and seams of coal (coal-measures) were laid down to the depth of several thousand feet. This long phase of gradual though intermittent depression, accompanied by the formation of some ten thousand feet of stratified rock, constitutes the first of the six phases of the geological history of the Mendips, to which allusion was made. We may describe it as the period of *the formation of the older rocks.*

At the close of this period England seems to have been caught in the grip of a squeeze which affected all this mass of newly formed strata and bent them into a series of waves or rolling curves with alternating arches and troughs. The sandstones, limestones, and coal measures of Mendip were thus thrown into the form of an arch—what geologists call an anticlinal fold—while to the north of this arch was the trough (synclinal) in which the Somersetshire coal-field now lies. This second phase, that of earth-throes and the formation through north and south pressure of the Mendip arch, we may describe as *the upheaval of the older rocks.*

Thus were the older strata of Mendip formed, and thus were they upheaved. Now comes the period of their earliest fashioning as part of the earth's surface. For the thrust which bent and ridged the strata, lifted the length and breadth of what is now England, with the possible exception of one or two small basins, into dry land. And this land was subject to the destructive and denuding effects of rain and the weather, of frost perhaps and ice, of streams and running water. By these agencies the back of the Mendip saddle was largely eaten away by denudation ; the coal-measures, millstone grit, and car-boniferous limestone, were in parts entirely removed, and the underlying old red sandstone exposed and eaten into. The solid arch of the hills was carved into something not very different from its present form, though the striking gorges of Ebbor, Burrington, and Cheddar,

Whatley Combe and Vallis Vale, had then probably no
existence. We may call this phase that of *the early
fashioning of the Mendip hills.*

This period of early Mendip sculpturing was of long
duration. During the slow fashioning of the hills from
the arched strata of the Mendip ridge, thousands of feet
of deposit (permian and triassic) were formed in the
region which is now central England, and in the region
which lies to the South over Devon and the English
Channel. Between these northern and southern areas
over which rolled the waters of salt lakes or inland seas,
there lay a stretch of land in which the Mendip hills must
have formed a striking and prominent feature. And the
next phase of Mendip history is that of the gradual
depression of this stretch of land between the waters and
the consequent submergence of the hills. When the
waves first washed the base of the older Mendips they were
still barren of life, like the waters of modern salt lakes ;
but before the hills were fully submerged the lake had,
through further depression of the land, become united
with a southern sea, and was tenanted with all the
abundant life that characterised the warm and shallow
waters of liassic and oolitic times—with ammonites and
belemnites and many kinds of bivalve shells, and with
the strange reptiles whose remains have been found at
Street. As the Mendips thus sank, they were gradually
smothered in the deposits of this sea, and before the
close of oolitic times were probably completely buried
beneath the newer strata.

Between the geological period during which the oolitic
strata of the hills round Bath were deposited, and that
during which the chalk of the Wiltshire Downs accumulated, the Mendips, with the newer strata by which they

Kaadar Cliffs

were enwrapped and smothered, were again uplifted to form a land surface subject to the denuding action of the weather, rain, and running water. I think it probable that during this period the newer rocks were stripped from the summits of the hills, and the older strata of old red sandstone and mountain limestone were exposed and perhaps further denuded. This is, however, to some extent conjectural. In any case the hills were again submerged beneath the waters of the chalk sea and were probably again smothered beneath the ooze produced by the abundant foraminiferal life of that period. Neglecting then the temporary re-emergence of the hills, we may speak of the fourth phase of Mendip history as *the submergence of the hills and their burial beneath newer strata*.

The fifth phase is that of *the re-elevation of the buried Mendips*, in common with the whole of what is now England, from beneath the waters of the chalk sea. This period, like that of the earlier formation of the Mendip fold, was one of severe earth pressures. England was, however, far from the main centre of the European squeeze ; and we must go to the Alps to appreciate the full effects of the tremendous lateral grip by which the rocks were held and crushed as in the tightening jaws of a vice. The squeeze was long-continued and lasted through the earlier part of the Tertiary or Cainozoic epoch of geologists. In the neighbourhood of the Mendips it gave to the oolitic and other mesozoic strata their easterly dip ; but further east it threw the beds of Alum Bay in the Isle of Wight into their vertical position and formed the arch of the Weald of Kent, Surrey and Sussex, now broken by denudation to form the North and South Downs.

P

The final phase of Mendip history is that of the removal by denudation of the overload of later deposits formed during the fourth stage, and *the refashioning of the hills* into the form which they now possess.

The deposition of the older rocks, their upheaval as a Mendip arch, their early sculpturing and fashioning under the hand of denudation ; their submergence and burial beneath the newer deposits of mesozoic age, their re-emergence buried beneath an overload of these latter rocks, and the final removal of this overload and the refashioning of the hills by denudation—these are the main phases of the geological history of the Mendips, concerning some of which I may now give some further details.

First, then, I must say something concerning *the formation of the older rocks.* The old red sandstone, the most ancient rock exposed to view in the Mendips, forms a little ridge to the south of Sidcot, which extending eastwards through Shipham, rises and broadens to form the elevated saddle of Black Down. On North Hill near Priddy, and again at Pen Hill, the same rock occurs ; while yet further south-east it forms the high ground stretching from Masbury Castle by Beacon Hill to Whatley. The beds are composed of red and reddish brown sandstones and conglomerates, and must have been formed in water which was shallow and troubled by swift currents. There are no remains of marine life, though fish scales have been found further north at Portishead. It is therefore inferred that the waters were not those of the open sea, but of a partially land-locked estuary.

Mantling round the edges of the old red sandstone are beds of dark shale with impure limestones. These are well seen in Burrington combe and in the cutting of the

Somerset and Dorset line near Masbury station. The marine fossils and the bands of limestone show us that the waters of the southern sea had gained freer access to the Mendip area ; while the shaly nature of the beds and the impurity of the limestones (due to an admixture of clayey matter) indicate that the rivers from the land were bringing down mud, silt, and clay, and rendering the water turbid. As the area sank, however, the water became clearer and brighter. This is shown by the

increasing purity of the limestones, as we pass up into the lower mountain limestone, which is well seen in the sharply scarped crags along the Shutshelf, and near the Eagle crag of the same escarpment further east. The brachiopod shell-fish *Spirifer* which is very abundant in the lowest limestones grows scarcer as we enter the massive beds of the mountain limestone proper, and the sea of that period seems to have been tenanted by great numbers of crinoids or sea-lilies, the joints or ossicles of which form a large proportion of the lower limestones, which in Burrington combe are not less than 1300 feet thick. Above these lower or crinoidal limestones we find a series of beds from two to three hundred feet thick in which the limestones generally have the structure called oolitic, because the weathered surface is covered with a vast number of little spheres about the size of, and somewhat resembling, the roe of a fish. These oolitic beds are of considerable interest. The purity of the limestone shows that they were formed in bright clear water; the not infrequent occurrence of current-bedding shows that the water was comparatively shallow and gently troubled to its bottom by currents; and the way in which the limestone in each oolitic or roe-like grain is arranged concentrically round a minute nucleus shows that the grains were kept a-dance in water which must have been highly charged with carbonate of lime in solution. Mr. E. Wethered has lately shown that in some cases the oolite grains, exhibit under the microscope a peculiar structure which seems to point to the presence of a minute organism (Girvanella) and he is inclined to believe that oolite is generally or always formed by the agency of this organism, a conclusion which is at present somewhat premature. This oolitic limestone from its close texture, its whiteness, and the massive beds in which it is apt to occur, forms a noteworthy feature of the hills. It is found near the entrance to Burrington combe (in the large quarry on the left hand side going up the combe); also just below the summit of Crooks

Peak, and in the upper part of Cheddar Gorge ; on the spurs of the hills lying to the west of Cheddar, and elsewhere.

Above these oolitic beds the character of the limestone changes. Whereas below them crinoidal remains are very abundant, above them crinoidal remains are scarce ; but instead of these organisms there are found in considerable abundance the remains of corals (chiefly species of Lithostrotion). How thick these upper beds of Litho-strotion limestone are I am unable to say with certainty. There are special difficulties (with which I need not trouble the reader) in forming a satisfactory estimate, but I think we may put it at about 1200 feet.

The old red sandstone and the mountain limestone, with the shaly beds which are transitional between these so different rock-masses, form the main mass of the Mendip upland. In this sketch of Mendip geology it is unnecessary to say anything here concerning the millstone grit and the coal-measnres, since they form no marked feature of the hills as they now exist.

Concerning the second phase, that of the upheaval of the older rocks, little need be added to that which has been already mentioned. Only two points require passing notice. In the first place it must be remembered that the formation of the Mendip arch was only one result of a widespread disturbance ; one which affected large areas of the earth's crust, which gave rise to the Pennine Hills, the backbone of Modern England, and which caused our coal-fields to lie in basin-shaped hollows. Secondly it should be noted that, though in a condensed description, we may speak generally of the Mendip arch as if it were one continuous saddle, it is more accurately a series of at least four arches the axes of which are arranged roughly thus :

Blackdown arch.
North Hill arch.

Pen Hill arch. ·

Beacon Hill arch.

Thus although the several ridges run nearly east and west the general trend of the hill range runs from about E.N.E. to W.S.W.

Coming now to the third phase, that of the early fashioning of the Mendip hills, I may explain that the nature and amount of this fashioning is ascertained by a careful study of the relationships of the later to the earlier series of Mendip strata.   The older strata were uplifted and sculptured by the forces of denudation before the newer series were laid down on their worn and eroded edges.   When we see, for example, in Vallis Vale, and near Shepton Mallet and elsewhere, the newer strata lying on the flatly planed edges of upturned strata of mountain limestone, we may be certain that the planing of these edges took place previous to the deposition of the later beds.   And when we see tongues of the newer strata penetrating to the heart of the hills, we may be sure that they were formed at the period of the early fashioning of the Mendips.   Such a tongue runs up at the western end of the range, and forms the charming valley (now partly occupied by beds of the newer strata) in which Christon, Winscombe, Shipham, and Rowberrow lie in the lap of the hills.   Another well-marked tongue runs into the northern flanks of the range from East Harptree, by the " Castle of Comfort,"

to Charter House Warren, thus cutting right across the
existing watershed of the hills.   The southern flank of
Mendip is indented by many minor tongues.   One of
these runs up from Wookey Hole to Durston ; others lie
on either side of Cheddar ; and it is interesting to notice
that the existing Cheddar Gorge lies in a promontory
between the older Mendip valleys.   Thus the evidence of
the early fashioning of the hills is abundant and con-
vincing.

The gently curved outline of the Mendip uplands often
differs markedly from the steep dip of the mountain limestone strata.   It seems as if the strata had been shaved
off so as to leave a surface which is nearly flat.   The
level planing of the upper edges of the strata is, I feel
convinced, due to the action of the sea.   When the waves
of the sea are advancing on and eating into a coast-line,
they remove the rocks down to about the level of low
water, shaving them off to that level, and forming a
" shore platform."   If this action were accompanied by a
slow and gradual subsidence of the land (as we know was
the case when the Mendips were sinking beneath the
waters of the mesozoic sea) the net result would be a
gently curved surface of marine erosion, such as we see
upon the present uplands of the Mendip hills.   I am,
therefore, strongly inclined to believe that the general
features of the uplands (irrespective, that is to say, of the
more recent valleys or gorges due to a later period of
denudation) received their impress from the waves of the
sea in which swam the strange reptiles whose remains
have been found at Street.

This planing went on during the gradual submergence
of the Mendips in the phase which succeeded that of
their early fashioning by denudation.   But, as I have

already stated, when first the waters began to lap the
shores of Mendip, the hills formed an island set in the
waters of an extensive lake, which was probably salt, and
was certainly barren of aquatic life.   The accompanying
map,* from the *Proceedings of the Bristol Naturalists'*
Society, shows the Mendips as an island in this triassic
lake.   It was in this lake that the tongues of deposit
which fill the ancient valleys on the flanks of the hills, and
which probably form parts of a sort of fringe all round
the range, were accumulated.   The deposit is known as
dolomitic conglomerate, and forms at Draycott and elsewhere valuable building stone.   It is variable in character,
but in general may be described as consisting of angular
or rounded fragments of the more ancient rocks em-
bedded in a red or reddish-brown matrix, containing
iron and carbonate of lime.   The fragments, especially in
the lower parts of the deposit, and in certain of the old
valleys, are often of large size.   They were probably
swept from the hills by torrential rains, for there is no
evidence that they were ice-borne.   Further from the
margin of the hills, the conglomerate gives place to red
and green marls deposited in the deeper and more open
waters of the lake.

Without break, that is to say by a quiet and orderly
sequence of stratified layers, the triassic marls pass upwards into dark strata, which contain marine fossils.
This shows that the waters of the lake had, through continued subsidence of the land, communicated with the
waters of the sea ; and there is little doubt that this sea
lay to the south.   These Rhœtic or Penarth beds, which
are not many feet in thickness, contain only a few marine

---

*Inserted by the Society's kind permission.

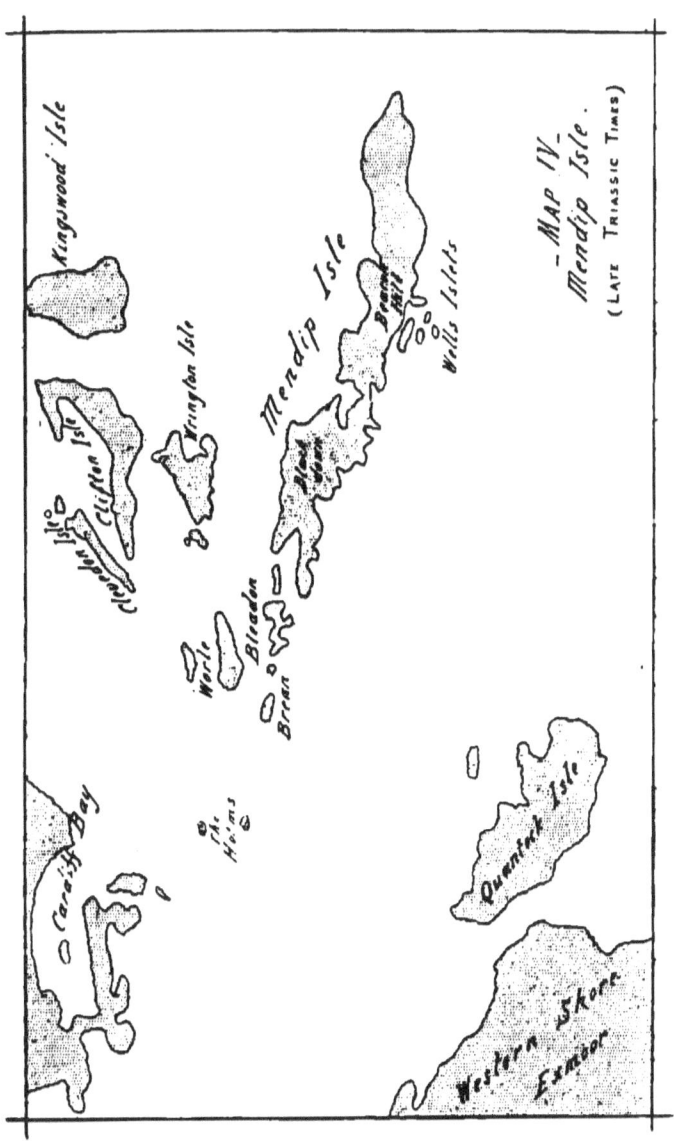

MAP IV.
Mendip Isle.
(LATE TRIASSIC TIMES)

Kingswood Isle

Wrington Isle

Mendip Isle

Wells Islets

Broadway Hill

Bleadon Isle

Clifton Isle

Clevedon Isle

Bleadon

Worle

Brean

Quantock Isle

The Holms

Cardiff Bay

Western Shore

Exmoor

shells, the lowest bed, being, however, sometimes crowded
with the bones and teeth of fishes and reptiles.   They
may be regarded as transitional beds from the barren
trias to the overlying lias with its teeming wealth of
shells, betokening a warm shallow sea.   Just on the
fringe of the land, the lias is peculiarly different in appearance from that which is found at a little distance
from the margin of the old island.   Above Shepton
Mallet, for example, it forms a white limestone (bastard
freestone) very different from the more normal lias beds
near Shepton Mallet station.   Above Harptree, it has
been converted into a silicious chert.   Near Nunney, and
in Vallis Vale, the whole of the lias is represented by
only a few feet of deposit.

    I must not linger over this gradual submergence of the
Mendip isle.   When the lias was succeeded by the oolites,
which form the hills round Bath, the Mendips had sunk
further beneath the waters of the sea; and in Vallis Vale
we may see the beds of inferior oolite resting upon the
upturned and planed edges of the limestone.   Whether the
Mendip island was completely submerged beneath the
sea and entirely smothered by the newer deposits
during oolitic times, is a disputed point.   I think that it
is probable that the submergence and smothering were
complete ;   that this was followed by temporary re-
emergence and the removal of some of the upper beds ;
and that then the hills sank beneath the chalk sea, and
were again smothered by mesozoic strata.   Thus ends
the fourth phase of Mendip History.

    With regard to the fifth phase—that of the final eleva-
tion of the Mendip area—we must again notice, as has
already been hinted, that the uplift of this region was no
isolated phenomenon, but resulted from earth-throes

which affected not only all England but all Europe. The range of hills, together with the strata beneath which they were buried, were given an easterly tilt. Hence as we go eastwards on Mendip, we find the hills gradually sinking beneath the oolites of Frome and its neighbourhood.

The final re-emergence—this new birth from the womb of the mesozoic sea—ushers in the last phase of the surely not uneventful history of the district. It must be remembered that the uplift of the area from beneath the waters of the chalk sea was not sudden but gradual. As the oozy bottom was slowly lifted to the surface, it was played upon by the waves, which would readily eat into the soft layers of recently deposited and little consolidated material. We may picture to ourselves a sort of battle of the forces. The forces of upheaval were striving by slow and uniform uplift to raise the sea-bottom into dry land. The forces of marine denudation lashed with their waves the oozy deposits as they came to the surface. Layer upon layer were lifted to the sea level; layer upon layer were gnawed away by the pitiless tooth of the sea. What eventually decided the struggle and gave to upheaval the victory, it is impossible to say. But it is not impossible that, so far as the Mendips are concerned, marine denudation, during the process of upheaval, held its own until the hard core of the old range was laid bare ; *then* upheaval slowly and steadily gained ground, for the older rocks offered greater resistance to the gnawing tooth of the sea. Thus the early Mendip range may have been freed from the wrappage of newer rocks as it rose from the sea in which those newer rocks had been formed.

Be this as it may, we know that upheaval did finally gain the mastery, and that by denudation, either marine

or sub-ærial, the wrappage of the newer rocks has been
removed. We know, too, that the combes, and gorges,
and wooded valleys, which give to the Mendips so much
of their charm, are, in many cases, the products of the
re-fashioning of the hills under the scalpel of a later
denudation. Some of them, such as Cheddar, Whatley
combe, and Vallis Vale, were cut (probably in great
part during the Glacial epoch) along new lines; others,
such as Burrington combe and Long Bottom, to the
east of Axbridge, along lines which were first established
by the earlier denudation. How extensive has been
the removal of the newer strata around the Mendips,
may be seen in the isolated fragments that remain in
Glastonbury Tor, in Brent Knoll, and, further north,
in Dundry Hill.

XV.—RICH AND POOR TOGETHER.

Freedom was there, and joy in every eye.
Such scenes were England's boast in days gone by

THE "fine old English gentleman" in days of yore gloried in rude hospitality. His manners might ring like the metal of his ancestral bucklers, but there was much in his honest kindly soul to raise him above the ostentatious mammon-worshiper, and prove him the true gentleman, in spite of some roughness of manners.

But times and seasons though they change, and customs pass away,
Yet English hands and English hearts are still Old England's stay.

And it is pleasant to find, that as each age has looked back to the " good old times " of its forefathers, each in its turn has become the same object of pleasant retrospection. 'Tis distance lends enchantment to the view ; and, in the mixture of good and evil in this mortal life, it is well that the good should be remembered when the evil is forgotten. " Look back!" said the good Archbishop Tait, "What age are you prepared to say it would have been more satisfactory to have lived in ?   For my part, I thank God, and take courage.*"

The hospitality of the old times, expressed in strong and abundant liquor, the benevolence of the " old buttery hatch," still linger in country places; but the accumulated mischief done by sottish habits has, at last, begun to force a change for the better.   Hospitality and benevolence are not lessened because an old porter is no longer kept at the gate to regale rogues and vagabonds ; and guests are no longer entertained with " old liquor able to make a cat speak, and a man dumb."   The modern English gentleman finds his hospitality and benevolence better applied in withholding that kind of entertainment. If the title *lord* originally meant a giver of bread, as distinct from a bread-winner, he must be a lord of high degree who gives the staff of life to the better part. Food for the mind which lasts is more precious than food for the body which perishes.   No " old courtier of the Queen,"† in the days of Elizabeth, ever won the gratitude of the honest poor more deservedly than the Earl of Shaftesbury in the reign of Victoria.   His charity was

* *Life of Archbishop C. Tait,* chapter xxvi, 1877.

† " The Old Courtier of the Queen " was the original song of " The Fine Old English Gentleman."

unconcerned in making cats speak and men dumb; he devoted himself to the task of providing homes where men might speak words of love and wisdom, and be kind to their dumb companions. No old courtier of the bear-baiting days of Queen Bess ever gave such noble entertainment as the late Earl of Carlisle, who spent his intellectual wealth for the profit and pleasure of " rich and poor one with another." The addresses of Lord Morpeth are models of good taste and the happy application of sound wisdom and right feeling to the condition of his audience. In one, on the marriage of Vulcan and Venus, he enlarged with the happiest eloquence on the union of the Useful and the Beautiful in the arts and hard work of daily life, and, urging the necessity of Religion as the guide and support of all, he said that he " did not so much care to what particular religious fold they might belong, so that there was a hope of learning that man is their brother, and that God is love."

If, in making a feast, the poor should be preferred to the rich neighbours, lest a recompense be made, the gospel rule applies more especially to feasts of higher than bodily kind. In these there is no risk of abuse. There is no danger in feeding the hungry soul with goodness and truth; the only danger is in feeding those who are full of their own conceits. Nor is there any danger in helping those who are maimed in the battle of life; in supporting those who limp in their efforts to walk uprightly, or in giving light to those who are conscious of blindness.

Feasts of this kind are given by many in our valley; sometimes the feast of charity and truth is accompanied by a corresponding feast for the body—as when the poor of the Union are regaled in a banquet expressive of

the good-will of benevolent neighbours—but more often
the entertainment is for the mind alone, such as a con-
cert or lecture, or the mixture of literature and music,
modestly called " Readings with Songs." These succeeded very well for several years ; but gradually sank,
as they have done elsewhere, into mere merriment ; which
however good in its way, is not a kind of good to engage
the services of those whose object is the moral and intellectual elevation of their neighbours.

Lectures on scientific subjects, with experiments and
diagrams, are highly interesting to our intelligent people,
and a ready way of gaining as much knowledge of such
subjects as can be practicable for the generality ; but
the rural intellect is only now becoming educated up to
this capacity. The audience at such lectures is select
and scanty, compared with the crowded room drawn by
music and comedy. After the day's work, tired Nature
seeks restoration, if not in sleep or creature comforts, in
amusement or music. That is natural and reasonable
enough ; yet in the long winter evenings, time might be
found for the pursuit of knowledge as well as amusement.
In fact, in all seasons, amusement and instruction can be
enjoyed by all who cultivate a taste for natural science,
and the arts of drawing, carving, and other handicrafts.

School Treats, of course, are given at Winscombe, as
well as in other places. Like everything else in this world
they are liable to abuse ; but they give much pleasure
to the children, and are a means of bringing old and
young, rich and poor together. Here, on the green-
sward, parson, squire and dame, join with cottagers and
village children in dances and games, as when

Such scenes were England's boast in days gone by.

Christmas Carols are still sung by the village children,
sometimes introducing the names of the inmates of the
house at whose threshold the carol is sung :

> The greeting given, the carol sung
> In honour of each household name
> Duly pronounced with lusty call,
> And "Merry Christmas" wished to all.

The *Bellringers*, too, come round at Christmas-time
and play on the hand-bells.   It would be well if other
villagers would cultivate their talents in this and other
ways.   There is no lack of ability in our Mendip valley.

An occasional festival of our valley is the *Cottagers'
Show ;* an exhibition of cottage industry and cottage-
garden produce, which has been very successful.   Modest
prizes have been given—enough to encourage without
causing heart-burning—for vegetables, fruit, flowers, and
handy work, such as machinery, woodwork, needlework,
maps and drawings, home-made bread, butter, honey, and
miscellaneous contributions.

Church Decoration is another opportunity for bringing
rich and poor together to celebrate the great feasts of the
church.   The Quaker and the cynic may regard this
custom more as a pious amusement than as an act of
serious piety.   But if the work be pleasant rather than
arduous, it need not be less pious.   With some pious
people religion is nothing if not melancholy.   We are not
only to deny ourselves the pomps and vanities of the
world, and the sinful indulgences of the flesh, but to reject the calls of the spirit to rejoice in the Lord, and give
thanks for all His benefits ; as if there were to be no

> Glad hearts without reproach or blot,
> Who do His work and know it not.

Q

Those who assist in decorating the House set apart for divine worship may not all be moved by ardent religious zeal, or suffer any mortification of the flesh or spirit, and yet their offerings may be acceptable. A sacrifice is not a penance, but a dedication, and may have some virtue in it, even though the pilgrim may shirk the suffering endured by more resolute martyrs, and may choose Peter Pindar's easier way :

> To walk a little more at ease,
> I took the liberty to *boil* my peas.

It is seemly to celebrate the beginning and ending of the work of Christ on earth, and the adornment of the place where he is worshipped is symbolic of the joy and thanksgiving which ought to be felt on such occasions. If the piety which prompts the custom be mixed, as it must be, with personal and social feelings, it need not be thereby contaminated. The gathering and wreathing of garlands, and arranging the various devices used in the decoration, may require much contrivance and attention to details, as no doubt it does; yet the work may go on in the spirit of " Glory to God in the highest, and on earth, peace, goodwill toward men."

I like, too, the Spring and Harvest Thanksgivings, and the bringing in and presenting to the Lord the best flowers and fruits of the earth, in token of the grateful acknowledgment that they are all His gifts, to be sacrificed to Him—dedicated to His service by using and not abusing them.

The exchange of the fruits of the garden and field and orchard, for other fruits of labour should be a business of mutual beneficence, not of mere selfishness and greed. It is one of the vulgarest of vulgar errors to set religion and business in opposition ; as if religion were opposed to industry and use, and business inconsistent with religion. On the contrary, what passes for religion is but a sentiment, a superstition, or a sham, when it does not rule in business and the affairs of daily life. We call it superstition in the peasants and market-women in Roman Catholic countries, when they bring their baskets to their chapels and shrines, and pray for help, or it may be for luck. To me it is more pleasing and hopeful than the practical atheism of our protestant places of business, where we are often tempted to say with Jack Falstaff, "Virtue is of so little regard in these costermongering times:"* " There is nothing but roguery to be found in villainous man."†

* II HENRY IV, Act II, scene 2.
† I HENRY IV, Act II, scene 4.

Whether in crowds or solitudes, in streets
Or shady groves, dwelt happiness, it seems
In vain to ask.

THE question rather is, where is happiness now to be found? Youth seeks it in pleasure, and imagines that the means of indulging every inclination will ensure a happy life in this world, if not in another. Health and wealth supply these means; but as health demands self-restraint, the chief object of human pursuit is wealth. And what says experience? Does what the world calls "success in life" insure happiness? Notoriously otherwise. There is an honourable success in life, the result of the divine blessing upon usefulness, which is attended with happiness ; but not when selfishness has been the leading end. The gratification of selfishness can never satisfy.

Crescit amor nummi quantum pecunia crescit.

The love of money is insatiable. Greed may be sick, but is never satisfied. Common-sense must agree with religious teaching, that happiness based upon selfishness is impossible. A community aiming at "the greatest happiness of the greatest number" can only succeed where the greatest number are governed by justice. The result would be anything but success in a community where the greatest number were rogues ; ruled only by Rob Roy's simple plan :

> For why ? because the good old rule,
> Sufficeth them, the simple plan,
> That they should take, who have the power,
> And they should keep--who can.

The philosophers would find themselves driven to the Bible for a still more simple plan ; though not one approved by the greatest number*—the plan of the gospel, to love and obey the God of justice,—to do unto others as we would they should do to us : the two-fold law upon which alone society can hold together.

The search for happiness is, therefore, the same as seeking the kingdom, or rule, of heaven. It is not here or there, but within ; not in earthly position, local or social; but in mental state, and mainly in the state of the affections. Where they are selfish, there will be discontent; where

* See St. Matt. vii. 13, 14.

they delight in useful service, there will be endless enjoyment ; mental health and happiness ; whether

> In streets, or shady groves ;

in a Golden City, or a Garden of Eden.   A City implies
citizenship and business, and a Garden daily work to
dress it and to keep it :

> If all the year were playing holidays,
> To sport would be as tedious as to work.

There can be no happiness on earth, or in heaven, apart
from useful employment.   Though an over-worked mind
and body may crave endless rest, a heaven with nothing
to do would be but a fools' paradise.

Samuel Johnson's paradise was the city of London,
where a man can enjoy both society and solitude at his
pleasure.   The elder Disraeli, in his paper on *The
Student in the Metropolis,*[*] refers to Gibbon, who says,
" While coaches are rattling through Bond Street, I have
passed many a solitary evening in my lodging with my
books ; '· and Rogers, who, in his *Epistle to a Friend,*
writes :

> When from his classic dreams the student steals
> Amid the buzz of crowds, the whir of wheels,
> To muse unnoticed, while around him press
> The meteor forms of equipage and dress ;
> Alone in wonder lost, he seems to stand,
> A very stranger in his native land.

Descartes is also quoted, who tells Balzac : " I would
rather advise you, if you wish to observe mankind, and at
the same time lose yourself in the deepest solitude, to

---

* *Curiosities of Literature.*

join me in Amsterdam." " If," he continues, " you con-
template with delight the fruits of your orchards, with all
the rich promise of abundance, do you think I feel less in
observing so many fleets that convey to me the productions of either India ? " And truly there is much rational
enjoyment in commercial cities and ports, and especially
in witnessing the arrival of ships, and the discharge of
their cargoes ; distributing the bounties of Providence in
food and raiment, and giving useful employment in the
business of civilized life.

If, according to common opinion, the best place to live
in is the place where most money can be made, it is not
because of the money-making, still less the money made;
but because, in the making of the money, there has been
employment—*work.*

> Get work, get work ;
> Be sure 'tis better than what you work to get.

The pleasures of walking or sitting in a garden, seeing
and smelling its flowers, and eating its fruits, are nothing
to the pleasures of *gardening.* Heaven itself, whether
Paradise or Golden City, would be no place of bliss
without useful occupation ; with that, and mutual goodwill,
and faith in the Lord, where cannot happiness be found ?

Look at that awful region in the heart of England,
where every green thing is smoke-dried, and nothing outside the abodes of industry offers the meanest " thing of
beauty;" where a black shroud of smoke hides from the
sun the hideous desolation of the leafless earth, and the
lover of nature shudders at the thought of living in such
a waste howling wilderness ; even there, in those dreary
regions of "the black country," wherever love is, there is
happiness, and the intellect finds more active exercise

than in Arcadian scenes, where shepherds are supposed
to be as innocent as lambs, and rural swains as harmless,
and, as simple as sheep.   Visions of opulence, no doubt,
break through the smoke of colliery and forge; parks and
pleasure grounds and sumptuous mansions are seen
beyond the mountains of slag and cinders;* and the
toiling thousands draw from the furnace comforts and
indulgences not to be gained by the plow.   But these
rewards of industry bring less happiness than the industry
itself.   There is no reason to suppose that men who toil
in the smoke and din for high wages are more selfish than
than those who prefer easier work.   Greater strength of
body and mind will draw men from the quiet of the
country, to the more stirring scenes of mechanical skill
and invention ;   where they can "get on in the world."
Under this prominent motive may be hidden, perhaps
even from themselves, the love of usefulness, which will
insure happiness in the black country as well as in the
green.

There is, really, much in these black regions which
a lover of rural scenes may admire.   The sublime and
beautiful are not confined to landscape scenery.   The
great seats of industry are full of them ; and South Lan-
cashire, the least attractive of all the counties in natural
beauty, abounds in sublimity of no mean order.   The
great factories of Manchester, and the Liverpool Docks
are among the grandest sights in England, and equal to
them, in its way, is "the Black Country" on a winter's
night, when the forges are in full swing.   In these realms
of Vulcan the forces of Nature are wonderfully employed

---

* These vast heaps are now used for the manufacture of *Ferrumite* for
paving, &c., a valuable new industry.

by human intelligence. Watch that huge hammer beating a lump of iron as if it were clay, yet so completely under control as to touch an egg without breaking it. See those men, stript to the waist, wielding their sledge hammers in rapid and regular succession ; what pictures of the manly form ! What Herculean muscles and shoulders ! See those great vessels of liquid iron poured into the sandy bed ; that long red bar of fire drawn from the furnace ; those plates of iron, six inches thick, rolled and pierced like soft paste ! And then examine the machinery that displays so marvellously the combined forces of mind and matter ; you cannot deny that in these Cyclopean workshops there is much of the sublime and beautiful.

Think too, of the heroism often found in that kind of life. We admire, and justly, the courage and sense of duty displayed by the soldier, and the firmness and skill of the military engineer : let us remember and admire, at the same time, the like virtues in the arts and services of peace. The heroism often displayed in saving life, both at sea and on shore, is at least as great, and as admirable, as that which is stimulated by the excitement of battle and the prospect of fame and reward. No military deeds have ever surpassed in fortitude and bravery those of the Fire Brigade and the Life-boat crews. Perhaps even those splendid services have not excelled the heroic courage and fortitude, in the midst of disheartening difficulties and dangers, displayed in the construction of the Severn Tunnel. The diver who, again and again, risked his life, and at last succeeded, in a task of extreme difficulty and necessity, deserves to rank with any hero of ancient or modern history.

The man of thought and feeling, bound by the claims of business to the confinement of the town, may sometimes envy the resident in the country, and look forward to the time when, "nursed at happy distance from the cares of a too-anxious world," he may enjoy the peaceful pleasures of the " gentleman farmer."

> O happy (thinks he) if he knew his happy state,
> The swain, who, free from business and debate,
> Receives his easy food from Nature's hand,
> And just returns of cultivated land.

And happy, doubtless, might he be, if content with food from Nature's hand, and sure of the just returns of cultivated land. Our gentleman-farmer, however, does not always enter upon his land on the Roman poet's easy terms. He generally has to pay pretty dear for it, and is seldom content with the simple fare dame Nature offers him in return for his attentions. He finds he must either sacrifice the leisure he hoped for, and accept Poor Richard's saying, " He that by the plow would thrive, himself must either hold or drive ;" or be content to farm as an expensive amusement. A few years' apprenticeship in the decline of life are seldom enough to make a successful farmer ; but they sometimes suffice to teach a lesson of wisdom, at the cost of the savings of many years' successful business.

The Son of Sirach said that " the wisdom of a learned man cometh by opportunity of leisure : and he that hath little business becometh wise." But this does not always happen. The idle man is often quite as foolish as the busy man. The ancient writer, however, does not regard the farmer as a man of leisure. " How can he get wisdom

that holdeth the plough, and that gloricth in the goad,
that driveth oxen, and is occupied in their labours, and
whose talk is of bullocks?" There may, perh'aps, be
wisdom even in talk about bullocks ; but one lesson of
wisdom is almost sure to be, learned by the man who
gives up a business in town to carry on a farm in the
country. He will learn the meaning of the proverb, *Ne
sutor ultra crepidam* : Let the cobbler stick to his last.

While the cobbler only left his last to return to it with
renewed health and vigour after a fairly-earned holiday,
he enjoyed his vacation rambles in the country with a
keenness rarely known to country residents. He could
sing to the sublime music of Handel's *Judas Maccabeus*,

> O, lovely peace, with plenty crown'd,
> Come, spread thy blessings all around.
> Let fleecy flocks the hills adorn,
> And valleys smile with wavy corn

The country was an *Arcadia*, "Each pasture stored with
sheep feeding in sober security ; while the pretty lambs,
with bleating oratory, craved the dam's comfort ; here a
shepherd's boy piping as though he should never be old ;
there a young shepherdess knitting, and withal singing,
and it seemed that her voice comforted her hands to work,
and her hands kept time to her voice music." Thus
wrote Sir Philip Sidney in the days of Elizabeth : in
those of Victoria, farmers find things rather different.
The youthful shepherd's pipe gives forth more tobacco-
smoke than music, and the young shepherdesses are too
busy within the pastoral enclosures of the Board Schools
to have leisure for knitting and singing in other fields.
The farmers cannot find weeders and scare-crows among
the school standards. Their fleecy flocks and wavy corn
are viewed with an eye to their price in the market ; the

pretty lambs, the flowery meads, and the golden harvest,
are all subjects of cold calculation ; their pictorial and
poetical charms are no more to the farmer with a rent to
pay, than are those of the picturesque cottage, with its
blue curling smoke among the trees, to the damp rheu-
matic tenant within.

Nevertheless, country life has its blessings, especially
for old age. Poor old Falstaff on his death-bed, played
with flowers, " and 'a babbled of green fields."*

> Sweet country life, to such unknown,
> Whose lives are others', not their own.

There may be more or less social and political bondage
in the country ; but on the whole, there is more freedom
from the trammels of "Society." Its pomps and vanities
are less pressing, and moderate means, both pecuniary
and intellectual, go further in country than in town.
There is always plenty to do for all who are willing to
help in improving the moral and social condition of their
neighbours, whether rich or poor ; for there is plenty of
room for improvement in both classes. " Life is not all
beer and skittles," nor is it all amusement of more
fashionable kinds. If those who have abundance would
spend more of it in the country, and support their
struggling neighbours, instead of distant City Stores, they
might increase their own happiness, while helping to cure
two of the most crying social evils—the over-crowding of
the great towns, and the desertion of the rural districts,
with all the deplorable consequences of a glut of labour
n the one, with starvation-wages, while the other is
starving for want of more labour, science, and capital.

* HENRY VI, Act II, scene. 3.

It is the old grievance complained of three centuries ago, in the days of Queen Elizabeth and her successor ; who protested against "those swarms of gentry, who, through the instigation of their wives, or to new-model and fashion their daughters, did neglect their country hospitality, and cumber the city, *a general nuisance to the Kingdom.*" To abate this nuisance, King James issued a proclamation commanding the country gentlemen to depart the court and city, and to look after the people near their own residences, "who had from such houses much comfort and ease toward their living."*

Mendip Miners' Cottages.

* Disraeli's *Curiosities of Literature.*

XVII.—OLD SHOES.

The Farmer's life displays in every part
A moral lesson to the sensual heart.
Though in the lap of plenty, thoughtful still,
He looks beyond the present good or ill.

ROBERT BLOOMFIELD'S *Farmer's Boy*.

SIR JOHN MALCOLM,
in his amusing Sket-
ches of Persia, men-
tions the report of a
young officer, who
being sent up the
country with orders
to take notes of the
manners and customs of the inhabitants, made this entry
in his journal,—"Manners they have none, and their
customs are beastly." This laconic report would be quite
untrue of the inhabitants of Winscombe, as our Sketches
will have shown. There is, however, one custom, which
they have in common with other country people, but
which struck us on first coming from London as curious
and unaccountable. Wherever we went along the rural
lanes, we always and everywhere met with cast-off boots
and shoes. By the roadside, down in the ditches, up in
the hedges, everywhere people seemed to have flung away
their worn-out shoe-leather, as utterly useless. We

thought of the nursery rhyme, "Whenc'er I take my walks abroad, how many poor I see ;" but here it would read—

> Whene'er I take my walks abroad,
> How many shoes I see ;
> Some lying on the dusty road,
> And some in ditch or tree.

Sometimes a pair might be seen on the road as if their last occupier, weary and footsore, had just quitted the premises, and left them vacant for a new tenant to take on a repairing lease, or at a corn rent. Whether all the left shoes are past setting to rights, or whether they have been cast off as mis-fits, in fits of mis-anthropy, we have never been able to settle, though the question often recurs, especially in winter, when the footless shoes in our rural lanes are apt to call to remembrance the many shoeless feet in the London alleys. It may be a bootless enquiry; yet there is a moral to it. Does the lack of thrifty saving knowledge, shown in this waste of shoe-leather, extend to other things ? Is it not of a piece with the notorious unthriftiness of poor people ?—poor, perhaps, because habitually and hereditarily wasteful. There are thrifty cottagers, who may be called poor people, but who are practically better off than many unthrifty reputed rich people. These thrifty poor can find uses for, or ways of disposing of, all kinds of things that the unthrifty throw away as "done with." London servants can generally find customers for all that is " done with :" in the country there are not the same facilities ; yet they might be found if there were a place for everything and everything were in its place.

There should be some better use for empty meat-tins, pots and bottles, broken glass, and old iron,—possibly even for old shoes, than to lie in a confused heap till carted away to fill up some hole, after wasting the time of a farm labourer in separating them from other refuse.

Where thistles, and nettles, and other weeds are suffered to grow and scatter their seeds, and blackberries and elderberries are left to the birds, we cannot wonder that old boots and shoes should share the general neglect. Yet one would suppose that there would be "nothing like leather" for durability and capacity for endless application. I once saw a piece of shoe-leather used for ends to a pair of braces, and a stout sole used for nailing up the branch of a vine.   Many a brokendown gate might be the better for hinges of shoe-leather, and old shoes cut into strips would probably be useful in the garden and farmyard in various ways.

When past use as leather, old shoes are still capable of service in the grand economy of nature.   If the cottager would take his old shoes to the farrier, when he takes his donkey for new ones, the leather and hoof-parings might be sent together to the chemist's laboratory, and used in the manufacture of ferro-cyanide of potash, from which is made the beautiful colour called Prussian blue.   Another economical use of old shoes has been found in America, where the leather is ground into pulp, and used in the handsome and costly wall decorations now in fashion.

The last and lowest of all uses is the grave of the dunghill, and here old shoes may play their last act with dignity ; being particularly nourishing to the grape-vine. Miraculous, indeed, are the conversions of matter.   The purest of perfumes, the loveliest of flowers created out of noxious refuse ! The delicious bunch of grapes nourished upon old shoes, without betraying the flavour of leather, though it may once have covered the form of your dear dog Tray! But this exalted use comes of humility; the leather must go through much tribulation, and be finally buried and reduced to its elements. It is useless while stuck up in a tree.

There is a worse waste than the neglect of turning things to use, or of preserving them for future service. Old shoes may be thrown away for want of thought, and they are generally thrown away by their owner. The act may be foolish, but is not dishonest. As much cannot be said in excuse of the culpable carelessness often shown in the treatment of other people's property. Lenders of books and drawings and implements know it too well: so do most employers of labour. You can seldom travel by railway in England without observing how little care is taken of your luggage. You see it thrown or kicked out of the van, the *guard* (?) and porters caring for nothing but to get rid of it with as little trouble as possible to themselves. If the owner does not approve of that mode of earning wages, he is told that " it makes good for trade." People of "limited income," presumably a large class of the community, are apt to reflect that what they have to spend in making good for the trade of a portmanteau-maker cannot be spent in making good for other trades. " Wilful waste makes woeful want ;" as people sometimes find out, too late, when they have wasted their own property as well as their employers'.

The Roman cobbler, in Julius Cæsar's days, had more reason in his political economy. He led the mob about the streets to make good for trade ; not to save himself trouble, but to get himself more work.

Why dost thou lead these men about the streets?
Truly sir, to wear out their shoes, to get myself into more work.*

* JULIUS CÆSAR, Act I, scene I.

R

Thus we come from the morals to the literature of
leather, about which much has been, and may still be
written. For there have been many famous cobblers
from St. Crispin to George Fox and Dr. Carey. Much
learned dust might be shaken out of Old Shoes : not to
mention the ashes of that famous "old woman who lived
in a shoe," and probably died there ; for her children
seemed likely to be the death of her. Certainly, if her
parental discipline was according to the wisdom of Solomon, her domestic economy was not so unquestionable.
But perhaps the story is allegorical, the living in a shoe
representing the life of a tribe always on the tramp, and
the old woman being only a typical gypsy.

How closely shoes are connected with industry and
economy is shown in the German story of *The Elves and
the Shoemaker*, where the hard-working cobbler finds that
" Heaven helps those who help themselves." The Elves
were loyal subjects of Queen Mab, whose people are
famous for rewarding industry, and punishing the reverse.

> If the house be foul,
> With platter, dish, or bowl,

the sleeping sluts are duly pinched ;

> But if the house be swept,
> And from uncleanness kept,
> We praise the household maid,
> And duly she is paid ;
> For we use, before we go,
> To drop a tester in her shoe.

Old shoes and cobblers figure also in the early history
of Christianity. It is related that St. Mark having burst
the stitches of his shoe at Alexandria, went into a

cobbler's stall to have it mended, and while the cobbler was at work the Evangelist preached the Gospel to him with such effect that the cordwainer became the first bishop of Alexandria. Two centuries later a shoemaker and his wife became the patron saints of their trade, and are still reverenced as St. Crispin and St. Crispinian. Upon St. Crispin's day, the 25th of October, 1415, was fought the famous battle of Agincourt, rendered more famous by Shakespear, in the well-known stirring speech of Henry V. to his soldiers,—

> This day is called the feast of Crispian,
> He that outlives this day, and comes safe home,
> Will stand on tip-toe when the day is named.
>
> And gentlemen in England now abed,
> Shall think themselves accurs'd they were not here,
> And hold their manhood cheap, while any speak,
> That fought with us upon St. Crispin's day.

Soldier or saint, every man must fight. Life is a battle, and the Church on earth is militant. Whoever is happy enough to gain the victory, and to end his days in peace, will say with the old soldier, that—

> The hardest engagement he ever was in
> Was the conquest of self, in the battle of sin.

We read that the Emperor Charles V., who sometimes went about in disguise to learn for himself the opinions and customs of his subjects, went one night to a cobbler's in Brussels to get his boot mended. It happened to be the feast of St. Crispin, and the cobbler, instead of being at work, was making merry with his friends. The Emperor requesting to have his boot repaired at once, "Why man!" said the cobbler, "don't you know better

than to ask one of my craft to work on Crispin's day?
Was it the Emperor himself, I would not do a stitch;
but if you will come and drink to St. Crispin, sit down
and welcome: we are as merry as kings."

The Emperor accepted the invitation, but soon became
a silent observer of the hilarity around him. This was
noticed by the jovial cobbler.—"What!" said he to his
guest, "I suppose from your long phiz you must be some
courtier; but whoever you are, you're welcome. Come,
drink the health of the Emperor!" "Then you like the
Emperor?" said the long-faced visitor. "Oh! aye, I
like his long-nose-ship well enough, but we should like
him better if he taxed us less,—but away with politics—
round with the flask, and let's be merry!" The next
day, the cobbler was sent for, and brought before the
Emperor, who told him that the *long phiz* he had seen
last night was that of *his long-nose-ship* the Emperor. At
this announcement the poor man was afraid that his
tongue might have endangered his life or liberty; but
the Emperor soon set him at ease; told him he had so
much enjoyed his good humour, as well as his feast to
St. Crispin, and he must come to him next day and tell
him what he could do to oblige him. Next morning,
accordingly, the cobbler arrived, and being asked by the
Emperor what he wished for, replied that he wished
nothing so much as the privilege for his craft, that the
cobblers of Flanders might bear for their banner a Boot
with the Imperial Crown upon it. The request was at
once granted, and the cobbler's ambition being so
moderate, he was told to ask something more. "Then,"
said he, "if I may have the height of my ambition, be
pleased to command that in future the cobblers march
before the shoemakers." And so it was ordained. To

this day the Cobbler's Arms in Flanders are the *Boot and Crown*, and [the shoemaker's guild walks in pro-cession behind the cobblers.*

Possibly, this connection of the boot and crown occurred to Charles XII., of Sweden, when in refusing to resume the crown, he told his countrymen he would send one of his boots to rule over them, which would answer the purpose just as well. The Duke of Wellington declared that battles were won by boots. They were nearly lost in the Crimea for want of them. " Extremes meet" with kings as well as cobblers. The last King of the French said, before the revolution of 1848, that if he should be driven from the throne, he should be better off than most of his fellows ; for he could clean his own boots, and had often done so. His imperial successor could probably say the same. Had they been wise men, they ought, according to the Stoic philosophers, to have been able to make their shoes as well as clean them ;

> Sapiens crepidas sibi nunquam
> Nec soleas fecit ; Sutor tamen est sapiens.
> .   .   .   .
> Sapiens operis sic optimus omnis
> Est opifex solus, sic rex.
>
> Though the wise man nor shoe nor sandal frame,
> Yet him a skilful shoemaker we name.
> .   .   .   .
> So every art the wise man knows alone,
> Skilful in all, and yet professing none ;
> And thus he is a king.

The wise man is both king and cobbler; a better answer than the usual one to the question, " Why is a

---

* Hone's *Every-day Book*, October 25th.

cobbler like a king?" In spite of Horace's irony, the
Stoics had some sense in their philosophy. The wise
man alone can say, "My mind to me a kingdom is."
Wisdom alone can rightly rule that kingdom. Where-
fore a Wiser than Solomon declared TRUTH to be king.*

What a royal cobbler was John Pounds ! Crippled in
a royal dockyard, he took to shoemaking ; rigged out his
crippled nephew with an apparatus made of old shoes and
shoe-leather, and then began his reign of love and wisdom ;
first by training birds, and then by undertaking the more
arduous task of teaching boys, until he established the
Ragged School Kingdom, which has since set up its
numerous colonies of shoe-blacks, and other useful and
flourishing dependencies.

Cobblers and kings are thus found to be old companions. Boots and shoes are connected with crowns,
and figuring as they do in the romance of history, it is
not surprising that poets also should be found among
the cobblers. It is a contemplative calling. *Ne sutor
ultra crepidam*, does not confine the cobbler's thoughts
to his last ; as the annals of cordwainery show. The
curious old town of Nuremberg boasts not only of its
cunning workmen in wood, and stone, metal and glass,
and in toys, but of its cobbler-poet, Hans Sachs. But we
need not go to the picturesque streets of Nuremberg to
find poetry connected with shoe-leather. Not to mention
Gifford and Coleridge, who both had a chance of adorning
the craft, we will end as we began, with Robert Bloomfield,
the shoe-maker poet. The son of a country tailor, he
began life as a cow-boy, in which occupation he showed
so much genius that his elder brother invited him to

---

* John xviii. 37.

London, where he learned the trade of a shoemaker, and practised the art of poetry; producing, among other pieces of more or less merit, his well-known rural poem, *The Farmer's Boy.* It is a pleasant review of his own experiences and observations while a farmer's boy, with the reflections of riper years.

> How wise, how noble was thy choice
>   To be the Bard of simple swains,—
> In all their pleasures to rejoice,
>   And soothe with sympathy their pains ;
> To paint with feeling in thy strains
>   The themes their thought and tongues discuss,
> And be, though free from classic chains,
>   Our own more chaste Theocritus.

Thus wrote Bernard Barton, on the rural poet's death in 1829, to

" The Bard who sang *The Farmer's Boy.*"

Cordwainer's Hall, Winscombe.

XVIII.—OLD COACHES.

Ah ! when the wold volk went abroad,
   They thought it vast enough
If your good hosses beat the road,
   Avore the coach's ruf.

BARNES'S *Dorset Poems.*

OME persons," says Hazlitt, "think the sublimest object in nature is a ship launched on the bosom of the ocean ; but give me, for my private satisfaction, the mail coaches that pour down Piccadilly of an evening, tear up the pavement, and devour the way before them to the Land's End." I rather prefer the sight of the fire-engines rushing along with their brave men, while all other traffic makes way at the cry of " Fire ! " But the mail coaches, with their fine horses and practised drivers, were worthy of all Hazlitt's admiration, and I never look down upon the now lonely village of Cross, on the sunny side of our hill, without thinking of the many four-horse coaches that used to stop there to change horses and refresh their passengers on the way between Bristol and Bridgwater.

In those old coaching days, travelling was a pleasure, as a drive in a four-in-hand is now, for its own sake, apart from any other object in view. If the pleasure increased with the speed, it was not from any wish to come to an end of the journey. The healthy excitement, the in-born desire *to go*, coupled, perhaps, with some semblance of taking part in the progress, as you watched the horses and their skilful driver, and listened to his talk of them and to them, the ever-varying passing scenes and views from the coach-top, and the fine open air—all gave a life and charm to the coach journey, unknown to railway travellers. Occasional hardships from weather, heat and cold, dust and rain and snow and wind—seldom more than enough to add vigour to body and mind—were better for both than the luxurious indulgence of the railway cars, in which vigorous manhood and decrepid old womanhood are carried from beginning to end of the journey with no more exertion of vital force than if they were parcels in the van. " Wold volk " may indeed be thankful for the ease and speed of railway travelling, enabling them to get about and visit friends long after the time of life when their own parents were laid on the shelf. They may admit, too, that distance lends enchantment to their views of the past ; giving beauty and picturesque effect to the far-off mist and shower and dust, which were not so enjoyable when present. Yet " fond memory " will dwell upon the pleasures, and forget the pains, of the old coach journey, and contrast its varied scenes, and scents, and sounds, with the tunnels and cuttings, the smoke and noise of the railway train ; doubting if that can be an un-mixed good, and a sign of the coming of the kingdom of heaven, which has brought in the steam-whistle in place of the old coach horn.

Quicker and cheaper means of intercourse are an undoubted good ; not so much for those who are making
haste to be rich, as for the poor, who can now meet
their absent kindred, and enjoy some change of scene.
The old stage wagon bore on its tedious journey many a
sad and anxious heart, and left many sorrowing behind.
Young girls leaving parents and home, "it may be for
years, and it may be for ever," and too often was so—left
the country village where they were known and cared
for, to go into a cold selfish world, in service among
strangers, with little prospect of ever returning to the
old home, unless in sickness, want, or woe.   The artist
has not drawn upon his imagination in depicting the parting scene of "Going to service," where the young country
girl, is quitting her cottage home, the wagon waiting
at the door, while she takes leave of her weeping parents
and the children.   Such partings on "going to service,"
and "going to school," are not now so choking since
steam power has shortened the distance from home.   To
send a young girl travelling day and night in a wagon,
or even a schoolboy night and day outside a coach, in
summer or winter, and all weathers, would now seem an
act of cruelty.   It was not so thought "in the brave
days of old."   There was a glory in mounting the top of
the Glasgow mail, and travelling all night and all day
and all night again, to the old grammar school at Sed-
bergh, where Dawson, the mathematician, taught Adam
Sedgwick and thirteen senior wranglers !   Schoolboys
can now indulge in a luxurious seat or couch in a Pulman
car !   The Glasgow mail is now the "Flying Scotsman,"
and the Devonport mail, one of the fastest coaches of the
old time, is now the "Cornishman."   Grand travelling it is,
no doubt; but what sort of men would modern schoolboys

make, if school life should become as luxurious as home life ; if the increase of brain work were not accompanied by cricket and football, running, jumping, swimming and rowing?

The starting of the mail-coaches from the General Post Office at eight o'clock every night was one of the "Sights of London," far surpassing in interest, and in some respects even in appearance, the ostentatious turn-out of the Four-in-hand Club. Here were seven-and-twenty four-horse coaches, all with first-rate teams and harness, driven and guarded by men in the king's livery, starting in regular and quick succession, as each received its bags of letters ; and starting, not on a mere show-off drive, but on a long journey to continue night and day, and of real importance. There was no pretence about it. The horses were fast and strong and well-fed, for no other purpose than to convey their loads at the greatest possible speed. True, this was not railway speed; but it was fast travelling for horses—ten miles an hour including stoppages. The Exeter mail ran 171 miles in 17 hours, the Glasgow mail, 187 to Leeds in 18 hours, and the whole journey of 396 miles in 42 hours, including stoppages for meals. London to Shrewsbury, 154 miles, was run in 15 hours ; to Manchester, with the long and steep hills of Derbyshire, 187 miles, in 19 hours; Holyhead, 261 miles, in 27 hours ; Devonport, 216 in 21¼.*

Travelling was pleasant enough by these night mails, especially on a midsummer night in fine weather and moonlight ; but, apart from the natural feeling of excitement in going by one of the "crack coaches," there was more real enjoyment in starting early in the morning,

* See more particulars in Lewin's *Her Majesty's Mails.*

with the day's journey before you, free from the fatigue
and sleepiness, inevitable after travelling all night.

Starting from London on a fine summer's morning,
behind four high-mettled horses, was more exhilarating
than going at four times the pace in the railway train.
Great was the delight as the coach bowled along, soon
leaving the smoke and din of London far behind; passing
the suburban houses and villas and gardens, and getting
into the real "country," with its fresh clean air and rural
scenes, before the first change of horses. The length of
the stages varied, according to the speed and the conveniences for stabling, from four or five miles to ten or
more. Each team would run from half-an-hour to an
hour. As we approach the stables, the horses prick their
ears and pull hard, while the guard gives the bugle call
to bring out the fresh team. Our smartly-harnessed and
well-groomed London horses, now hot and dusty, are
rapidly nearing the end of their run. Their successors are standing ready to begin theirs. The coach
stops ; the coachman has already unbuckled the ends of
his reins, and now throws them across the wheelers'
backs, keeping his seat on the box, while the fresh horses
are quickly put to. The reins, thrown up by the horse-
keepers, are dexterously caught on the whip-handle,
buckled and grasped in professional style, and at the
guard's signal of " Right," followed by the coachman's
" Let 'em go," the horse-cloths are pulled off, and the
fresh horses start with a plunge :

> And gaily rode old age and youth,
> When summer light did fall
> On woods in leaf or trees in blooth,
> Or great folks' parkside wall.

And they thought they past
    The places 'fast
Along the dusty ground,
    When the whip did smack
    On the horses' back,
And the wheels spun swiftly round.   Those days
    The wheels spun swiftly round.*

Stage after stage, we get more and more into country
scenes, rustic manners, and provincial talk. We are fifty
miles from London, and the coach now stops for dinner.
The civil innkeeper receives his welcome guests at the
door, supplies the conveniences for washing after the
dusty ride, while dinner is laid in the "passengers'
room." The meal over, the smart London coachman
appears, hat in hand, to receive the customary remem-
brances, and takes leave, wishing us a pleasant journey.
His successor is already on the box, whip and reins in
hand ; his style, from hat to whip, as different from
the last, as his team is from the fine iron-greys that came
out of London with rosettes and blackened hoofs. He
and his horses, however, are well up to their work. We
have not gone far when a sign-post half-a-mile ahead
marks the junction of another road with our own, and
looking back a cloud of dust tells our guard of the
approach of a rival coach galloping to get before us. A
word is enough : our coachman puts his horses to full
speed, and we keep in front—a decided advantage on a
dusty road, if it did not give the guard an occasion to
celebrate his coach's superiority by playing on his bugle,
"The lass I left behind me." The other driver keeps his

* *Dorset Poems.* I have taken the liberty of using the common spelling,
as my recollections of the old coaching are not of Dorsetshire, but the road
from London to the North.

passengers in the dust rather than miss a chance of passing us. The day is hot, and a long hill is before us; the pace
moderates by common consent or necessity, and when we
stop at the top to rest our foaming horses, the rival is in
no condition to rush past.

As we slide down the hill, we leave him at the top, his
·cattle more distressed than ours. The race is over, and
the rival coachmen have leisure to reflect on the subject
of cruelty to animals, and the probable sentiments of the
respective owners of their horses. We have crossed a
ridge of hills and entered a different valley. Clouds are
seen gathering and distant thunder is heard. The whole
sky becomes overcast; we are getting into a storm.
Large drops of rain warn the " outsides " to put on over-
·coats and wrappers. The coachman turns up his coat
collar, and draws up the leather apron. A dazzling
flash of lightning, followed in a moment by a rattling
peel of thunder, and down comes the rain in a torrent.
It is only a summer storm and soon passes over, as we
drive rapidly through it. At the next change of horses,
the sun shines again. Wet wraps are cast off, and the
road is again dry. But the sun is going down and the
air is cooled by the storm. Towards evening, we observe
the cows gathering to the milking grounds ; the poultry
go to roost, rabbits appear on the heaths, and hares play
in the meadows. The pheasant's graceful form and
splendid plumage are seen on the skirts of the wood, and
squirrels leap among the trees. Now a slim weazel or a
stoat bounds across the road. The sun has set, " The
chough and crow to roost have gone," and now Reynard
is descried on the look-out for game, stealthily wend-
ing his way to the farm-yard, where Farmer Dobson's

geese have long helped to maintain the families of
Dobson and Fox, and " the pleasures of the chase."

> Now fades the glimmering landscape on the sight,
> And all the air a solemn stillness holds,
> Save where the beetle wheels his droning flight,
> And drowsy tinklings lull the distant folds.

Summer is too far advanced, and we are too far from
the home counties to hear the nightingale. The even-
song of the thrush may sometimes be mistaken for it.
The cries of the nightjar and owl, as they flit past, alone
join the music of hoofs and wheels. " We're a' nod-
ding," when the guard's horn rouses us to the fact that
we are nearing the market-town where the coach stops a
few minutes for refreshments, and to change our second
coachman. We have travelled a hundred miles, through
several counties, each having its peculiarities of scenery,
houses, breeds of cattle, productions, vehicles, costume,
and dialect, to say nothing of its historical scenes, each
full of interest to the well-informed traveller. We now
start again for six hours of moonlight, with leisure and
opportunity to watch the magnificent procession of the
heavens, and the beauty of the landscape bathed in
silvery light ; the glittering river, the dark woods, the
quiet hamlets :

> In such a night as this,
> When the sweet wind did gently kiss the trees,
> And they did make no noise.

Our reveries are broken by the guard's bugle, calling
up the turnpike man to open the gate he has closed for
the night. The sleepy janitor appears in his nightcap,
sulkily lets the coach through, and retires again to bed.
But not to undisturbed slumber ; for we have not gone

far before we meet a long drove of cattle on their way
to Smithfield, filling up the road, and reaching as far as
can be seen.   After much shouting, and many blows,
a passage is cleared for the coach ; the lowing of the
herd dies away in the distance, and again all is still
but the roll of wheels and the clanking of hoofs.   Passengers, guard, and coachman are all drowsy ; whip and
reins hang slack, grasped automatically by the accustomed hands.⁻   The horses slacken their pace ; visions
of friends and scenes left behind mingle in a midsummer
night's dream, with the glimmering landscape and star-
spangled sky.

> Sounds of music
> Creep in our ears ; soft stillness and the night
> Become the touches of sweet harmony.
> Look how the floor of heaven
> Is thick inlaid with patins of bright gold.

The sounds of music, however, that mingle with our
reveries, are not the harmony of the spheres, but the
breath of the guard's horn.   We are behind time.   The
horn wakes up the coachman, and the crack of his whip
the leaders 'and drowsy passengers.   A brisk gallop
brings us to the county town, where coffee and other
" hot rebellious liquors " are taken "to keep out the
cold," felt even in summer before dawn.

> What time the shepherd blowing of his nails,
> Can neither call it perfect day nor night.

Our third coachman leaves us.   The coach alone disturbs
the silent streets ; unless, perchance, the awakened watch-
man proclaims his vigilance by " calling the hour,"—the
first he happens to think of.   As we pass through the

streets, a night-capped head is seen, here and there, peeping at the side of the blind, curious to see the passing
coach. But "Nature's soft nurse," is in charge of the
town, and to her we leave it ; even the fresh horses
leaving the dark stable and the sleepy ostlers sleepily.
Streets and suburban houses are left in the quiet moonlight, and we are again in the open country.

A few stages more, and the light, which has never
left the northern horizon now sensibly increases toward
the east. The cock's shrill clarion is heard from the
roost :

> And now o'er valley, hill, and lake,
> The day begins to break.

Nature awakes, refreshed by the restoring influence of
that rest which All-wise Beneficence has ordained to save
creation from the wear of constant light and activity.
No created being can bear incessant sunshine, either
physical or mental. "Evening and morning" must ever
be the order of nature and life. To each new arising of
light in the mind, as to the body, the previous state is
as the dimness of evening. As the present day, or state,
wears away, and the light grows dim, "the night cometh,
wherein no man can work," until, at a fresh sunrise, again
"man goeth forth to his labour until the evening."

> Sweet is the breath of morn, her rising sweet,
> With charm of earliest birds ; pleasant the sun
> When first on this delightful land he spreads
> His orient beams on herb, tree, fruit and flower,
> Glist'ning with dew ; fragrant the fertile earth.

S

YORK Four Days Stage-Coach.

Begins on Friday *the* 12*th. of* April, 1706.

ALL that are defirous to pafs from *London* to *York,* or from *York* to *London,* or any other Place on that Road; Let them Repair to the *Black Swan* in *Holbourn* in *London*, and to the *Black Swan* in *Coney-ftreet* in *York.*

At both which Places, they may be received in a Stage Coach every *Monday,* *Wednefday* and *Friday,* which performs the whole Journey in Four Days. (*if* God permits.) And fets forth at Five in the Morning.

And returns from *York* to *Stamford* in two days, and from *Stamford* by *Huntington* to *London* in two days more. And the like Stages on their return.

Allowing each Paffenger 14¼ weight, and all above 3d a Pound.

Performed By {
Benjamin Kingman,
Henry Harrifon,
Walter Baynes,

Alfo this gives Notice that Newcaftle Stage Coach, fets out from York, every Monday, and Friday, and from Newcaftle every Monday, and Friday.

Copy of an old Coach advertisement still to be seen in one of the old inns at York.

The world is once more astir. The mowers are early afield. Giles fetches the cows to the yard :

> Forth comes the maid, and, like the morning, smiles,
> The mistress too, and followed close by Giles ;
> A friendly tripod forms their humble seat,
> With pails bright scoured, and delicately sweet.

The farm-yard is alive with poultry ; the horses are brought to the water ; the blue smoke curls from the farm-house chimney, and rises among the trees. All is astir in the homestead.

But we are nearing the end of our journey. The smoke of the city for which we are bound is seen in the distance. Cottages and houses come nearer together ; suburban villas with flowery gardens and well-kept lawns, the abodes of thriving citizens ; then market-gardens for the supply of the city, and, all too soon, brickfields to help forward its encroachments on the country ; presently, rows of newly-built houses, " Mount-Pleasant," and " Prospect-Place," facing each other, and hard by, a fine new Union-workhouse ; sometimes a grand new gaol, considered by the town council "a credit to the town!" We pass rapidly by farmers' and nursery-men's carts, and people on horse-back and on foot, for it is a market day, and soon the coach wheels and horses' hoofs clatter on the well-paved streets of the busy town. The guard's horn sounds for the last time, the carts and people get out of the way, and the coach, all soiled with the dust and mud of many counties, weather-beaten, like a ship after a long voyage, pulls up at the old-fashioned inn. Landlord and landlady, with head-waiter and chamber-maid, welcome the dusty passengers, while the ostlers quickly release the tired horses. The fourth coachman,. and the guard, who has come the whole journey, touch their hats and receive their accustomed fees, and the way-worn travellers go to breakfast.

Those coaching days are gone, and cannot be brought back by the modern four-in-hand stages for a few hours' drive in summer-time. Such trips are pleasant enough in their way, but they have none of the excitement of the old coaching, when there were no railway trains rushing by and leaving the coach far behind. Recollections of the old journeys are pleasant memories, now that the wind and rain and dust are forgotten ; but, perhaps, if we could now travel all day in the heat and wet, and all night in the wind and snow, the stern reality would make us all thankful for the comfort and speed of the railway car.

XIX.—SIDCOT SCHOOL.

In the heart of the Mendips old Sidcot stands,
    How her name like music thrills !
Long, long may she rest like a white-robed queen
    In the arms of those grand old hills.

SCHOOL SONG.

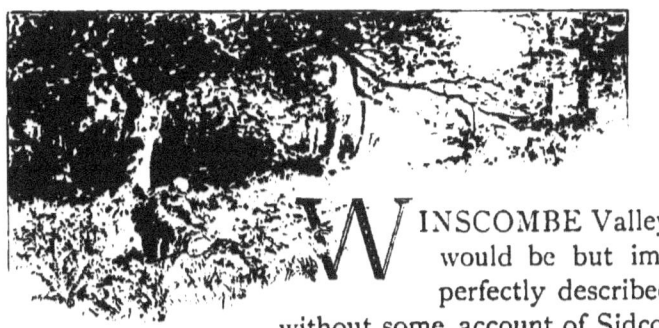

INSCOMBE Valley would be but imperfectly described without some account of Sidcot School, which forms so important a part of our population, and is so conspicuous an object in the landscape.

The Society of Friends, if it has lost much of its primitive spirituality, has lost also the narrow and

exclusive spirit which claimed for its members the title of
" The People of God," and looked down upon all others
as " the world." Friends have learnt that the distinction
between the people of God and the children of the world
is not drawn by the limits of any religious denomination,
however godly its rules, or spiritual its creed ; while, on
the other hand, the improved education, reputed wealth,
and social influence of the Society, have changed the old
vulgar contempt for the *Quakers* into a general respect
for the *Friends.* The Schools have largely partaken of
the altered state of the Society, and are no longer the
half monastic institutions of former days.

From the natural advantages of its position, Sidcot
School is particularly noted for the pursuit of natural
history. Most of the boys and girls are, more or less,
" field naturalists." It is pleasant on a fine day to meet
a troop of them on their rambles in search of the
" common objects of the country ; " some with botanic
and other boxes, others with butterfly nets ; almost all
carrying some specimen or other of the animal, vegetable,
or mineral creation. Butterfly-catching and bird-nesting
are not allowed for mere sport. Every one taking such
specimens is required to keep a record of observations as
well as captures.

All boys and girls, however, are not naturalists, and
customs change, as well as times and seasons, at Schools
as well as elsewhere. More boisterous sports are sometimes favoured : fir-cone fights on Banwell hill have been
connived at by teachers, who remember they were once
boys themselves, and who, perhaps, have found benefit
from the exercise of temper and fortitude in those mimic
fights that prepare for the harder battles of life all have
to endure in some shape or other. I do not know that

the girls have yet taken to fighting with fir-cones, and the
sport is, perhaps, going out of fashion with the boys.
Both boys and girls get more exercise now in the gymnasium and cricket field, as well as in rambles in the
fields and lanes with much more freedom than was
allowed in the olden time. In early spring, when Lent
lilies are in bloom, you may meet troops of girls returning
from Daffodil Valley, so loaded and bedecked with
flowers and willow-palms, as to look as if the flowery vale
itself were coming to Sidcot School, as " Birnam wood
did come to Dunsinane," in the fatal day of Macbeth.
The golden treasures deck the schoolrooms like a flower-
show ; while hampers full and boxes without number are
sent to hospitals and distant homes, cheering many
hearts, and bringing back blessings to the happy
gatherers.

But the greatest floral festivals are on the School Anni-
versaries, especially those of the Boys' and Girls' Literary
Societies, when the rooms are decorated with excellent
taste and skill.

Sidcot School, as at present constituted, was established
in 1808, by the purchase of a school and premises, the
property of John Benwell, who remained for some time
superintendent of the newly-endowed institution. There
had been a much older school on the same premises,
under the patronage of the Society of Friends, though
not under its direct control. In 1699, one, William
Jenkins, of Hertford, was invited by the Friends at
Bristol to set up a school " for teaching Greek, Latin,
Writing, and Arithmetic." It would seem that the English tongue was not then considered classical, or to need
teaching. The terms were to be 30s. per annum for the
full course, or 20s. for Reading, Writing, and Arithmetic

the charge for board, £9 per annum. The School was
"to reside at *Sithcott, a very healthy, serene air.*"
This School was kept up till 1729, when William
Jenkins sold the premises, and they do not appear to have
been again used for a school, till bought by John Benwell
in 1790.

The following letter, the original of which is preserved
in the present School, must have been written by a pupil
of William Jenkins. Whether the sentiments and mode
of expressing them were spontaneous in the school-boy
of the period, or whether the "Mr." may not have had
something to do with the composition, must be left to the
judgment of the reader. W. J. may not be answerable
for the punctuation.

Sidcott, yᵉ 21st of ye 6th mo., 1714.

Dear Grandfather and Grandmother,

I present mine and my Brother's Humble Duty to you and Parents
my kind Love to my Brother, and Sisters, Uncles, and Aunts, Cousins,
Relations, and Friends, I write these few Lines to let you know that I and
my Brother, Mr. and Mrs., and all yᵉ Family, are in good health, hoping
you and all yᵉ Family are Partakers of the Like Mercy, Letting you know
I have learnt in Grammar, Latine Testament, Corderius, Castalion, Textor,
and Tully, and am got through Arithmetick, except one Rule, and also have
learn'd Merchts Accots., In learning of which these 5 Years no doubt but
I have cost my Dr. Father a pretty Deal of Money, But hope to be so diligent to Imploy my Learning and Dutiful that my Father may never repent
yᵉ Charge bestowed upon me, I have now near finished my Learning intended and expect my Father here to fetch me Home, yᵉ Beginning of the
Next Month, I remain, with my Mr. and Mrs. their kind love to you, your
Dutiful Son,

ROBERT SCANTLEBURY.

My Mr. and Mrs. desire yʳᵉ Dr. Love to Thomas Quin, &c.

Among John Benwell's pupils were Jonathan Dymond,
the essayist; and Joseph Sturge, the philanthropist; and

his cousin, Jacob Player Sturge, the eminent land sur-
veyor, of whom John Benwell wrote to his father as
follows :

Sidcot, 6th month, 7th, 1803.

Esteemed Frd.,
    I am sorry to part with Jacob as he has been a good boy, and has
improved, I think, considerably in his learning.   ⋅
    Few lads of his age appear to have a clearer knowledge of figures ; he
has also a tolerable idea of grammar, and seemed to be getting into the
knack of writing free.*

This letter may give some idea of the range of learning
in a Friends' School at the beginning of the nineteenth
century, when boys left at fourteen years of age, and began their seven years' apprenticeship.   J. P. Sturge says,
in a letter to his father, that he was "in the twentieth pro-
position of Euclid's Elements, and learned Grammar and
Spelling, &c."
    The present School opened 1st September, 1808, with
twenty boys and nine girls, there being room for six more
girls.
    The diet was pudding and meat daily for dinner, milk
for breakfast, except when milk was scarce, when some
substitute was to be supplied ; bread, with cheese, or
butter, or milk, for supper.   " The drink to be beer of
two and a half bushels of malt to the hogshead."
    The books used were Murray's Grammar and Reader,
Walker's Gazetteer, Goldsmith's Geography and His-
tories, and Vyce's and Joyce's Arithmetic, with Barclay's
and Cowpers' Poems, and a copious list of Friend's
books.   Such was the mental dietary of that day and
generation.

* Copied from the *Sidcot Quarterly* for June, 1891.

The Rules for the Christian education of the children were chiefly these :

" To endeavour to feel the disposition of mind which craves protection from evil."

" To go soberly to their meals, and endeavour to feel gratitude and thankfulness to Him who is the giver of every blessing."

" On lying down to rest, to recollect the transactions of the day, and to cherish a humbling sense of sorrow for any deviation from rectitude of conduct, of which they may be sensible."

" Finally, they are earnestly requested to seek an acquaintance, with the principle of Truth in their own minds, which alone can enable them to live in the fear of the Lord, which is the beginning of wisdom, and to depart from evil which is a good understanding."

Much difficulty seems to have been met with in finding a suitable master and mistress. John Benwell continued from time to time to act as superintendent, apparently without salary ; for in 1810, the " officers' and servants' wages " came to no more than £39 9s., including the wages of an assistant master at the rate of eighteen guineas, he finding his own washing. In this year, the boys " were released from the employment of mending stockings."

No suitable master and mistress being found, it was concluded to combine the offices of superintendent and master ; a conjunction which seemed propitious ; for " a suitable man friend " and wife were soon discovered at "Ives, Hunts." They were appointed master and matron at a salary of £120 the pair. There were then sixty-five children in the School. The household expenses were £1089 13s. 5d. besides £277 7s. 9d. for clothing, and £42 10s. 4d. for conveyance of children. The salaries and wages amounted to £257 8s. 5d. There was also an extraordinary outlay of £637 14s. 5d. for a well and pump, though £210 had been laid out for the same purpose the year before. These water-works are no longer available.

By the end of a year and a half, the suitable man friend is found to be "not in all respects as suitable as is desirable;" and Robert and Lydia Gregory take charge of the School. The salaries and wages fell to £125 18s. 1d. The item for clothing was £316. The charge to parents was raised from £14 to £16. The annual subscriptions in support of the School were £402 7s. 6d. In 1814 they amounted to £481. That year the salaries were £75, and the "ale, beer, and cyder, £72 1s. 6d."

Two years later the charge for schooling was again reduced to £14 ; and the number of children rose from sixty-nine to eighty. The average cost per child was £27, including clothing, conveyance, and beer. The last item steadily diminished till 1843, when it finally disappeared.

In the earlier years of the School, though a large amount had been sunk in wells, the use of water seems to have been pretty much limited to the kitchen and washhouse. The forty and odd boys all washed in a stone trough, twelve feet long, and filled once a day.

At the jubilee meeting in 1873, an old scholar of the ruder times expressed his astonishment at the contrast between the present Sidcot School and what it was in his own day, sixty years ago. His only pleasant recollections were of the occasional rambles over the hills— "almost the only objects unchanged in their outlines." The rest of the time, he says, the boys "were shut in by high walls and gates ; scarcely a window looking on the wicked world without." This was called "a *guarded* education : " but the high walls and gates did not keep out those demons who rush into places found " empty, swept, and garnished."

Another old scholar at the same meeting, after contrasting the refinement and kindliness of the School as it is now with the rough usage he endured, said that, after all, "the pleasant memories preponderate over those of an opposite kind;" particularly those of "the delightful walks through fields and green lanes, and over the beautiful hills of this lovely neighbourhood." A scholar of rather later date does not complain of cruel usage, but says the boys were not taught what boys as boys ought to learn. They were not taught to swim, or to play cricket, or football ; nor were they taught " that all action should be guided by a strict sense of honour and right."

> Say what is *Honour ?* 'Tis the finest sense
> Of *Justice* which the human mind can frame.

The old pedagogue, who might be propitiated, but could not be loved, is a creature of the past. If not of pre-historic and fabulous times, he may be, at least, figuratively referred to the stone period, with his pachydermatous scholars. The liberal arts have softened men's manners. Schoolboys of the present softer times have no notion of what schools were in the days of their grandfathers. Some old gentlemen are said to regret the change. They prefer the wisdom of Solomon to the tickle-trout system of this thin-skinned generation. Perhaps they prefer the virtues of Spartans to the humanitarianism of Christianity. Fortitude and courage are, indeed, admirable manly qualities; but there is a fortitude

nobler than that of the Spartan, a courage more manly
than that of the bull-dog and stoat : the fortitude that
withstands the temptations of folly and vice; the courage
to uphold what is just and true against numbers and
fashion.

Boys cannot be expected to have a very high idea of
manliness ; a big brother, or some indulgent, sporting
uncle, may be the standard for emulation. Smoking
tobacco, and shaving, are objects of ambition to some
youthful minds. The cockerel spirit begins early in the
schoolboy life ; it is well if it pass without serious fighting. Later on, the pagan notion of " honour " prevails—
or did in my schooldays ; it was unmanly and disgraceful
to receive an insult without retaliation. The schoolboy
gospel was that of the Scottish thistle : *Nemo me impune
lacessit.*

Sheepishness is of all things despised by young people
of both sexes ; humility and meekness are as much out
of fashion as obedience and veneration. And yet the
only perfect MAN, the Hero of heroes, was meek and
lowly ; and when reviled, reviled not again.

A late amiable master of Sidcot School held that
where discipline cannot be maintained without severity,
it is the masters' own fault. If the opinion be slightly
flattering to the modern schoolboy, it is at least a wholesome one for a school·master to hold, if not to publish,
and one which his scholars will not often dispute.

On the 5th of November, 1823, a meeting of some of
the boys was held at the School, and the following
resolution agreed to : " That a society be formed, to
consist of boys of the best character in point of diligence
and propriety of conduct, to be entitled, *The Juvenile
Society for Mutual Improvement in Useful Knowledge.*"

Though the wording of the resolution betrays the school-master, the scheme is said to have really originated with one or two of the boys. The names of nine boys are recorded as members at the beginning, and three more the following week. This society was kept up for six years. Many of its members are, or have been, well-known and honoured members of the Society of Friends, and some are more widely known—Charles Gilpin, after-wards M.P., and Secretary to the Poor Law Board, and George Palmer, M.P. for Reading, who was the last of the original society left in 1831, and was the means of remodelling it, by turning its efforts more in the direc-tion of natural philosophy.

A small periodical was printed in the School in 1832, called the *Juvenile Miscellany ;* but it does not seem to have succeeded.* Nor did the revival of the Mutual Improvement Society prove permanent, though another revival lasted from 1841 to 1843. From this date the case seems to have been one of suspended animation, till 1852, from which time to the present the proceedings are recorded without further break.

While a taste for literature and science has thus been kept up in the Boys' School, the Girls have shown no less commendable zeal in the same good cause. A Report of the *Girls' Literary Society*, printed in 1874, contains the following statement : " From an old book in our possession we find that a 'Girls' Juvenile Association for the promotion of Useful Knowledge' was established on the 22nd of 8th month, 1824. The volume contains a miscellaneous collection of poems, essays, and letters to the Society, all with a decided

---

* A copy of No. 1 is owned by Francis Fox, C.E., of Bristol.

moral or religious tendency. The Juvenile Association
seems to have died out after a few years' existence, and
we have no further records until the year 1847, when the
Society was re-established under the title of the Girls'
Juvenile Literary Society, which, to judge from memorials
left us, seems to have continued in a flourishing condition
until the year 1870, when the name was changed to the
Girls' Literary Society, which it still bears."

There seems to have been considerable zeal in the
School for the formation of societies.' An old scholar*
at the school between 1828 and 1832, speaks of a *Thee
and Thou Society*, which fined its members for saying
Thee instead of *Thou*, a practice then common with all
but north-country Friends. There was also an *Anti-
trash Society*, which seems to have laboured rather
against bodily than mental " goody," to the serious loss
of the local vendor of lollipops, jumbles, and parliaments.
The same writer's reminiscences refer also to the local
tailor and druggist, who repaired both clothes and con-
stitutions, assisted in the cure of soles by a neighbouring
cobbler. These worthies are alluded to in an addition to
Mrs. Hemans's negative views of The Better Land:

> Is it where Miller, the cobbler, lives,
> And Dr. Strode his medicine gives?
> Not there, not there, my child!

Once a year, " Dr. Strode fitted the boys with new
suits of brown or claret cloth with cord trowsers ; the
older boys with Friends' coats ready for General Meeting." " The girls wore a uniform dress of cotton or stuff,
white tippets and sleeves, and Friends' silk bonnets; and

* Robert Harding, at the Jubilee Meeting in 1873.

it was a pretty sight," says an old scholar, " to see them, dressed alike, drop into their seats at Meeting." The uniformity of dress, perhaps, set off the variety of personal charms, but the silk bonnets must have been rather an expensive sacrifice for the sake of "consistency !" Our old scholar speaks with affection of "dear old Arnee Frank," and of "dear Mary Tanner," and "the gentle pleadings of her melodious voice ;" of "the General Meetings, with their examinations, hopes, and fears ; the kindly visitors ; Joseph John Gurney, with his anecdotes, and 'six rules to be remembered'; the happy deaf and dumb servant, who loved to have a chat on her fingers with those she thought did not tease her ; the tall boy,* now an M.P., who would run from any part of the playground at the cry of distress from the little one under his care, just come to school ; the slender, loving lad, a close friend, now under Catholic vows as Father F————†: with a few shades to these pleasant pictures, in those who have proved that the way of transgressors is hard."

The Minutes of the Committee of Sidcot School‡ are an interesting record of the gradual progress of more humane and liberal views of education. In 1825 it was decided to give prizes or "rewards, as a means of stimulating to exertion, and preventing, in a great measure, the necessity for positive punishment." The next year it is ordered that no child shall be struck by a teacher under any circumstances, and that no corporal punishment shall be given but in the presence of the

---

* The late Charles Gilpin ; through life a champion of the oppressed.

† Charles Prideaux Fox, afterwards a member of the Friends' Essay Club in London, and now a priest in Dublin.

‡ Of which I have been kindly allowed the perusal.

Sidcot School in 1831

head master, who shall "prevent too much rigour for the offence." In 1844 the master is required to report to the committee, quarterly, every case of corporal punishment; and at last it is found that such punishments can be wholly dispensed with.

The religious instruction of the School for some years consisted chiefly of learning and repeating a *Catechism*, compiled for the purpose. In 1825 it was decided that those who were perfect in the Catechism need only say it occasionally; but should "be introduced to the further knowledge of the Scriptures, and the principles and writings of Friends." A thorough acquaintance with Holy Scripture was prescribed, under four heads: 1. The Books individually; 2. Bible History; 3. Prophecies; 4. Doctrines—the Divine Attributes, the Fall of Man, Redemption by Jesus Christ, and the Work of the Holy Spirit. "More especially—the Scriptural grounds for the peculiarities of Friends, as regards forms of worship, the vain customs of the world, and the immediate and sensible influence of the Holy Spirit."

The Catechism was discontinued in 1835, experience having proved that religious principles can be better impressed than by learning answers by rote.

The growing spirit of liberty and reform was further shown in 1837, by the permission of trowsers instead of the orthodox breeches. The former, having been introduced into the gallery by Joseph John Gurney, could no longer be denounced as a vanity of the corrupt world.

For thirty years, from 1808 to 1838, the boys' and girls' schools were in separate houses. By the end of 1834, the old buildings were found to require such · extensive repairs, that it was concluded to erect a new house to accommodate the whole united School. A large sum

T

was raised for that purpose, and in 1838 the present building was completed.

The family being now under one roof, it was thought suitable that the master and mistress should be man and wife, which was not at present the case. A year elapsed, however, before a suitable couple could be found.

The boys were still employed in the garden, and the girls in the laundry ; but there seems to have been a growing taste for the more refined arts, which arc said to soften manners. Thus we find in 1839 the boys had raised a fund, according to their small means, for the purchase of drawing materials, and the Committee, with the kindness that runs through all their Minutes, add £2 to the fund, and order " a land-measuring apparatus " for the use and instruction of the School. In 1841 it was concluded that the frequent companionship of gardeners and laundry women was not improving to the children employed, and those occupations were discontinued. Education was aiming higher. The " march of intellect " was advancing, and everything in its way must give place to the standards of science and art.

Nor was the demand for more light for the mind without a corresponding craving on the part of the body. If the light of other days had not really faded, its glory had relatively gone. As dips had succeeded rush-lights, and argand lamps mould-candles, oil-lamps must now give place to gas. Accordingly, at the end of 1841, gas-works were erected at Sidcot School; the engineers being Edwin Octavius Tregelles, a well-known minister in the Society of Friends, and his partner Francis Fox, an old Sidcot scholar, who in 1867, with his brother John as resident engineer, constructed the Cheddar Valley's Railway.

The project of the World's Fair, in 1851, which stirred up the nations to an emulation worthy of rational beings, was not without its influence upon Sidcot School. An " Exhibition of Industry" was projected by some of the more enterprizing boys, to include the whole of their little world—both boys and girls : a bold stroke for those days when the boys had no more dealings with the girls than Jews with Samaritans. So rapid were the movements of these young Commissioners, that they were enabled to anticipate the Hyde Park exhibition by three months. *An Account of the Sidcot Exhibition of Industry* is preserved, and was lately reviewed by one of the projectors in a humorous paper, which, unfortunately, will not bear the curtailment necessary to bring it within the limits of this chapter.

The hopes of universal peace and good-will among the nations were soon crushed by the Crimean war ; but the spirit of liberty was shedding its influence upon Sidcot School. From the date of the Great Exhibition, the monastic separation of boys and girls was relaxed. In 1853 we read that " on the day usually called Christmas day" (there being then no winter vacation) " after tea the boys and girls assembled in the girls' schoolroom, and amused themselves with games of a more or less intellectual character;" and early in the following year, "the boys took a pleasant walk round by Shipham, Rowberrow, Churchill Batch, and afterwards *they and the girls* partook of a treat of tea and cake, kindly provided for them, to commemorate there being the full number of scholars in both wings." There were ninety-two scholars, though the School was considered full with fifty boys and forty girls.

Up to this time and a year later, the School had only one vacation, that at Midsummer ; but in 1857 it was decided to permit parents, if they pleased, to take their children home for a fortnight in the winter. A majority did so, but as a large number of children were left at school, their care-takers gained little by the change, until a winter vacation was gradually established. The increasing strain of modern competitive schooling absolutely requires at least two periods of rest; most schools find three expedient.

The Jubilee of the School's foundation was celebrated on the 1st of September, 1857. "No lessons; but the decking of the rooms with gay flowers; a ramble through the valley, and over the hills; a visit to an interesting collection of fossil bones, the property of a peculiar old man;* a repast of tea and cake in the evening, and then an interesting account of the establishment of the School, and of various particulars in its history, followed by a little reading of poetry, were the proceedings of the Jubilee day."†

On the 20th October, 1852, the Boys' Juvenile Society, which seems to have been asleep since 1843, was awakened with the title of the *Boys' Literary Society*, for the promotion of literature and general intellectual improvement. A library was formed, a series of drawing copies procured, and encouragement given to art and handicraft. This latter division, however, was in 1860 handed over to a separate *Society of Arts;* the Literary Society giving its attention more to essays, natural history, and the forming of collections of plants, insects, birds' eggs, and mineral specimens. "Curators" were appointed

---

* William Beard, of the Banwell "Bone Cottage."

† Budget by H. Lees. The account of the School does not seem to be available.

for the special care and reporting of progress in each department. The meetings became more lively, and often required adjournment. Two years later a report of proceedings was printed, and has been continued from that date. In 1865 a large cabinet with shelves and drawers for specimens was procured at a cost of £40. The Boys' Literary Society had become an important part of Sidcot School.

The Society of Arts also flourished. Though drawing was not, as now, systematically taught, it had been encouraged as a recreation, and exhibitions were held half-yearly, containing a variety of more or less creditable work for young amateurs. The girls also contributed equally well to these exhibitions of out-of-school work.

An Association of *Old Scholars* was founded in 1871 "to facilitate communication, and keep up a friendly connection and interest among those who have been scholars at Sidcot : to meet annually on the occasion of the " General Meeting." This association, equally creditable to the school and its scholars, is a means of keeping up a kindly feeling towards *Alma Mater*, and of exercising that feeling in various practical ways ; by which the present scholars are encouraged in the pursuit of science, literature, and art, and animated with the same grateful affection. The Old Scholars' Association has given liberal prizes for excellence in many departments, including swimming and athletic sports, and was the means of placing the drawing classes, which had gradually become less of a leisure amusement and more a part of the school work, upon the footing of a regular school of art. The improvement in drawing has been highly satisfactory.

Besides the liberality of the Association, the School has received, from time to time, munificent gifts from individual scholars. Conspicuous among these are the additions made to the premises by the brothers Tangye, of Birmingham, who have provided class-rooms on both sides of the School, besides many other liberal benefactions.

Great, indeed, have been the recent improvements in Sidcot School. The systematic teaching of drawing, carpentry, carving, and chemistry, has been followed by that of music. The singing of hymns gradually developed into part-singing ; the permission to have lessons on the piano-forte, from a teacher outside the school, was speedily extended to general music lessons on the premises. Music-rooms have been built, pianos and teachers provided, and a large proportion of both boys and girls are now under competent instruction.

An extensive and well-furnished gymnasium is one of the latest additions to the premises, where both boys and girls are drilled by an experienced master. A new and enlarged laboratory, with other improvements continually in progress attest the growing prosperity of the School ; which has for some years past been freed from old encumbrances, and is in the enjoyment of an excess of income over the ordinary expenses of the institution.

In the summer of 1890, some enterprizing spirits among the Old Scholars, started a periodical, called *The Sidcot Quarterly*, which is ably kept up, being edited, printed and published, as well as supplied with literary and artistic matter, by Sidcot Scholars, present and past. and it is to be hoped that the publication will continue to receive the support of scholars present and future. The

following extract is abridged from an article in the London
Daily News :

> THE SIDCOT SCHOOL—A delightful and unmistakably genuine
> letter of a young Quakeress school-girl appears in the new number
> of the organ of the Friends' School at Sidcot. The writer, having
> been asked to tell the latest news, relates how a problem in social
> ethics was satisfactorily settled. " Some friends (she writes) have
> just been here from the yearly meeting, and one of them told us not
> to spend our pennies at Mrs. Durston's, but to save them up for the
> missionaries ; but one of the teachers told her that if we all left off
> going to Mrs. Dursron's, Mrs. Durston would have to go to the
> workhouse, and that we were doing good near home. So then the
> Friend said she'd go 'right away and buy some chocolate '; and she
> did." Then we hear that ' another day a great bundle of walking-
> sticks came from Weston, and Miss Davis got them and put them
> in the store-room, but Mrs. Ashby sent them to the study, and the
> teachers gave them to us, and the girls started a hockey club, and
> everybody played hockey after that." It will have been observed
> that, in spite of the outside world's notion of—
>
> > The Quaker rule
> > That doth the human feeling cool,
>
> this flourishing Quaker school among the Mendip Hills does not set
> its face against innocent pleasures. "

Some "Old Scholars" of Sidcot School have distinguished themselves in Art, Science, and Literature, as
well as in Philanthropy and Politics. Whether the school
may be the Alma Mater of any guiltless Cromwells, of
Miltons or Newtons, is still in the womb of futurity. Its
children are diligently picking up pebbles on the shore
of the ocean of Truth, and we may hope are not mis-
taking those pebbles for the *Bread of Life,* or that ocean
for the *Living Water.* We know that, while the ocean
is useful as a means of transit for the ships, which it
bears upon its bosom, and as the abode of the living

creatures that swim in its depths, its water is not drink-
able, and is of little direct use to Man, until it is raised
up by the Sun, and brought down again as rain and dew,
to refresh vegetation and supply the rivers and springs.
So is it with the ocean of natural truth or Science. It
must be navigated in vessels that will float—as our
Saviour taught from a ship—and its waters must be
first mentally elevated by the influence of the Sun of
Righteousness, and then brought down to practical life, in
the fertilizing streams of the River of Life, and in the
living water of the Wells of Salvation. The woman of
Samaria had come many times to Jacob's Well, before
she found One sitting there who told her all things that
ever she did, and convinced those who listened to Him,
that He was indeed the Christ, the Saviour of the world.

Fir-cone fight at Banwell Tower.

WINSCOMBE PARISH.

HOUGH our Valley is chiefly occupied with the parish of Winscombe, with its hamlets of Woodborough and Barton, the hill-sides include not only Sidcot and Hale, but part of the parish of Banwell and the small parish of Christon, divided from Winscombe by the brook below Max. Shipham parish also comes into this valley, approaching within a few acres the boundary of Banwell ; a narrow strip of land, at Slough·pits, connecting Woodborough with the outlying hamlet of Sandford on the north side of the hill.

The Tithe Rent-charge apportionment and Map, made in 1840, show that the parish of Winscombe contains 4140 acres, divided into about 1300 holdings or enclosures; of which about 860 were less than three acres, many consisting of small plots of cottage ground. Seventy-six freeholders held less than an acre each, forty held between one and three, and sixteen from three to four—with or without the corresponding cow. There were twenty-seven owners of four to ten acres, forty owning from ten to fifty, fifteen from fifty to a hundred, and ten above one hundred. Only two possessed two hundred acres; the largest landowner holding two hundred and forty-five.

These proportions have changed much in the half century, especially in the last few years. The inevitable tendency of land is to gravitate together. Ruined cottages have been bought and re-built by those who had the means, and their plots of ground have gone with them. The picturesque and poetical have been sacrificed to the utilitarian and inevitable, and neither laws nor lamentations can prevent the change.

The total rent-charge in lieu of tithes on the 4140 acres was £462—of which £253 10s. went to the Vicar, and £208 10s. to the lessee under the Dean and Chapter.

POPULATION.

THE population of Winscombe Parish at the last census (1891) consisted of 648 males and 731 females, total 1379, being an increase of 26 males and 94 females, since 1882. At Sidcot School there is an excess of males; but throughout the Parish female servants and others must exceed the males. In the absence of factories and large employers, the young men find work elsewhere.

NAMES OF MEADOWS, &c.

THE following are some of the curious names of enclosures in Winscombe Parish :—

Jackamoors, Jackaman's yards, Farthing Olds, Fidling Wells, Clapper, Clails, Cockles, Burnt Cockles, Butter Cliffs, Froglands, Duck's Nest, Heale Croft, The Legg, The Foot, Lugfall, Blunderhedge, Benges, Pullings, Vardles, Nalguss, Ditchet, Tinings, Sliders Lay, Tippets, Stook Pie corner, Yeovill, Yeolm, Barrow-mead, Brook-mead, Blockmead, Hardmead, Pope mead, Sandmead, Mill mead, Penny mead.

Leland, in 1540, speaks of the pastures and fields in Somerset as "much enclosed with hedge-row elms." The small enclosures and hedgerow elms are still conspicuous in this valley and neighbourhood.

ST. CONGAR—p. 18.

THE legend of this Saint may be at least as true as that of Joseph of Arimathea. He is said to have fled from the attractions of empire—remembering, perhaps, who it was that claimed the disposal of the kingdoms of this world—and to have been brought from the Levant in some vessel trading with Britain ; probably for the Mendip metals. Desiring solitude, he settled in the Marshes by the Severn sea, and made himself a hermitage where Congresbury church now stands. Here he turned the swamp into flowery meads, and planted his yew wand as St. Joseph had planted his thorn. The trunk of the yew remains in the church-yard, and the village tradition is that the bones of the Saint are underneath, in a golden coffin !

A Mendip Valley.

CHURCHILL.

THE tradition mentioned in page 18, is rejected by recent authorities. In the *Arch. Proceedings*, 1885, Mr. Green, F.S.A., shows that Rutter mistook the John Churchill, who purchased the manor of Churchill in 1652, for the John Churchill of Sedgemoor. The manor belonged to the Jenyngs family from 1563 to 1652, when Richard Jenyngs sold it to John Churchill of Lincoln's Inn. He was a nephew of John Churchill of Wotton Glanville in Dorset, one of the Deputy Registers in Chancery, and succeeded his uncle in that office, retaining it under the Commonwealth and the Restoration, and being knighted in 1670, and made Master of the Rolls in 1685, in which year he died. The property was then involved in many years of litigation, being finally sold to several purchasers; among others William Arney, John Lewis, James Brookman, Samuel Foord, and John Gregory—all names well known in this neighbourhood.

John Churchill of Wotton was the direct ancestor of Lord Churchill, who became Duke of Marlborough, and who married Sarah the daughter and heiress of Richard Jenyngs, his sons having died before him ; but it does not appear that Lord Churchill had anything to do with Churchill manor or its manor-house, and the tradition of the troop of horses kept there seems to be a mistake.

VALUE OF MONEY—p. 10.

THE following are some of the prices, taken from a Churchwarden's account of a Somersetshire Village from A.D. 1433 to 1645 :—

1433. For a Bullock, 2s., for a Cow, 2s.
   Mowing ½ acre of Wheat, 6d.
   For a Capon, 3d.

Sale of a Calf, 2s 6d.
Cow and Calf bought, 13d.
The fleece of the Ewe, 3d.
The Ewe sold, 1s.4d.
1462. Wintering and Summering the Church Cowe, 11d.
Hive of Bees, 3d.
Wheat, 12d. per bushel.
1483. The winter keep of the Cow, 1s.4d.
A Surplice for the Priest, 9s.8d.
For the Clerk, 2s.4d.
1497. Cow and Calf sold for 9s.4d.
A Book, 45s.4d.
Pair of Vestments, 18s.4d.
Allowances for one new Clock this year bought, 33s.4d.
For the half-price of the Bible this year, bought 6s.5d.
1614. Paid for a Bible 48s., and for a Communion book 8s.
1615. Received for the Old Church Bible, sold by consent of the
Parishioners, 12s.4d.

The same curious record has the following entries :—

1614. The first Rate made 1d. the Acre.
Churchwardens excommunicated.
To Peter Tucker, for whipping the Dogs out of Church——
1629. 2½ quarts of Wine at 16d. a quart, and one penny loaf, against
Whit-Sunday.
A Rate for Bread and Wine made and collected.
Churchwarden excommunicated again.
1634. Setting up the King's Arms and sentences of Scripture.
1648. Striking out the King's Arms——
1645. Two Surplices, the troopers did take them out of the Church
and cut them in pieces, and the poor of the parish had the
pieces.

(*Vide* Arch. Pro., 1886.)

MODERN RISE IN PRICES.

DR. JOHNSON said of the fast coaches, that they would
leave no cheap places for genteel poverty: prices of

commodities would be equalized. This has been the
effect of the Cheddar Valleys Railway. It has opened
an increased traffic in dairy produce and early vegetables,
taking our milk and butter, and the Cheddar cheese, and
the early peas and potatoes of the southern side of the
hills, to London, Bristol, and South Wales, and considerably raising prices here. Milk has risen from 2d.
delivered, to 4d. in the dairy; butter made at Winscombe
fetches as much as that brought from Lombardy. Veal,
which, thirty years ago, was 6d. or less, and beef and
mutton, are fully half as dear again.

THE CHURCH PORCH—p. 57.

EVELYN'S "first rudiments of learning were acquired from
the village schoolmaster, *over the porch* of Wootton church"
(*Evelyn's Diary—Preface, p. ix*). The room over the
Porch of Winscombe Church may have been used, perhaps, as a parish schoolroom; there being no other.

MENDIP FOREST—p.p. 14, 28.

THE term *Forest* includes open hunting ground as well
as woods. The tyranny of the Norman Kings, especially
John, extended these forest-lands to the cruel oppression
of the people. The "Perambulation of Mendip Forest" in
the reign of Edward I, in 1298, considerably reduced the
extent of the royal encroachments, and the following
"vills and woods" were declared "disafforested," viz :—
Chewton, Priddy, Stoke Gifford, Compton, Loxton, Uphill,
Worle, Chricheston (Christon), Hutton, Banwell, Church-
ford (Churchill) and Langford, Wynescumbe, Shipham,
Robergh, Burrynton, Blakedon (Blagdon), Harptre, and

Whatleigh : leaving little more as forest than the parishes of Axbridge and Cheddar.

The Forest, as a mining country, though owned by the King as supreme lord, was divided into four lordships or royalties, viz :—The Bishop of Bath, the Abbot of Glaston, the Lord of the Manor of Richmond in East Harptree, and the Lord of Chewton Mendip.

Each of these lords had a minery jurisdiction, under a steward and *lead-reeve.* It was not till 1773 that calamine, manganese and ochre were added to the list of minerals touched by the laws. Coal is not mentioned, not being found within the limits of the mining forest. At Harptree, the latest minery court recorded was in 1819; at Chewton, the lead-reeve was in operation as late as 1834. These particulars are taken from an interesting paper on *Somerset Forest Bounds*, by Bishop Hobhouse, in the *Archæological Proceedings* of 1891. They throw a doubt on the supposition at p. 39, that calamine was one of the metals dealt in by the ancients. The Dolbury *Gold* was probably only lead.

Leland's account of Dolbury, so often quoted, is as follows :—"There is upon the Tope of one of Mendipe Hills a Place encamped caulyd Dolbyri, famous to the People, thus saynge :

> If Dolbyri dygyd ware
> Of Golde shuld be the share."

SNOWDROPS.

I am reminded by Mr. Knight's *Rambles of a Dominie*, that the old Botanist *Gerarde*, in his famous *Herbal* published in 1597, mentions Snowdrops as having been lately established in England beyond the bounds of cultivation. His words are: "These plants do grow wilde in Italy and the places adiacent. Notwithstanding our London gardens have taken possession of most of them many yeares past. In English we may call it the bulbous Violet. Some call them also *Snowdrops.*"

The end of the Avenue.　The Field Naturalists' return.